Bess smiled r...

Whatever doubts ... ... and ... journey were blo... ... ... by Harry's reception of her. No one could pretend such passion...

His eyes travelled over her. 'You are beautiful, Bess.'

It was scarcely decent, he thought, to be brought to the edge of such ecstasy by the touch of a woman — and that woman a wife of five years!

Dear Reader

Bonfire Night lights up the November sky, and this month we have books which create their own fireworks! Francesca Shaw is back with a frothy Regency, MISS WESTON'S MASQUERADE, and in MAIDEN COURT Laura Cassidy follows up on Bess and Harry's marriage from her first novel THE BLACK PEARL. Our American offerings are the second part of the Ferguson brothers duo, THE HELL RAISER by Dorothy Glenn, and then we have ROSE RED, ROSE WHITE by Marianne Willman, set in the days of Edward IV. Enjoy!

The Editor

Laura Cassidy followed careers in both publishing and advertising before becoming a freelance writer, when her first son was born. She has since had numerous short stories and articles published, as well as four novels. She began writing for Legacy of Love after discovering sixteenth-century romantic poetry, and very much enjoys the research involved in writing in the historical genre. She lives with her husband, who is a creative consultant, and their two teenage sons, near London.

Recent titles by the same author:

THE BLACK PEARL

MAIDEN COURT

Laura Cassidy

MILLS & BOON

MILLS & BOON LIMITED
ETON HOUSE, 18–24 PARADISE ROAD
RICHMOND, SURREY, TW9 1SR

> **DID YOU PURCHASE THIS BOOK WITHOUT A COVER?**
>
> If you did, you should be aware it is **stolen property** as it was reported *unsold and destroyed* by a retailer. Neither the Author nor the publisher has received any payment for this book.

All the characters in this book have no existence outside the imagination of the Author, and have no relation whatsoever to anyone bearing the same name or names. They are not even distantly inspired by any individual known or unknown to the Author, and all the incidents are pure invention.

All Rights Reserved. The text of this publication or any part thereof may not be reproduced or transmitted in any form or by any means, electronic or mechanical, including photocopying, recording, storage in an information retrieval system, or otherwise, without the written permission of the publisher.

This book is sold subject to the condition that it shall not, by way of trade or otherwise, be lent, resold, hired out or otherwise circulated without the prior consent of the publisher in any form of binding or cover other than that in which it is published and without a similar condition including this condition being imposed on the subsequent purchaser.

MILLS & BOON, the Rose Device and LEGACY OF LOVE are trademarks of the publisher.

First published in Great Britain 1994 by Mills & Boon Limited

© Laura Cassidy 1994

*Australian copyright 1994   Philippine copyright 1994
This edition 1994*

ISBN 0 263 78857 1

*Set in 10½ on 12½ pt Linotron Times
04-9411-74206*

Typeset in Great Britain by Centracet, Cambridge
Printed in Great Britain by
BPC Paperbacks Ltd

CHAPTER ONE

IN THE first month of 1541 Bess Latimar triumphantly bore her husband his first son, followed twenty minutes later by his first daughter. Nine months later she announced her intention of joining her absent husband at Richmond Palace, where he, in the train of his king and new queen, was to spend the last summer month following his inclusion in the royal tour of the North. For this announcement Bess had needed to summon almost as much strength as she had during her confinement, her mother being emphatically opposed to the idea.

''Twould be quite wrong to go, Bess,' Joan de Cheyne insisted, having supervised the feeding of her grandchildren, helped change their soiled napkins, re-dressed them in the complicated constricting clothing little babes wore, and sent them away with their nurse to sleep. 'The little ones need you far more than Harry does.'

Bess, still in the blissful dreamlike state feeding Harry's babies always induced in her, settled back on the plumped pillows for a protracted argument.

She was truly glad to have her mother with her in these days — there was much that was puzzling about tending infants. Why they cried for no reason was a worry and an aggravation to her; on the other hand the darlings, so perfect, so entrancing, were a delight to admire in company and Joan was the most adoring of grandmothers. Of course, Bess thought, Joan was especially blessed in her daughter's offspring, for they were beautiful with their pale, lovely skin, dark blue black-lashed eyes and shining black hair. If Joan had one criticism, it was that both children were the image of their father — there was nothing of Bess in their handsome looks.

But motherhood was not all the proverbial bed of roses, Bess decided, for everyone appeared to think she should now settle down to a life of domesticity, content to care for her family, oversee the running of her manor house with its carefully husbanded acres, become overnight a mother first and last; and she was simply not that kind of woman.

True, it had been the greatest sorrow to her for four long years that she had not become pregnant. It was five years since her marriage in the little church in Devon, surrounded by her childhood friends, supported by her aristocratic father and country-born mother, five years since she had married in joy the outsider Harry Latimar. Sir Henry Latimar, to give him his official title. And his unofficial? Well, gambler, profligate, rake, with long-legged, black-haired good looks and boundless charm that had established for him a place in the Tudor court, a long-established friendship with its monarch, and an attraction for any lady who strayed within his vicinity.

Good blood and impeccable heritage combined

with the above had produced for him a contract to marry an heiress promoted by his royal master, which Harry had inexplicably thrown up to take instead the penniless little fair-haired girl from the West Country who had entered court life only on the invitation of a well-connected cousin. The little Devon duchess, as some nobles teasingly called her, had for a brief, sparkling time been a part of the most exciting heyday of the Tudor years, the time when Anne Boleyn had reigned supreme. She had also played a small but dramatic part in the tragedy of that queen, having become her friend and confidante, and had finally carried off one of the premier jewels of the court in the shape of Latimar.

But she had not, in the first years of their marriage, given him a child. She could still remember with a sense of elation how she had felt the day when she had known for sure that at last she would give Harry the child they both desired so much. The following months had not been easy; Bess was sick at first, then ungainly with her double burden. Harry had been sympathetic during her malaise and tender during her last weeks.

Called to court in the final days, he had not been in their manor when her pains had begun, nor been below in the hall when his babes' first cries had been heard. He had, of course, come in the next hours. On his wild black horse he had clattered into the stable yard and, taking the broad stairs three at a time, viewed his wife's effort with a joy which left nothing to be desired. He had taken her hand and kissed her flushed cheek and spoken words of love and she had thought in that moment that she had never before been so completely happy. The christening, held one month later, had been a very grand affair attended by the king of England and his favourite courtiers, the godparents luminaries of the court. Bess and Harry then had two idyllic months together, until Harry was summoned to join the king and queen on their royal progress. He had been gone for five months now and Bess's burning desire was to be with him.

'Did he ask you to come?' Joan enquired, folding and putting away the little padded silk cape Bess had worn for the recent ceremony.

'No, he probably thinks as you do that the babes are too young to be left.' Bess had read and reread Harry's letter advising her that he was now at Richmond, but, loving though it had been, there had been no mention of her joining him.

'Which they are! Really, Bess, you have been such an exemplary wife, despite some provocation — although we will not dwell on that; Harry has the right to expect you to excel in motherhood as well.'

'I was a wife before I was a mother,' Bess said stubbornly. 'And I want to be with him. In truth I cannot bear to be parted from him,' she added thoughtfully. It was painfully true. She loved her little ones fiercely; her interest and attention to their welfare was almost unseemly in a lady of her class, some thought; if anyone had attempted to harm them she would have given her life in their defence, but — what she felt for them could never be fairly weighed against what she felt for their father. Bess had loved Harry Latimar from the moment she laid eyes on him in the falling rain outside Greenwich Palace when she had travelled from her poor home in the west to the exotic splendour of a new life, and that love had grown and spread and flourished like a freely blossoming plant in the years of their marriage. That plant needed the sustenance only to be got from the man who had given it life.

'Do you have some special reason for wanting to go to him — some reason you feel you ought to go?' Joan asked.

'Why, Mother, what do you mean?' Bess asked coldly. 'Is it not natural for a wife to want to be with her husband?'

'Oh, of course.' Joan blushed and, glancing at the bed, saw she had annoyed her daughter. For such an intensely feminine creature, Bess could on occasion wear an expression similar to that of a man looking at an adversary along the gleaming length of a drawn sword. She turned away and busied herself with more tidying.

Bess simmered. She knew what was in her mother's mind: Harry attracted members of her sex as a honeypot attracted wasps. Had he been faithful to her for the past five years? Bess could not answer that, hardly dared answer that, even in the privacy of her own thoughts, but it angered her that any other should refer to it. . . Was that why she wanted to go to Richmond? She hoped it was not, for she would be ashamed to own to such disloyalty. She directed these unsettling speculations into annoyance and with angry blue eyes watched Joan adding another log to the already mountainous fire.

There was little point in her mother's trying to judge Harry by the men she knew and had known in her own rural community, by her father and brothers. Or by her husband. Robert de Cheyne, Bess's father, had been a member of the young King Henry's court, then, crippled in a tournament, had fled into the West Country to farm poor acres and marry a farmer's daughter. Robert had worked his land, cherished his wife, and helped to bring up his daughter without causing Joan a moment's anxiety in that respect. He had died two years ago as quietly and bravely as he had lived his life and Joan had left the farm in the care of her nephews and made her permanent home with Bess. But there had been a bond between the dead knight and his son-in-law, a bond of kinship not to do with blood. They had had the same roots, deeply spread during their youth in court life and revealed to Joan the day her beloved husband had died.

By chance Robert and Joan had been visiting Bess. It was high summer, the days broiling hot, and Robert had been in the stables with Harry viewing a recent acquisition. Robert's disabilities—his legs had been irrevocably damaged after he had fallen from his destrier at the tournament—did not allow him to ride, but he was enjoying the sight of Harry showing off the chestnut's paces, when he felt suddenly dizzy. He slipped first to his knees, then fell prone on the dusty cobbles. Harry, leaping from his horse, had picked him up and carried him bodily into the house where he lay for two days without waking from his coma. On the third, as night fell, he opened his eyes and his lips moved.

Bess, tending him while Joan took a little rest, bent closer to hear what her father strained to say. She caught only the one word, 'Henry', and turned to Harry who was keeping vigil with her.

'Come nearer the bed, Harry, he is asking for you.'

''Tis not me he wants, sweetheart,' Harry had said from the shadows. 'It is the king he is needing now.' Harry had then left the room, saddled up and ridden through the night to where the royal court was being kept at Whitehall. How he had persuaded the king to ride back with him, he did not say. But persuade him he did and Henry Tudor came to Maiden Court as the sun rose over its mellow roof and entered the room where the man he had not seen for a quarter-century lay dying. He filled the small chamber with his vast bulk, and almost overturned the bed as he sat and took Robert's hand.

'Now, de Cheyne,' he said rallyingly. 'What is this? I have never seen a tumble such as you took at Windsor, and yet rose up from. Will this little affair down you?'

Robert had smiled crookedly, for whatever had struck him in the stables had pulled down one side of his face, numbed one side of his body. 'It is over for me, Hal. I was just holding to the light a space to see if you would come to bid me farewell.'

'I will not say it! Come, man, 'twould be hard indeed for me to have come this long way and not see you better. Look at me—a crock, with this damned leg, but still up and around. Only try a little and in a week or so we shall sup together and talk of old times—good times.'

'The best of times,' Robert had agreed with difficulty. He tried to return the pressure on his hand, but the numbness was creeping over the whole of his body now, and the king's massive body shut out the growing light of the dawn. It was not difficult or painful as he had always imagined death to be, but easy and peaceful like drifting into sleep.

One last effort and he moved his eyes to the wall where Harry stood, his back flat against the dark wood, his face impassive, to Bess beside him, her blue eyes sparkling with tears—everything all right there, Robert thought gratefully. If he had had the choosing of the man for Bess, if he had scoured the length and breadth of England for a husband to make her happy, he could not have done better... Robert reserved his last glance for Joan, beside the bed, twisting her hands, then allowed the everlasting rest to take him.

'So...' The king stood up. He looked down at the man in the bed, thinking of a summer's day twenty-five years ago when Robert de Cheyne had mounted his fine horse, clad in gleaming armour, and ridden out into the lists to do mock battle for the last time. He had been as fair a man as any had seen, tall and blond and straight. Henry had thought of him in that way ever since, although he knew he had been carried from the field twisted and broken. Now he was dead and a full five years younger than himself. . . Henry turned abruptly away and Joan dropped a curtsy, unable to prevent the tears running down her face and on to the hand he offered her. She faltered her thanks that he should have come and given her husband such pleasure at the last.

'Nay, lady,' Henry interrupted her. 'Don't thank me for coming — I am glad to have seen Robert this last time.' As if to himself he added, 'Those friends we make in our youth become more real to us as we grow older, and I am sad indeed this day that Robert is no more. He was, after all, five years younger than myself.' He turned to Harry, an expression very like fear in his eyes. Harry gave him an ironic smile.

'Don't worry, Hal. Only the good die young, or so we are told.'

The king did not stay for refreshment, but took the road again, apparently intent on putting as many miles between himself and the evidence of mortality as possible, but Bess thought more kindly of him after.

'What are you thinking of?' Joan asked, coming back to the bed.

'Of Father. I miss him very much.'

'As I do,' Joan sighed. 'I am sure, were he here

today, he too would question your desire to abandon your babies.'

'Oh, Mother! Abandon? They will be safe in my home with the best of care — are you not their slave? Is not Annie, their nurse, the best and most competent of women? Please try to understand why I must go.'

'I don't understand! They are not yet weaned, after all——'

'But will be,' Bess said determinedly. 'We will begin upon that this coming week. A little fresh stewed meat, and ewes' milk — come, Mother, will it not be delightful for you to take charge of the lambs' bottle?'

'Well. . . Shall you send a message to Harry to advise him of your coming?'

Bess deliberated. 'I don't believe I shall. I shall simply arrive.'

'But, my dear, will that be wise?'

'Why should it not be?' Again Joan received the straight blue stare.

Two weeks later Bess was on her way to Richmond Palace. Richmond, originally named Shene from the old word meaning 'beautiful place', deserved that title. It was set like a jewel in vast majestic forest, close to the broad ribbon of the Thames, and boasted a fantastic number of towers and turrets along its boundary walls, creating an exotic outline against the sky. Its gardens were a playground for the king and his friends, with archery rows, bowling greens, tennis courts and a selection of the most spectacular plants and shrubs which could be persuaded to grow in its lush soil. It had always been Bess's favourite royal residence, and she was looking forward to being there again.

She had intended leaving Maiden Court at first light that day, but a number of things had prevented her. Over the years those in the manor, and living on the surrounding estate, had come to regard Lady Bess as their friend as well as their mistress. They all, young and old, now brought her their troubles and their joys and had grown accustomed to having the lovely wife of their liege lord attend to them.

Harry had brought his young bride here straight from their Devon marriage. Bess, riding up the drive flanked by silver birch, had been entranced from the start by the old house. Inside it was sorely outdated—the great hall with its central fire hearth was draughty in winter; its stone walls, uncovered and lacking the new and fashionably glazed windows, were black with smoke and contrived to let in the chill cold from November to March, but keep out the warmth in the summer months. Its kitchens were overrun with vermin, its bedchambers mouldy and comfortless. But, oh, how beautiful the design and structure of the building, the graceful sweep of its broad stairs. How lush and fertile the acres beyond the overgrown lawns. . . Bess had set to work immediately to clean and polish all.

For a month the ancient manor was a hive of activity as its debris was removed, its floors scrubbed, its furnishings renewed. Not content with renovating the actual house, she put her mind to bringing the gardens back to life, to trimming and pruning and shaving the green lawns. Then she turned her attention to its acres—after all, she was a farmer's daughter. Much of the land had lain fallow for many years and must be coaxed gently back to productivity, the orchards pruned and cosseted to provide fruit, the fields ploughed and sown for the future. The home farm must be cultivated and nurtured to provide produce for the kitchens of the house. The land blossomed under her loving care, the house returned to former grace and seemed to envelop her with affection.

Harry looked on in amusement as his new wife revolved like quicksilver around her new home. He was frequently absent, called to his royal friend's side, but each time he returned to Maiden Court he marvelled at the amount of work his delicate Bess had generated. Within a half-year he had a home worthy of a premier knight of England. He had borrowed money for these improvements and Bess had spent it well.

'Where did it come from—our home?' Bess asked him once. 'I mean, when I married you, you did not mention you had a manor house in Kew.'

'No more I did,' agreed Harry. ''Twas a gift.'

They were having this conversation on the little rise overlooking Maiden Court. It was late afternoon and Harry had come unexpectedly, and Bess had taken him out to view his estate. He had been complimentary upon her efforts and she was so happy, her arm entwined in his, as they looked down upon their home.

'It's a strange name,' she had mused, 'but charming.'

''Tis from the French,' Harry had said absently. 'Mispronounced over the years. The Norman commander who laid the foundations called his house *Mille un acres* — one thousand acres and one — for this is what he was granted in payment for conquering the intransigent Saxons. Over the years the English whittled away at the name until it resembled something they understood, so — Maiden Court.'

'Oh,' Bess had frowned. 'I had imagined it called for some beloved daughter of its first owner. Who gave it to you? The king?'

'No, not Henry,' Harry was evasive. 'Come, sweetheart, let us go in — it grows cold out here.'

Rural areas were not known for their easy acceptance of newcomers, but Bess managed to find a place in the villagers' hearts very quickly, mainly because she did not press for it, but went about the task in a roundabout way on advice from her father.

'You'll be a foreigner,' Robert had smiled. 'For years to come probably. I know, because I was so regarded when I first came to Devon. Keep yourself aloof for a little, but be ready with an open hand and a kind heart if occasion presents itself.'

Bess had found this good advice, but for a time it seemed that an occasion for her to show her willingness to be a part of the life here at Kew would never come about. When she rode out the men would doff their caps, the women bob a respectful curtsy, but they did not speak personally to her — however long she lingered at the fairs and other gatherings all country people indulged in at every opportunity. They did not seek her out and allow her to love them and care for them as she so longed to do.

Harry they treated very differently. After a bare few months in residence at Maiden Court he became important in their lives. The men would seek his counsel on the smallest of matters, the women would hold up their babes in the fields for his inspection, invite him into their poor cottages to drink cowslip wine. Little tokens of their absolute acceptance began arriving daily at Maiden Court. A fine fresh fish wrapped in green leaves 'for my Lord Harry who has a taste for trout'; an oven-fresh batch of honey cakes 'for my Lord Harry who has a sweet tooth'. . . In her heart Bess resented this show of affection, for she was the one who was prepared to put her soul into caring for her 'people'; to Harry they were a very minor part of his life.

The thaw had come one Christmas. Bess had been provided with competent household servants — an ancient crook-backed woman, Margery, who had turned out to be an excellent housekeeper with an iron devotion to 'things being right', a cook who, although unimaginative, was unusually clean and industrious, and some assorted little maids, all of whom were related in some way or other to Margery. One of these, Mary, was assigned to Bess as her personal maid. She would not have pleased a more demanding mistress — her hand was heavy both on her lady's waterfall of silvery hair, and on the dainty linen Bess's cousin Meg had given her as a wedding gift, but she was willing and Bess liked her. One night when Harry had already left to keep Yuletide at Whitehall and Bess was preparing to join him, she found Mary dripping large tears into the trunk she was packing for her mistress. Questioning had revealed that Mary's sister was nursing a new babe, and that babe not expected to live the night.

''Twill be her tenth,' Mary had gulped.

'She has ten children?' Bess had enquired.

'No, m'lady, 'twill be the tenth she has lost.'

'Ten lost?' Bess was horrified. Two or three little ones dead, yes, for the times were not kind in poor places to infants, but ten. . .

''Tis the one thing or another, you see,' Mary had sobbed. 'The winter months are cruel on little ones, and Joseph has the croup. . .'

'Well, we must see what we can do,' Bess had said with more assurance than she had felt. Her mother had been renowned for her remedies in times of sickness; before Bess had married, Joan had passed on some of her sovereign aids, indeed had made her daughter write them in a little book, and made sure she packed a cedar box of ointments and pastes and bottles of musty-smelling medicines. Now Bess searched her mind for any reference to the croup. Yes, she believed she remembered what her mother had said on this particular problem. She hurried to her chest, found the book and, holding it to the candlelight, read the words of wisdom. Despite Mary's protests, both girls then donned sturdy shoes and warm cloaks and went immediately to the little hovel on the outskirts of the village.

'Boil your kettle,' Bess had said to the desperate woman. 'And fill as many of your pots and pans as possible with water and set them on your fire. Give me the babe and don't worry.' Bess in that moment had looked so like the angel Mary's sister remembered in her childhood seeing depicted in the stained glass windows of the local church standing above the virgin Mary that she had handed over her precious son and gone instantly to carry out her instructions. Bess had hugged the child to her breast and carried it out into the night air.

When the cottage was full of steam Bess had come back in and, seating herself beside the fire, rocked the child and waited.

'A miracle!' the villagers declared the next day, when the news spread abroad and little Joseph, able to take his breath without difficulty, was a different child from the one on the brink of eternity the previous night, and lay peacefully in his cradle. 'My mistress wrought the miracle!' Mary declared proudly.

Bess's stock had soared. Within a short time, my lady Latimar was deemed to be both sympathetic and practical, and so her reputation grew throughout the outlying villages and no one was happier about this state of affairs than Bess herself. Her days were filled with such incidents—a septic finger, swiftly returned to health by the green ointment she made, a struggling heart, greatly helped by the infusion of foxglove leaves she recommended... But such fame brought with it certain responsibilities, and she was delayed this fine morning by a number of small crises. It was just after noon when she left her home.

It was hard to leave Maiden Court; harder still to leave her babies in spite of Joan's assurances that she would care for them as her own. Bess had bent for a long time over both little cribs, kissed all four chubby hands a hundred times and eventually torn herself away. Looking back along the now immaculate drive, the call of her home and family was strong, but stronger by an immeasurable distance was Richmond Palace—for there Harry was...

Harry's instructions were always that his wife rode on the public highway in the care of at least two sturdy grooms, but she disobeyed him this day, taking only one lad, Walter, from the stables and her maid, Mary. She did not want a great gaggle with her when she joined Harry, wanted in fact just to slip back into his life with the minimum of fuss, after what had been almost two years' absence from court.

Of course Bess was more worldly now than she had been when she had first come to a palace as an innocent seventeen-year-old from a country background, capable of being horrified by the events which had occurred while she made a place for herself among the uneasy glitter of a society comprised of the aristocratic, the wealthy, the beautiful and witty, but foremost the ambitious. But with a greater knowledge of how this society revolved, there had not come a compromise of integrity, or a careless cynicism which others, in particular Harry, wore like armour beneath their skin. Bess was still the forthright girl she had been five years ago, the girl who had declared it a scandal and an injustice that an innocent lady could be accused and convicted of crimes she did not commit, that her close friends and brother could be similarly accused and convicted, that they all could be despatched with such arrogance upon the whim of one man.

Her strong character had made her both friends and enemies in the Tudor court. Surprisingly, Henry Tudor was not among the latter, though he had so often smarted beneath her gentle and honest tongue. Speculation on the reasons for this had abounded in Bess's first years; some felt it was because she was married to one of Henry's greatest friends — an old and tried relationship, forged when Harry was a boy and his sovereign a young man — others declared it was so because, however much Bess abhorred the removal of one queen and the substitution of another, she had become a friend to Jane Seymour during her brief reign. It had been a friendship built on ashes, but firm nevertheless — for Bess had loved Jane and been very upset when she had died. Henry, whose son was his pride and joy, was very sentimental regarding his mother's memory and inclined to favour those she had cared for.

Most, however, believed it was because Henry could never resist a pretty face, and Bess Latimar was not merely pretty but beautiful. When Harry had brought his bride back to court for long periods after their marriage, she soon acquired a legion of admirers, both male and female. Of course few of the ladies could aspire to her dazzling fairness, but many attempted to copy her individual style of dress. Also, she was witty company with her new-found confidence — after all, if Harry loved her, she reasoned, she must be special — and the jaded palates of the gentlemen were intrigued by her intelligent humour. Yes, Bess had achieved a certain greatness, admirable among so many gracious and beautiful women.

It did not hurt her case, either, that her husband appeared changed overnight. It was hard to remember in those days that Harry Latimar had once been the most promiscuous of men, a handsome free spirit apparently unbound by any convention, taking his own debonair way, a magnet for lovely women, a hawk at the card tables, beloved of his royal master, showered with privileges — a powerful force to be reckoned with should he ever choose to exert his influence, which was rarely. Now, careless Latimar had been apparently brought to heel and worshipped at just the one shrine — his wife's.

Bess, riding with easy pleasure upon her little roan mare along the dusty roads, thought back on those days, brought abruptly to a halt by her pregnancy. Her condition had necessarily curtailed her time at court—she must be safe within her own four walls, lead a more sedate existance. No more wild rides with her husband, no late nights at the masked balls, no more all-night vigils at the gaming tables. So had declared her husband, and had there not been a hint of relief in his eyes when they had decided upon this? wondered Bess now as she glanced over one slim shoulder to ensure that Mary and Walter, taking this opportunity to further the romance they had begun lately, kept up the pace she set.

Before their marriage, on the occasion of their engagement, before accepting the magnificent ring he gave her, Bess had delivered an ultimatum to Latimar: I will not, she had declared, wander the outskirts of your life, bearing your children, tending your home and acres, being a wife, but will be a part of your life—a vital and indispensable part. She had meant it, and he had agreed. But how firm had been his resolution? Used as he was to the wives of his friends being kept very much much in the background, as they pursued the game of life? In the last year and a half she could count on one hand the number of months Harry had spent with her. Certainly, he had been loving and attentive on these visits to Maiden Court, certainly he had praised her efforts to make the house a home, and—her lips curved in a lovely smile—he had been more than passionate during the nights in the comfortable linen-decked bed. But his real life, she felt, was contained wherever the court was. She had not expected him to be the kind of husband who never set foot off his estate, indeed she was quite sure the king would not allow him to be, but she would not permit him to relegate her to a corner of the world where he might visit when the mood took him.

Her blue eyes on the dusty road ahead, she considered the word 'permit'. Not one easily used in connection with Harry—outwardly the most easy-going of men, but actually very resistant to influence of any kind. His friends might laugh indulgently and say that pretty Bess had tamed Latimar, but Bess knew this was not so. Harry allowed her to rule on any decision other than his personal freedom, and it seemed increasingly that this was the area frequently in dispute.

'A gentleman of the court may not choose where he goes and what he does,' he would protest. 'And I swear you are with me more than any other lady of my companions.'

'You make it sound as if I am pressing myself upon you,' she would accuse him in return.

'No such thing! But you must necessarily divide your time between our home and the cares of attending your unruly husband—let us not waste our time together in disharmony.' He would then smile and take her into his arms, thus stopping her mouth with his kisses.

We never get to the end of any argument, she would sometimes think despairingly; nothing is ever resolved, nothing ever changes. Well, she thought now, the time has come for change. Naturally Harry had to obey his orders to be with the king on his progress, naturally her twins were too young to be left, but. . . She was free again now and determined to take her rightful place. Half unconsciously she urged her mount to a faster pace.

CHAPTER TWO

WHEN Richmond Palace lay before them, dreaming under the still bright sun, they had been in the saddle an hour. Many were making the trip along the roads to offer their confirmed allegiance to their monarch, and the last miles had been slow indeed. Bess eased her aching back as she and Walter and Mary rode single file over the narrow bridge which forded the dry moat. As they threaded their way through those on foot, Bess's beauty-loving eyes caught sight of a black-haired, brilliantly costumed lady being lifted from her horse by a gentleman in grey. The lady, no more than a girl, laughed up into the face of her companion whom, even at this distance, Bess instantly identified as her husband. The crush of new arrivals to the palace prevented her from immediately hastening to his side and, with frustration, she had to watch the pair go arm-in-arm into the open doorway leading to the central courtyard.

Walter helped her to dismount. He looked around him with startled eyes. He had never been from his village before he sought employment in the Maiden Court stables, and since then never far from the manor. He had never before seen so many people in one place. He gave Bess a glance both shamefaced and fearful, and she smiled encouragingly.

'Take the horses into the stables, Walter. Tell them there that you are Lady Latimar's groom and they will advise you where to put our mounts and where you should go for food and shelter. Mary — we will go in.' She began her graceful way to the main steps.

Bess was not as cool as she looked; it was a long time since she had arrived at any grand residence without Harry by her side to swing her down from her saddle, toss their reins to the nearest groom and sweep her into the colour and light within. This day it had been some other girl he had been escorting between the wide oak doors. . . She took an impatient breath. Was she to begin at once with her jealous, possessive thoughts? No, she would retire to one of the waiting-rooms and send a page to inform Harry she was in the palace; he would come for her and their reunion would be as rapturous as she had imagined in the days since she had decided to come. She would not allow any suspicions to interfere with that dream.

In the cool, velvet-draped room she surreptitiously shook some of the dust from her skirts and readjusted her hat. There was a glass in one dim corner and she examined her face for signs of the hot dusty ride. Mary hastened to her side and dabbed at the delicate skin of one cheek with her handkerchief. 'Excuse me, my lady, a little speck of dirt.' Mary sensed a tension about her young mistress not usually present. Lady Bess was always so *sure* in all she said and did; she never lost her temper, never raged, or struck her servants, was never less than her own reasonable, softly spoken, sweet-natured self. Now Mary could see the blood moving under the enviably perfect skin of Bess's face, see the dilation of her blue eyes and the nervous clenching and unclenching of her hands. Not used to seeing her lady in this vulnerable state, Mary's instinct was to protect and encourage.

'No one would guess you had just ridden an hour under the hot sun, my lady.' She was rewarded with an absent-minded smile, then the door behind them opened and Harry Latimar came into the room. Both women turned to look at him.

Harry Latimar was thirty-one years old in this, the fourth decade of Henry Tudor's reign. He had come to the royal court as a page in the retinue of the Earl of Stanford when he was seven. As a young squire he had attracted the attention of the new king of England who was married at that time to a princess of Spain and anxious already for a male heir. To King Hal, Harry Latimar had seemed to embody all the desirable characteristics in a boy: he was tall and well-made, intelligent at his studies despite excelling in the tiltyard and exercise field, charming of manner, with an appreciation of music and poetry at odds with his physical ability.

By the time Harry was knighted at twenty-one years of age, he had acquired a reputation for being a womaniser, a gambler, a man whom careful fathers steered their impressionable sons and daughters away from, but he also now had the powerful patronage of the most important noble in England. Once Henry had been asked to declare who among his gentlemen he would place his absolute trust in. He had named but two: Thomas More, and — Latimar.

In 1533 Henry had at last married his obsession, Anne Boleyn, and there had come a change in his relationship with Lord Harry. Harry had an affection for the mercurial Anne, both as queen and woman, and had loved her brother, Viscount Rochford, intensely. The two men, so different, had been as brothers, and when Henry had executed both brother and sister three years later he had sown the seed of a bitter plant in Harry's heart.

During this time Bess de Cheyne had come into Harry's life as a fresh breeze from the sea might blow through a stuffy room. Trying to deny the instant hold she laid on him, he had at first tried to seduce her, to put her conveniently into the place he reserved for such emotions as she aroused. Failing in this, he had then tried to ignore her, but had found this impossible. The whole affair had reached its climax at the same time as the royal drama was being brought to its conclusion around them. Anne had been murdered, Bess had returned to her home and Harry had thought himself free of her. Instead, unable to forget her, a few months later he took the road to Devon, prepared to admit to her and to himself that he could not now live without her.

Returning after their wedding, she had, with her gentle love, helped him through the uneasy time of a new queen on the throne, new stars in the Tudor court, and it had been Bess who was mainly responsible for healing the rift between her new husband and the man who had so disappointed him. That rift was never thought of by Henry now, and if Latimar ever felt again the sharp pain of that time, he never spoke of it.

He and Bess had had several delightful years before she bowed to her confinement and remained permanently at Maiden Court, and all changed again. Harry truly loved his wife, he delighted in her company, but—perversely—was not sorry when she was forced to stay in his home. Domesticity had been a hard lesson for him to learn, and without Bess with him every day he had quickly reverted to happy bachelorhood. Not in all ways—whatever impression Bess had, or any of their intimates, Harry had been physically faithful to her for the duration of their marriage. But—how pleasant it had been in the past year to sit up all night in a card game without censure, to choose to lie abed all day without a gentle reminder that his duties awaited him, to empty his purse on a foolish bet without a dismayed look. . . Also, suddenly to miss her so much that he must mount his horse at any hour of the day or night and spur for Maiden Court, knowing she would greet him at the door with—even in the last weeks of her confinement—an embrace which would set his pulses racing. Now she was here and, looking at her in the abstract way any really masculine man viewed a female, he saw that maternity had not changed the slender, virginal body, or left its mark on the ethereally beautiful face, or changed the expression in her clear blue gaze. It had been five months since he had last seen her and in that time Bess had managed to erase any claim to matronship. He crossed the floor in half a dozen steps and took her in his arms. Mary Weeks averted her eyes from such a display of affection.

'Darling Bess,' Harry murmured at last. 'Why are you here? Why did you not advise me you were coming?'

'I wanted to surprise you. A pleasant surprise, I thought. Is it so?'

'Of course! You know it is. But—there is nought amiss, the babes. . .?'

'Hearty, and in my mother's care. I simply had a fancy to see my husband, so I came.' She smiled radiantly. Whatever doubts she had had before the journey, or during it, were blown away by his reception of her. No one could pretend such passion—really, if Mary had not been present. . . She turned a little from him and patted her disarranged hair. 'I have a new costume; you have not commented upon it yet. . .'

His eyes travelled over her. 'I have had no time to consider anything but how happy I am to see you. But now I see it becomes you very well. You are beautiful, Bess.' He touched his own black hair, which held hints of copper within its shining depths, slightly disconcerted. It was scarcely decent, he thought, to be brought to the edge of such ecstasy by the touch of a woman — and that woman a wife of five years!

'Thank you.' Satisfied, Bess took one of his hands and raised it to her lips. 'So — I am unannounced and have not even asked the king if I may enter his palace! A shameful breach of manners, I know, which must be put right immediately.'

'Henry will be pleased to see you, of course. His new queen also. You have not yet met Catherine.'

'She is beautiful, I hear, and a cousin to Anne——'

Harry took back his hand. 'Indeed,' he said coldly. 'But as unlike that lady as is possible... Bess, I am transported by your appearance, but must tell you that Richmond is packed to the rafters. I am sharing room and bed with three others. I have no idea where you will lay your head tonight.'

Bess smiled again. 'If it be under the same roof as you, Harry, I am content. But I would like to change my clothes now — 'twill be the supper hour shortly and I would not disgrace you by attending the table in this dusty suit.'

'You may descend to the great hall in sackcloth and never do that, darling, but there will be a place for you in the ladies' dorter and I will arrange it immediately.' He went to the door and opened it. Shouting for a page, he informed the boy who came running that my lady Latimar must be taken to the west wing and her trunks sent there forthwith.

Bess followed the child, Mary in her wake. Richmond was no more really than a large country mansion, she thought. There had always been a palace on this site, until, in the first Henry Tudor's time it had been burned to the ground in a violent fire from which the present king's father had been lucky to escape with his life. Surviving the smoke and licking flames, Henry VII had at once rebuilt on the foundations of the ruin a fanciful red brick structure with copper cupolas, onion domes and luxurious apartments, and renamed it Richmond, to commemorate his first title as Earl of Richmond in Yorkshire, before he attained for himself the grander title of King of England. In its days as Shene Palace the place had enjoyed the dubious reputation as being a palace for dying in. Edward III had taken his last breath there, Anne of Bohemia too. . .

Its gardens, reclaimed from the surrounding forest, were a joy, its walls very grand, but its interior — composed of small apartments — luxurious but not equipped to contain a vast number of occupants. Henry used it mainly for sporting weekends and the holding of the tournaments he so enjoyed. Bess had always experienced overcrowding in this place, and apparently nothing had changed in that respect.

At the end of one of the long winding passages the page threw open a door and announced in treble tones, 'My lady Latimar.' The four or more young ladies within turned startled faces towards Bess. One rose from her chair and dropped an impeccable curtsy.

'My lady — welcome to Richmond.'

Bess came into the room. 'Thank you. I am so sorry if I put you out in any way.' The room was small; two beds occupied most of the space, a giant fireplace the remainder.

'You do not,' the girl who had greeted her assured her. 'We are honoured to have you share our poor accommodation.'

Candles had recently been lit in the chamber. They illuminated the dark corners and shone their light on the girls seated at ease on the beds. But Bess's eyes were fixed on her welcomer. She was, she saw with a thrill of recognition, the girl that Harry had lifted from the rangy grey mare and taken into the palace earlier. The girl stood impassively under her appraisal, head up, hands loosely clasped before her.

'May I know your name?' Bess asked politely. The girl inclined her head a second time.

'I am the Lady Madrilene.'

A beautiful, exotic name, thought Bess, well matched to its owner. For Madrilene was beautiful; black-haired, the shining strands with a bluish sheen, doe-eyed with lids luminous, creamy skinned and — young. So young that her excessively sophisticated gown gave the impression of a little girl dressed up in her mother's clothes.

'An unusual name,' Bess murmured. 'I believe I have never heard it before.'

The girl smiled. Her face was triangular; when she smiled, showing perfect white teeth, one got the fleeting picture of a kitten smiling. 'My mother was

French — from the royal court of King Francis — but my father was a Spaniard. He died soon after I was made, and *ma mère* named me for him. Madrilene — it means literally "of Madrid", for it was from that fair city he came.'

She might be young, thought Bess, but she had the self-assurance of a mature woman — that and the pride of expression and movement Spanish daughters of the nobility possessed. Her smiling friendliness was no doubt inherited from her French mother.

'But we are not hospitable!' Madrilene exclaimed, taking Bess's hand and leading her forward. 'I will perform the introductions, then show you our poor amenities.' The other girls smiled politely when named, then left the room leaving Madrilene to carry out the last of her promise. Bess wished she would go too; she did not want Mary to begin unpacking under this girl's curious eyes. She regretted now that she had not delayed a little longer at home and ordered several new gowns, as well as the fashionable riding habit. Fashions changed so quickly in this stylish company, and she knew that what she had brought was sorely out of date.

Oblivious of these distressing thoughts, Mary opened the trunk and began reverently to take out her mistress's gowns. She took them from their tissue shrouds and shook them to remove the creases. Madrilene's bright eyes roved over each one.

'But how charming are your gowns, my lady. You

obviously have your own style, and do not follow like the sheep us other silly hens.'

As good a way as any of informing me of what I already suspect, thought Bess wryly. Perhaps Harry would be ashamed of his provincial wife; he was one of those men who always noticed what women wore. However, there was little she could do about the situation. She removed her hat and began to unbutton her jacket.

Madrilene helped her. 'So you are Harry's wife,' she said, as Bess in her underblouse began to wash her face and hands in the bowl of water on the dressing-table. 'And just as beautiful as he said you were.'

A nice compliment, thought Bess, but I am not pleased with it. Instead I am annoyed that Harry should have discussed me with this girl. She dried her hands and face and moved to the glass and bent, looking into it. Beside her, Madrilene examined her own face and Bess felt like a ghost beside the vivid looks of the Spanish girl. She straightened up and said, 'It will soon be the supper hour — you must not let me delay you if you wish to go down.'

'Oh, let us go down together. I feel the duties of a hostess for you! It will be strange for you here, will it not?'

'Not at all! I know Richmond well, and have many friends here at court.' Bess could not help the touch of frost which invaded her voice. Madrilene gave her a speculative glance from her slanting eyes.

'To be sure, to be sure. . .but you have been away

some time, have you not? And people forget so quickly.'

Determined not to find any double meaning in the other girl's words, Bess turned briskly from the mirror. 'I think I will wear the white silk tonight, Mary. Harry always declares he likes me best in white.'

'Harry has such definite ideas on such things, does he not? For me he always prefers jewel colours — ruby, rich sapphire and emerald.' Having delivered this statement in purring tones, Madrilene went away and left Bess to her toilette.

Descending the stairs half an hour later, Bess found Thomas Seymour at the foot. He watched her, his fine blue eyes appreciative, and when she was beside him bowed gravely and lifted her hand to his lips.

'Lady Bess — welcome to Richmond. Harry has kept your coming a close secret.'

'He was unaware of it until an hour ago,' Bess replied. She had always rather liked Tom Seymour — brother-in-law to the king, uncle to Edward, the little heir to the throne — but he and Harry were often at odds with each other. Harry thought Tom and his brother, Edward, prime movers in the fall of Anne Boleyn that their sister, Jane, could take her place. Certainly, since that event both during Jane's reign and after, the brothers had been in high favour with the king, Edward created Earl of Hertford, and Tom a privileged gentleman of the privy chamber and expectant of other honours. Thomas had early shown himself willing to proffer the olive branch to Latimar, and Bess thought Harry contrary in appearing to forgive the king for his part in the affair, but not Thomas. Probably it was the female in her that desired a cessation of hostilities between two of the king's favourites because, of course, Tom was a very attractive man and it was hard to remain immune to him when he chose to exert his charm.

He said now, 'May I take you into supper, Bess?'

'I had hoped Harry would do so,' she said, looking around at those entering the hall.

'Ah. . . I believe there is a game in progress which has his full attention at present. Please allow me the pleasure of escorting you.'

'You are very kind,' Bess said stiffly. Surely it was not too much to expect Harry to make himself available to her on this, the first night of her arrival!

The hot colour rose in her face, and Thomas said quickly, 'Come, Bess, our friend does not change — but his charm is such we forgive him, do we not?'

The king was already on the royal dais when Bess came into the hall on Thomas Seymour's arm. She hesitated, feeling she should present herself to him and ask for shelter in his palace as etiquette demanded. Tom pressed her arm.

'Later, Bess, he is not so well lately and tonight is the first time he has appeared in the great hall for a sennight. Also, you will have none of his attention with his new bride at his side.'

When they had taken their seats, Bess looked up

for her first sight of the young girl who had so enchanted Henry that he had divorced a royal princess before she was even properly his wife.

Bess had met Anne of Cleves briefly before she left court and had thought her both gracious and sweet. She had also surveyed the famous Holbein miniature of the lady which had brought Henry to the point of marriage, and she had thought it, although flattering, not entirely lacking in honesty. The artist had portrayed the kindness of his subject with great faithfulness. But perhaps, Bess thought, Henry did not wish for kindness in his life, but instead preferred the heady drug of youth. Howsoever, my lady of Cleves was now discarded, called a sister to the king, and would shortly occupy this very palace as her own establishment. Her supplanter sat next to her ageing husband this soft autumn night and Bess saw that she had all the Howard beauty, although none of her cousin Anne's striking attraction, her main attribute being her shining youth.

For some reason Madrilene came into Bess's mind, and she glanced around the hall to see where the girl was sitting. Her bedchamber companions were present, laughing and chattering, but the black-haired Spanish girl was not there. She said idly, 'Thomas — do you know the Lady Madrilene? She is to be my room-mate for a while.'

'Lady Madrilene de Santos? Yes, I know her — who does not?'

'Why do you say that?'

'She came here but six months ago, but has already — as the saying goes — taken the court by storm.'

Bess moved her food around her plate; it was rich and spicy, but already fat congealed on the meat, and the accompaniments were half cold. One of her improvements at Maiden Court had been to extend the kitchen area into an ante-chamber adjoining her hall; each meal served was consequently piping hot. She said thoughtfully, 'She is very lovely.'

'Oh, yes, that, but also the richest heiress England has ever welcomed to her shores. Her parents are both dead, no other relative survives the family and the girl is the inheritor of a fabulous amount of gold and vast lands in Spain and France. Henry is her guardian here and every gentleman within a hundred miles an ardent suitor for her hand.'

'Are you one of those suitors?'

Thomas laughed. 'No, indeed, for my affections are engaged elsewhere. . . Besides, despite Henry's negotiations the girl has a mind of her own — I suspect she will choose her own mate.'

Bess pushed away her plate; an eager page removed it, another refilled her wine goblet. She drank a little and said, 'From the way she spoke it appeared she and Harry are good friends — she spoke of him in the most intimate way.'

Thomas raised his own goblet without speaking. He thought Bess Latimar the most attractive of women, and Latimar a lucky man. Also Bess was a lady one did not attempt to cozen. If she were to remain at court for any length of time, she would soon know what was common knowledge: that Madrilene de Santos had apparently fallen headlong in love with Lord Latimar, and was hunting him tooth and nail. He lowered the silver cup, at a loss to know what to say.

Bess glanced at the handsome profile of her supper companion. So, Lady Madrilene had a mind of her own and it was set on Harry... She could scarcely ask Tom if he thought the emotion was returned. A deadly depression seized her. She should never have come here, but stayed in her rightful place in her country manor.

'Bess — I have not yet congratulated you upon the birth of your twins,' Thomas said kindly. 'I wish I could have attended their christening — how clever you are to produce not one but two offspring. I am sure they are beautiful, if they resemble their mother at all.'

'Thank you,' Bess murmured. 'But both Anne and George are the image of their father.'

Thomas raised his eyebrows. 'Anne and George? I fancy it may have been more politic to name them for more current favourites.'

Bess did not answer. Through the wide doors of the hall she saw Harry and Madrilene enter. They both approached the dais to apologise for their late arrival and received an indulgent nod from the king. Harry scanned the diners and his dark blue eyes found Bess. He came swiftly towards her with the girl behind him. He bowed.

'Bess—I am so sorry I could not take you in to the meal.'

His gaze shifted to Thomas, who rose and said easily, 'I inadequately filled your shoes, Harry, and retire now, having spent a delightful hour in your wife's sweet company. Lady Madrilene, earlier you expressed a wish to see the players set up their theatre—let us go there now.' He took the girl firmly by the arm and led her away. Harry sat down.

'Why do you show that man favour?' he demanded, helping himself to the cold food.

"Twas entirely the other way around,' Bess returned. 'I was missing an escort, and he kindly filled the role.'

'I am sure he did,' Harry said, cutting his meat with deft and angry despatch.

'Oh, I beg your pardon, I thought you were in the wrong for not considering it important to show your wife the courtesy of attending her at the first meal she has taken at court for more than a year. But apparently I am at fault for allowing myself to be rescued by a kind friend.'

'He is neither a friend, nor kind,' Harry said. 'If you had but waited in one of the ante-chambers I would have come for you.'

'I do not like to wait! Especially when I know my husband finds the gaming tables more of a draw than myself.'

Harry laid down his knife. 'Bess—are we arguing? After being separated for long months?'

'I believe we are. I notice you could find the time

to entertain the Lady Madrilene and escort her into the great hall.'

'She came to me while I was finishing my game,' Harry said sulkily. 'I could hardly refuse to bring her down with me.'

'No, indeed, when I hear she is such a close friend of yours.'

The king had now finished his meal and rose with difficulty to take his queen to the dancing. Harry stood up and gripped Bess's arm. 'Do you wish to dance now?' he asked abruptly.

'Why not? Although I am sure I shall not know the latest steps, any more than I know the latest fashions. Are you not afraid I shall shame you before your new friends, Harry?'

Sighing inwardly, Harry led her from the hall and up the stairs. Who could have told her so soon about Madrilene? Tom Seymour, he supposed. Why couldn't people mind their own damned business, and why couldn't Bess use her common sense when confronted with such gossip?

As they turned the square landing she said, 'I thought we were to dance.'

'We will dance, but later,' he said, propelling her along the broad stone passageway. He opened a door in the west turret.

The room was octagonal and richly appointed. Through the square windows could be glimpsed trees and beyond them the slow-moving river. Harry closed the door and turned the key in the lock. It was dark and Bess stumbled against a footstool.

'Wait while I light the room,' Harry said. She heard the strike of tinder then one candle bloomed, then another. She turned in the yellow light.

'What are we about, Harry?'

'What I have been dreaming of for a twelve-month,' he said, turning back the covers of one of the wide beds. 'Do you not know how much I have missed you, sweetheart? While you were carrying and caring for my children?' He lifted one of the silver candlesticks and carried it to the table by the bed. It shed its light on the satin sheets.

'This is your room?'

'It is,' he agreed, coming to her and raising a hand to release her hair. It fell about her shoulders, shining silver in the flickering light. 'Shared with three others—but they are dancing at present. Up here—alone—we shall make our own music.'

'Harry—'

'What?' He took her face in both his hands. 'You don't want me?'

She raised her lips to his. 'I always want you, Harry. You know that.'

An hour later she turned to face him. 'I can truly believe it is as you said—that you have missed me.'

He drew up the coverlet to protect them against the night chill now stealing into the room. 'Can you doubt it? Why? There is no one but you, Bess, and has not been since I surrendered to you on the Devon seashore. Is it five—six years ago?'

'Almost six... But times change, I know that. Life moves on.'

'Not mine — at least it does not move away from you. You are my touchstone, Bess, my light in the dark night — I would be lost without you.'

They lay in silence for a while, and the unwelcome thought crept into her mind that Harry always solved the disputes between them in this way — and she let him.

'Tell me about my babes. They are well, you said?'

'More than well — flourishing, growing each day into more beauty.'

He sighed. 'I find I miss them. I could wish I were able to spend more time watching their progress.'

'Can it not be arranged?'

'I fear not. I am appointed a gentleman of the privy chamber now. Henry is a sick man in spite of his attempts to prove otherwise to his new bride, and demands that his friends be in evidence at all times.'

Bess raised herself on one elbow; she was a distracting sight with her slender pale limbs agleam in the candlelight, but Harry fixed his eyes on the moulded ceiling and went on, 'Those ulcers on his legs — they are not healing. There is little relief from the surgeons for the pain they cause him. It is a special agony for those who knew him when he was young, for me — who love him — to witness his decline.'

'We all must grow old,' Bess said gently. 'And he is a half-century already.'

He turned his dark blue eyes on her. 'Is that supposed to be of comfort to me? Bess — he is the nearest to a father I have ever known. When he is gone I shall be more bereft than his real son.'

She took him in her arms. 'Why think of that now? Henry is newly married; he is happy in spite of his infirmities. And we have our own lives after all, Harry.'

He turned his head against her breast. What she said was reasonable and true. He had a life now to live away from court, he had responsibilities outside his allegiance to Henry. Not for the first time Harry thought with regret of his careless youth, when friends had been congenial and amusing, but not necessary to him, when women had been fascinating and desirable — at least for a short time — but not essential to his happiness. He moved uneasily in Bess's soft arms. All this dependence on others was bewildering and sometimes painful. So it had been when his greatest friend had died. For a time after George Boleyn had been shorn of his handsome head, Harry had found himself in a dark and unfamiliar place, his actions unpredictable, his thoughts difficult to live with.

Bess had rescued him from this frightening land, but had he not then simply exchanged one dependency for another? And now two more insistent strands attached him to his son and daughter. Other men did not appear to feel as he did, did not hold their babes in their arms and find their breath shortened from the pure love induced. At least, if they did, they showed no sign of it. The trouble is I am not *used* to loving and being loved, Harry thought. His mother had died when he was a baby, his father when he was eight, he had no brothers or sisters to care for him in that special way a family did. . . .

'Are you sleeping?' Bess asked.

Harry sat up. 'At this hour? No, indeed, the night is just begun and I have not yet danced with the prettiest lady in the assembly.'

'Who might that be?' Bess rose too and began to dress. She struggled to lace her stays.

'Let me do that.' Harry pulled the strings and Bess gasped.

'Careful, dearest, I am no longer the sylph you married.'

'Nonsense, you are skin and bone.'

'Are you complaining? I was ugly for so long.'

'You were never ugly! Just beautiful in a different way,' Harry insisted.

Sparring in this very married way, they came down to find the play in progress. One of the things Bess had missed during her spell at Maiden Court had been these performances. One of those she had been pleased to do without was the cockfighting which came later.

As Harry could not resist any opportunity to gamble, she sat bravely through the first bout, then retired, averting her eyes from the blood-soaked sand, and found a seat at the back of the chamber where others were dancing. She signalled for a steadying glass of wine and sipped it, watching the complicated weaving movement of the dancers.

Presently the seat beside her was taken by a slim man in black. He gave her an appraising look, then said, 'Forgive me for speaking without introduction—but you are the Lady Bess Latimar, are you not?'

'I am, but I don't think. . .'

'No, we have never met. I am William Christowe and Harry is an old friend of mine.' The man stood and bowed.

'In that case I am happy to know you, sir,' Bess said with her warm smile. 'I have not heard your name, I think.'

'I have been absent some years in the French court.'

'Indeed? On the king's business, or your own?'

'Both. My mother's family is French. I am on cordial terms with King Francis—he has been prepared to overlook my English heritage, and 'tis useful for Henry to have a foot in his rival's camp, so to speak.' In fact, the treaty of peace and friendship between King Francis and Emperor Charles—the two rulers of France—signed so recently, was now hardly worth the paper it was written on, and Will had come home to tell of this.

'Is your home to be in England now?' Bess accepted more wine.

He gave her a considering look. 'My home? At

this moment I have no home other than my share of a rather damp bed in the east wing of this palace.'

She was taken aback by his tone, which was a mixture of humour and bitterness. There was a brief pause, then he said, 'You really do not know who I am, do you?' When she only looked puzzled, he laughed. 'Well, why should you? However, a decade ago I would have introduced myself as William Christowe of Maiden Court. Are you wiser now?'

'I am not. Maiden Court was once yours?'

'Harry won Maiden Court from me in a card game eight years ago,' he said bluntly.

'Harry won Maiden Court from you in a card game. . .' Bess repeated slowly. 'But he said 'twas a gift. . .'

'I suppose that is one way of putting it — certainly I gave it away that night, along with the lands and gold inherited from my dead father.' Bess made a swift gesture and some of her wine spilled on to her lap. She dabbed absently at the red stain with her handkerchief.

William took the linen and she looked up. He said quickly, 'Ah, please do not look like that, Lady Bess. I am sorry, that was rather brutal of me. . . 'Twas all quite fair, I assure you. I was young and foolish. . . I wish now I had never mentioned the matter at all. In fact when we sat down to play, I remember Harry warned me I was playing out of my league — it could equally well have been one of the other gentlemen indulging that evening who took what I so carelessly laid upon the table ——'

'But it was not, was it? It was Harry who took your home. And kept it.'

'If one gave back what one was lucky enough to win, there would be little point in playing at all,' William said gravely. He looked at her in consternation. She had been pointed out to him as Latimar's wife and he had come casually to introduce himself. Now he found he had apparently deeply upset her. And she was so lovely...

'Even so...' Bess looked down at her soiled white gown. The mark would not be removed easily; the dress was spoiled. She said, 'I love Maiden Court, I have from the start. We have been so happy there.'

'I am glad,' he said swiftly. 'You know, for some years after I lost it it seemed Harry intended no care for it. I would ride over sometimes and see how the land was lying barren, the house becoming derelict, and my heart would be sore indeed. I went to France just after this time and there received a letter from a friend informing me that Latimar was wed and now living at the manor. Soon came the news that Maiden Court had been reclaimed from its limbo and was beautiful again. Also that its new mistress showed an intense interest in its welfare... I was very happy that day, for 'twas a Norman ancestor of mine who laid the foundations for the house, and wrested its fields and pastures from the forest.' He broke off as Harry came up to them. His eyes travelled over Bess; knowing her so well he could tell instantly that something had distressed her. Will rose.

'Harry—I am glad to see you, my friend.' He extended his hand.

'Christowe—I did not know you were back in England.' Harry hesitated before gripping the offered hand.

'I arrived only an hour ago and now must seek my bed, being scarcely able to keep my eyes open.' He bowed to Bess. 'Goodnight, my lady, and once again forgive me if I upset you.' He moved swiftly away.

'In what way did he upset you?' demanded Harry.

'You should have told me you won Maiden Court in a game of cards!' Bess said angrily.

'So that is what you were discussing so intimately—practically reclining in the man's lap.'

'Reclining...! Do not attempt to put me in the wrong, when we are discussing a misdeed of yours!'

'What misdeed? Some years ago I sat in on some mildly amusing entertainment—if we were to discuss everything I have gained in this manner over the years we would have time for little else! I sold much of the jewellery I had acquired to renovate Maiden Court: I have not observed you spilling tears over the owners of those baubles.'

'It is obviously different! 'Twas his family home... Can you not imagine what it was like for him to lose it?'

'I am afraid I can't. I had neither family nor home at the age he sat down with me—I prefer to think, however, that if I had been so fortunate, I would have possessed the sense not to toss the deeds of such on to a gaming table!'

'He was but a boy then; he can be little more than five and twenty now!'

'He was eighteen and full grown — I do not strip children of their goods now, and did not then. I wonder if your emotions would have been quite so engaged had he not been such a personable young man——'

'Harry! That is beneath you!'

'Nothing concerning you is beneath me, Bess. It is of the minutest interest to me, and I did not like the way he looked at you, nor the way you looked at him.'

'I looked at him in no special way — other than in sympathy. You are determined to put me in the wrong to divert me from taking you to task for such a shabby act!'

They had both raised their voices in this heated exchange, others looked now in curiosity and amusement. Bess, flushed already, turned a deeper colour, suddenly remembering where she was. She said breathlessly, 'I have spilled wine on my dress, Harry, I think I should change it.'

'I think you should,' Harry said more quietly. He too was abruptly aware of their surroundings. Only Bess could have brought him to behave so in a public place, he thought bitterly.

'Will you take me to my chamber?' she asked, filled with embarrassment. What had she been saying to him? And with half the assembly looking on! No wonder he looked so cold, and spoke so distantly. She laid a hand on his arm. 'Please.'

He removed her hand. 'I must forgo that pleasure as the king awaits me in the gaming room.' He looked over his shoulder and, seeing his squire hovering, beckoned to him. 'Richard, please take Lady Bess to her chamber.'

Richard de Vere had only recently been appointed Latimar's squire and did not know Bess. He had been shocked to hear her sharp words to the master he already adored, but the lady now looked so distressed. . . He bowed and offered her his arm. Bess took it and straightened her back as she walked away. Harry looked after her with narrowed eyes.

'Harry?' Madrilene was at his elbow. 'My bird tries next — I am come to advise you to put your purse on him.' She too had been an interested spectator of the sight of the Latimars conducting a private argument in full view, and felt that Harry had carried the honours and done exactly the right thing in sending his wife from the room. She gave him a brilliant smile which he did not see, so intent was his gaze on Bess's retreating back.

They had had their share of disagreements in the past — theirs was a passionate liaison and storms were inevitable — but Bess had never, *never*, used quite that combative tone to him before, had never criticised his actions in that way. How much was the obvious impression young Christowe had made on her responsible for her outburst? She had never before given him cause for jealousy in their marriage either, but now he felt its cold fire attack him. Felt it and bitterly resented it.

'Harry! Did you hear what I said?' He turned to Madrilene.

'Yes, I heard. Your bird tries next and you advise me to lay my purse on his victory.' He followed her back to the cockpit, where her bird was being fitted with its wicked spurs. Harry looked it over — it was a likely contestant and he fingered the gold in his purse, considering his bet.

But concentration — that vital tool of the gambler — eluded him tonight. The pit, full of yellow sand, the circle of sweating faces and the colour and movement dissolved. He could see only Bess's face, troubled and distressed, eyes shining with tears as she upbraided him for a careless manoeuvre made before he had even met her.

He could scarcely remember the event after all this time, but recalled it had been a deep game, its participants more than a little tipsy after a long night. He could remember Will Christowe — boyishly proud to be included in the most élite group of wealthy gamblers. He had recently come into his inheritance, in fact he had been wearing mourning black that night. But surely — Harry frowned in the effort of remembering — he had remonstrated with the boy at some point over his recklessness. Yes, he knew definitely he had. Even so, as the dawn had crept into the stale room, the deeds to Maiden Court had lain before him, Christowe's gold distributed in equal measure before the others. . .

Harry had put away those deeds in his jewel box and a few years later had been glad enough to take them out. He had a young bride and needed a home for her. The day he had brought Bess to Maiden Court, she had been in raptures, had fallen in love with the place, and he had not wanted to tell her how he had come by it. Now that particular chicken had come home to roost and caused dissension between them. Apart from the old sin, if sin it was — and he did not entirely agree with Bess about that — there was another aspect to the affair. Will Christowe had been a handsome boy, an interesting and attractive boy. Actually, he supposed Will had considered them friends — as much as could be in view of their different positions at court. Indeed it had been Harry who had suggested to the king that he send Will off on his diplomatic mission in the French court. Tonight Harry, who noticed such things, had seen that Will had grown into a handsome man. No woman could fail to be aware of such male beauty and Bess had looked at him... Harry shifted his stance. It was unthinkable that his Bess could find any other man appealing — she belonged to him! But she had looked at him...

'Harry.' Madrilene touched his arm. 'The contest is about to begin. Shall you not make your bet?'

Harry stood up. 'I think not. The air in here is foul. I shall take a turn about the gardens to clear my head.'

Under the black sky, pricked with stars and hung with a pale yellow moon, Harry took a breath, then another. The path leading through the courtyard and out into the gardens was lined with yew fashioned into fantastic animals; lions and dragons were incongruously stationary against the blaze of flowers in the carefully tended beds. Harry heard light footsteps behind him and turned to find Madrilene.

'Did you not wait to see how your protégé performed?'

''Twas over in a few seconds.' Her black eyes glittered in the moonlight. She was wearing violet tonight, the smooth silk of the skirts of her gown parted to reveal a deeper purple beneath, the arms slashed to show the same rich colour. Above the modest neckline her face was a perfect creamy oval. 'He was named for a matchless prince and proved so tonight.'

'What is his name?' Harry wished she would take herself away and let him brood on his problems. He liked Madrilene well enough — what man would not enjoy the company of such beauty? — but lately she had made her preference for him so obvious that he was beginning to feel. . .hunted.

'Ferdinand! Is that not amusing?'

'I doubt if it would amuse his namesake who was, by all accounts, the most stiff-necked of Spanish grandees,' Harry said idly. He sat down on one of the moss-strewn walls. 'You should not be out here alone with me,' he remarked. 'Tongues will wag.'

She took a seat beside him. 'I care nought for that. In fact, I care for nothing but you, Harry. You know that, do you not?'

They had been on the brink of this conversation for some weeks now. Harry, his mind still on his wife, thought it as good a time as any to have it. He said gently, 'Madrilene—you are very young, and you are in a strange country. You have shown me friendship and I return the compliment in advising you of this: I am married. Not married in such a way as some of the gentlemen you see around you in this place. But married in the heart of me. In simple terms, I love my wife and see no other woman.'

Madrilene considered this. She was very intelligent, and perceptive as well. She said, 'But you were not pleased with her tonight.'

Harry crossed one leg over the other; a shaft of moonlight struck fire in the diamond set into the buckle of his silk shoe. 'No, indeed. I am frequently displeased with her, and she with me. That is the way with lovers.'

'And she railed at you for some imagined fault. I find this hard to understand: in Spain what a man does is his own concern—his wife supports him howsoever he acts.'

'Does she indeed? That must be pleasant. . . Here in England a man grants his wife a status above the rank of servant. Or at least I do.' His words were repressive but Madrilene was not deterred.

'Naturally you would defend her. You are a gentleman.'

Harry raised his eyebrows. 'I am not defending her, nor would do so to any man—or woman. But your attentions—flattering though they might be—are not welcome to me, lady. Am I plain enough for you now?'

Madrilene crinkled her smooth brow. 'Plain? That is to be unhandsome? No, you are not plain, but the reverse.' Harry's proximity and the seductive moonlight combined to make her quite mad. 'I love you, Harry. From the moment I saw you, I loved you, and——'

Harry stood up. 'You must not say such things to me,' he said quietly. 'Come, let me take you back to the hall where you must find another gallant for your inclinations.'

She looked up at him. 'You pretend that I mean nothing to you, but I cannot believe it is so. I tell you, Harry, we were made for each other and in time you will see that.'

'I can only repeat that I am not available,' Harry said, exasperated. 'Come.' He took her hand to help her to rise. She remained seated, then suddenly stood up, the impetus of his pulling hand causing her to fall against him. She slipped an arm around his neck and kissed him.

He neither responded nor resisted her, but stood impassive in her embrace. He registered that her advances, although fervent, were very inexperienced and thought, Poor child, I should deal with this gently.

It was unfortunate that his thoughts were not communicated to Bess, coming suddenly along the path to witness what appeared to be a passionate encounter between her husband and the beautiful Spanish girl.

Bess had been up in her room for half an hour

battling with her conscience. She had been horrified by what Will Christowe had told her, sympathetic to his wry acceptance of the matter, and eager to put her point of view to Harry. His casual dismissal of the whole affair had infuriated her and there had followed the acrimonious exchange in the dancing chamber. He had banished her to her room, and she accepted that she should go there, for she had broken the golden rule. She had opposed her man before his peers and must therefore be ashamed and punished.

In the quiet bedchamber she had reviewed the situation and found her strongest emtoion was one of regret. She cared nothing really for William; she cared little for Harry's past exploits. What she cared about was that Harry couldn't see how he had damaged Will's life, and she didn't want to think less of Harry. However, she was not at odds with him and anxious to rectify the situation at once. Harry, she reasoned, must feel the same. Skimming down the staircase, she paused at the entrance to the great hall. It was still crowded. She touched the shoulder of a sleepy page.

'Have you seen my lord Latimar, child?'

The boy thought, then said, 'I have, my lady. A quarter-hour since he went out into the gardens.'

Into the gardens, thought Bess. Poor Harry, out in the dark to escape from his shrewish wife. Disconsolate — as she was — following the discord between them.

But Harry was not disconsolate, she saw, as she rounded one of the palely lit paths. Instead he was consoled, and by the young lady to whom Bess had taken such an instant dislike. Bess stood on the damp ground and felt the chill rise up through her body until it reached her heart.

She turned abruptly away and ran back through the dusk to the palace. Inside the doors she paused. Why had she run away? She should have marched on them and demanded an explanation. But what explanation could there be for those entwined bodies, other than the obvious: that Harry was unfaithful to her? Her only half acknowledged suspicions were apparently true. She was outraged, she was angry, but more than either of those she was regretful for something precious spoiled.

She had been entirely innocent when they married, Harry the reverse, but between them they had achieved a physical joy in each other almost tangible in its strength. Now she felt as if, possessing a gift cherished and admired by both giver and recipient, that gift had now been broken by the careless handling of one of its owners. Harry was entirely responsible for that conclusion; she had watched him turn away enough women over the years to know that what she had just seen would not have been possible without his consent, however determined the woman. Bess went slowly back to her room and undressed and got into the cold bed. She had no wish to be up and around when Madrilene finally sought her bed, but had no confidence she would sleep at all that night. Surprisingly, within a few minutes, she drifted into a deep sleep.

CHAPTER THREE

WHEN she awoke the next day, for a moment she remembered nothing of her dilemma. She turned on her side and watched the sun slanting through the windows and along her bare arm. Her skin, with her hair the most noticeable feature of her beauty, gleamed in the brilliant light. She lay on her back, listening to the regulated snores of the girls beside her, and memory came hastening back. She sat up and surveyed the sleeping women. Madrilene was not among them and Bess got quietly out of bed, a bitter cold invading her in spite of the warmth of the room. She dressed quickly and opened the door.

The passageways were silent and she guessed it was but a few hours after dawn. She felt she must have air, and trod softly down the stairs and out into the grounds.

She had always loved Richmond Palace, so rural and surrounded by breathtakingly beautiful countryside. Many of the rare plants and shrubs in her own garden had been grown from cuttings from here, and now she thought she would seek out the head gardener and tell him of their progress. They were old friends and Jonathon Pearce was wreathed in smiles when she approached him. They spent an enjoyable hour discussing the intricacies of horticulature before Bess turned reluctantly back into the palace to break her fast.

Harry was already in the hall when she entered; he rose immediately and came to her side.

'Bess? I came to your rooms and was told you had disappeared. Where have you been?'

Without looking at him she said, 'In the gardens. Old Jonathon was showing me some of his latest successes.'

He smiled. 'You are like a flower yourself this morning, darling. I trust you slept well.'

Now she raised her eyes to his face. How strange, she thought, that betrayal was not written clear upon another's face as was so when one brushed against any other thing which was dirty.

'I am hungry now,' she said shortly. 'Have you eaten?'

'Of course not. Naturally, I was waiting for you.' He stared at her, trying to assess her mood. 'Is aught amiss?'

'Why should there be? A pleasant walk in the gardens would disturb no one, surely. Unless, of course, one took it at midnight yester evening.'

Some sixth sense warned him immediately of what she was referring to. He said gently, 'Come — let us find a place.'

He ignored the greetings from his friends and found them a corner of one of the tables by the fire — which was lit and fiercely burning in spite of the heat of the day. Bess looked at the licking flames.

'Really—'tis a waste of fuel to have such a blaze on a mild day, and I am hot enough already.'

'So I see. But others feel the same and have avoided the hearth, so we may have a little private conversation.'

Bess sat down and arranged her skirts. 'What would you wish to speak of privately?'

'I think you know.' Harry signalled for ale and waited while their mugs were filled. He drank from his, then said, 'You obviously saw the embarrassing situation I found myself in last night.'

'I saw no embarrassment,' Bess said, trying her own ale. She thought it not as good as that which she brewed herself at Maiden Court. 'I saw, on the contrary, the shameful sight of a husband straying.' She put down the cup with a clatter.

Harry sighed. 'Now, Bess,' he said soothingly, ''twas not as it appeared. Had you granted me the knowledge of your presence, I would have explained there and then.'

'What would you have said, I wonder? Someone—I forget who—once said that a picture was worth a thousand words, and so it was for me.'

Harry refilled his mug. 'What exactly did you see?'

'I saw you and the Lady Madrilene just one step away from satisfying your passion for each other,' she said baldly.

Harry turned the diamond in his earlobe. 'You saw no such thing, sweetheart. What you saw was a silly child attempting to play grown-up games.'

'Who was cast in the role of the child, I wonder? You, or she?'

Harry restrained his temper with difficulty. 'If you wish me to explain what happened,' he said softly, 'I will do so. But I will not be spoken to in that manner.'

A platter of beef had been placed before Bess; she looked at it without enthusiasm and drank more of her ale. Harry took her mug from her.

'Such bitter stuff lies badly on an empty belly, and will make you more out of sorts, love. But perhaps you have been in that state for some time, even before you came upon Madrilene and myself in the gardens. Perhaps you have been seeking an argument with me to cover the guilt you feel after your passage with Will Christowe last night.'

'Passage! What passage? I was engaged in simple conversation with him — as I might be with any gentleman. You were not in similar case with the Spanish woman!'

'I was trying to convince her that I was not in the market for her advances,' Harry said patiently.

'With a kiss? I do not suppose that convinced her — it would certainly not convince me!'

'I hope not, Bess. For the kisses I give to you are of an entirely different nature — but maybe you have forgotten what passed between *us* last night? Or perhaps it meant little to you?'

She looked at him, stricken. 'Meant nothing to me? How can you say that, when you must know differently?'

'How can I know differently, when you attack me in this way? Were this conversation repeated to any other man here, he must laugh at it. Your unsophistication is charming, Bess—I have always found it so, but in this situation it is ridiculous.' The cold words, delivered in casual tone, were the greatest insult to her. All during their association she had felt herself to some extent inferior to him. Her beginnings were humble, she knew that. Her father, certainly, had been a knight and a friend of royalty, but her mother had been from yeoman stock, and her home a poor farm. Harry's parents had been from the class which had ruled in England since Saxon times. How cruel of him to raise that issue now. . .

Tears pricked her eyelids. She could never win an exchange of this nature with Harry. He had turned around her grievance to make it appear trivial and gauche, for what he said was only the truth: the closely confined courtiers exchanged kisses often. What had happened between him and Madrilene was different, she knew, but could not find the words to convey that knowledge. Nimble-tongued with any other, she could never best Harry when he wished to confound her. A ridiculous game, she thought, when what was at stake was so important to them both.

Harry moved uneasily on the bench. He disliked seeing any woman cry, but when it was Bess. . . He had no defence against her tears. He took her hand

and pressed it. 'Bess——' He was interrupted by a man coming to them; it was Will Christowe.

'May I join you, Harry, Lady Bess?' He smiled.

Before Harry could tell him to take his smiles and himself elsewhere, Richard de Vere came to his side.

'Sir, excuse me — the king is asking for you.'

Harry kept hold of Bess's hand. 'Come with me, Bess. Henry would like to see you.'

Richard cleared his throat. He said tentatively, 'His Grace is not so well today, sir. I think perhaps. . .'

Harry rose. 'Very well. Bess — I must leave you briefly. I will be back as soon as I am able.'

Will took his place and drew the meat platter towards him. 'Don't worry, Harry,' he said cheerfully. 'I will look after her as if she were my own.'

Harry hesitated. Richard said, 'The king is in much pain, sir——'

'I am coming,' Harry said irritably. He turned with his swift light stride and left Bess staring after him. Will cleared his plate, showing astonishingly white teeth as he consumed the good food.

'You have eaten?' he asked Bess.

'I am not hungry.'

'You are not unwell, I hope?' He had very clear grey eyes, and a forthright gaze.

'No, not at all.'

'Then you must eat — here, I will help you to some of this excellent beef.' He did so. 'I imagine Harry was very much annoyed with me for speaking of. . .

of the past last night. I am surprised he has not taken me to task for such ungallant behaviour.'

'On the contrary—*I* took *him* to task,' Bess said drily.

Will looked dismayed. 'Oh, surely not! I am very fond of Harry—I would not for the world be the cause of argument between you.'

'Why are you fond of him?'

'Why?' Will frowned. 'Why not? I can recall a hundred kindnesses Latimar has done me over the years.'

'I have only heard of one act—not kind at all.'

Will looked around for the jug of ale. When it was passed up the long table he poured for himself and refilled her mug. He said quietly, 'Lady Bess, I think I explained how it was—that affair? You will make me feel sad indeed if you hold any of this against Harry. After all,' he laughed wryly, 'the first advice a young man receives on coming to this court is not to take Latimar on in any pursuit involving a game of chance.'

The ale was working in Bess now; she said caustically, 'What a fine claim to greatness! Holbein for his brilliance with brush and oil, Cecil for his statesmanship, and Latimar for his ability to lay cards in a certain order to achieve financial stability!'

Will was silent. He had not examined his motives for raising the subject of Maiden Court with its mistress. Now he found he was unsure of what those motives might be. He had not lied when he said he was fond of Harry, but neither could he deny that what had happened eight years ago had always rankled with him.

Added to this confusion of facts was the strong attraction he felt to Bess Latimar. An attraction he had felt when he had looked across the crowded dancing chamber and seen her for the first time. That instant quickening of the senses had been reinforced by his brief conversation with her. She was beautiful, yes, in a very unusual way—all that silver-gilt hair, that perfect cameo-pure face and startling blue eyes, the mature but oddly virginal body beneath her outdated gown. But her personality, too, was intriguing. Will had grown up with the spoiled and highly bred girls of the Tudor court who had little more on their minds than their clothes or their love affairs and paid only lip service to another's feelings. Last night Will had felt Bess's genuine concern for him and it had fired his interest even more than her looks.

Even so, she was Latimar's wife, a new mother, and any deep interest on his part must be resisted. Will looked around the hall for inspiration. Henry was confined to his bed that morning, but his queen was present. Catherine was seated on the royal dais, surrounded by the dignitaries of her husband's government, but she leaned forward, her bright hair hanging over her shoulders, to speak with her secretary, Francis Dereham. Will had been at Richmond Palace but a few hours before gossip told him of the relationship between Dereham and the queen of England. . .

Bess did not notice his preoccupation. She was feeling guilty again. Never in the past had she criticised Harry in any way—to his friends or acquaintances. But last night she had reviled him in public, this morning she did so to Will Christowe. . . She was ashamed. But nagging at her constantly was the mental image of Harry and the Lady Madrilene as they had been under the moon last night. She started when Will spoke.

'I beg your pardon, I did not hear you.'

'I was asking,' Will said, 'if you liked to ride, Lady Bess. In France I was too much confined to the stuffy court gatherings. I have a desire to feel English wind in my hair once more. When Harry returns, I shall ask him if I may take you for a brief ride out into the countryside.'

'Why wait for Harry's return?' Bess asked coolly. 'If the king is indisposed I imagine he will wish my husband's company for the remainder of the morning. I doubt we shall see Harry again until the midday meal, and I should like to ride with you.'

Changed and ready, Bess waited in the stables for her escort. As Will came over the cobbled ground with a groom leading two horses, she had the irrelevant thought that anyone observing them might well take them for brother and sister. Will had the same ash-blond hair and delicately modelled facial structure as she possessed herself. Their bodies, too, were similar: slender, but giving the impression of strength. Only their eyes were different—his a light grey and wary, hers a striking blue and expressive of her innermost feelings. Will helped her into her saddle, leaped on to his own mount and they set off.

September was hot that year; already the fields were hastening towards harvest and the skies above stretched endlessly blue and empty of cloud. Along the western horizon, however, a concentration of purple clouds held the promise of rain before nightfall.

'Do you know what I would love to do now?' Will asked as they slowed their horses after an hour.

'What?' The breeze lifted Bess's loose hair from her shoulders and put colour into her cheeks.

'Visit Maiden Court,' he said, drawing up and allowing his horse to crop the grass beneath his hooves.

'Maiden Court? But, Will, 'tis an hour's ride away.'

'Not if we leave the road and go across country,' Will said persuasively. 'Come, Lady Bess, would you not enjoy a brief reunion with your babes? And we would be back at Richmond before the midday meal was over.'

'Well. . .' Bess looked into his eager face. A reunion with her babes? Yes, she would like that, but. . . 'Will it not upset you to go there?' she asked, her voice gentle.

'I don't believe it would. I would like to see the old place cared for and lived in by your family. What do you say?'

'What can I say?' she asked, smiling. 'Except — all speed for Maiden Court, sir.'

Joan was in the nursery when she heard hoofbeats below in the courtyard. Carrying George on her shoulder, she peered out of the window in time to see Bess lifted down from her horse by a tall fair man. She replaced the little boy in his crib and, ignoring his loud protests, hurried down to greet her daughter. The two women embraced fondly.

'May I introduce William Christowe, Mother?' Bess said. 'Will — my mother, the Lady Joan de Cheyne.'

Will bowed. 'I am honoured, my lady.'

Joan surveyed him with interested eyes. 'Welcome to Maiden Court, sir,' she said shyly. 'I will order refreshment immediately. It is such a hot day, is it not?'

'Indeed; for so late in the year we are most fortunate.' In one sweeping glance Will took in the familiar walls of the hall, the broad glossy boards of the floor, the view of his grandmother's rose garden through the windows. He lifted his grey eyes to the lofty ceiling. Why — there was the dent he had made with a pig's bladder while playing with his brother one wet afternoon! He had been proud to have kicked the ball up so high, but his father had beaten him soundly for the injury to the decoration. . . Now the earl was long in his grave, his older son, too, dead of plague. . . Bess laid a hand on his arm.

'Let us sit down, Will,' she said gently, concerned

by the expression on his face. 'My mother's blackcurrant cordial is the best I have ever tasted. It will be cool from the well and we shall enjoy it on this warm day. Mother—what is that disturbance above?'

''Tis your son, my dear. Much annoyed to be interrupted during a cuddle with his grandmother.'

'Bring him down,' Bess said. 'Also Anne—I want to show them off to our visitor.'

Will admired both babies when they were brought for his inspection, although he thought it a shame neither resembled their lovely mother. He drank and complimented Joan on her cordial, then Bess suggested a tour of the estate.

'You should not have come,' she said as they dismounted later in the stable-yard. Will had been courteous about all he saw, but her heart was wrung by the sadness he could not hide. 'I am sorry for you.'

'You really are, aren't you?' he said impulsively. 'But your sympathy is wasted. I was a fool and, like all fools, punished in the severest way.'

'I regret it very much that my joy in Maiden Court is built upon your unhappiness.'

'Ah, don't say that. It gives me the greatest comfort to know you love my old home.' There was a silence between them, broken by Will.

'Now I think we must return to Richmond. Are you rested enough?'

Bess sighed. 'Of course. I will just go in and bid farewell to my mother.'

As they rode away the first drops of rain began to fall. Will looked anxiously up into the sky. ''Twill be a heavy shower, I think.'

Bess raised the hood of her cloak. 'A little water will not harm us — let us ride on.'

Half a mile further the downpour became torrential and Will peered through the driving rain for a place of shelter. 'The church just ahead, Lady Bess.' He pointed with his crop.

They tethered the horses under a spreading oak tree outside the little church and hurried inside. It was a modest place, but even so had lost its one beauty — stained glass windows above the altar. The openings had not been reglazed and shards of ruby and violet glass still clung to the window frames. One of the things Bess regretted most about the loss of the old Catholic religion was the absence now of colour and grandeur in places of worship. There was nothing wrong, she felt, in having a little luxury in a dwelling dedicated to God. She said thoughtfully,

'Do you ever think of the old religion, William?'

'Sometimes — I love beauty, and the Protestant faith has little of that, either in its services or its churches.' He wondered if she caught the intonation in his voice as he said the first words, his eyes full on her face.

Bess had not noticed it, but some acute sense warned her that there was more in his manner than there should be for a gentleman in casual conversation with a lady. As one of the red deer which roamed the forest around Maiden Court might lift her pretty head and scent huntsmen at the fringe of the trees, so Bess was suddenly on her guard. She had been courted and pursued by many since her marriage, and their attention had meant nothing to her. Now, today, for some reason, she was not quite immune.

His eyes still roving over her face, Will said softly, 'You are not afraid to be here alone with me—Bess?'

'Of course not.'

He moved a little closer; the light coming in through the high windows was poor but enough to bring out the gleam in his fair hair. She walked to one of the pews and sat down, clasping her hands loosely on her lap, apparently at ease. He remained where he was and said, 'You might do well to be afraid. From our moment of meeting I have found you enchanting, now—after a few hours in your company—I am your slave. You know what I am saying?'

'I do. And must take half the blame that you should feel so. I have obviously given you reason for it.'

He laughed. 'Well said, Bess! No lady at court could have been more diplomatic.'

'Well, I am a lady of the court,' she said sharply.

'Indeed you are,' he returned. 'But you are not like them. You are. . .different.'

She fixed her eyes on the bare altar. Only a plain

white cloth covered the marble block on which stood a wooden cross. How Will's words took her back half a decade! So had Harry described her in the early days of their relationship. You are, he had said, different. . . That difference had attracted the jaded palate of sophisticated Latimar, as apparently now it attracted the slim young man beside her. She said, 'At risk of sounding again like one of those ladies of the court, I would say, Thank you for the compliment of your regard, but——'

'But. . .?'

'But I love my husband. Love him so greatly that I am in despair at this moment——' She stopped.

'Because of Madrilene de Santos?'

Bess rose and walked a little way down the aisle. The sky had lightened outside, the drumming of the rain on the roof was less heavy. 'I should not be having this conversation with you—with anyone.'

'If we can be nought else,' Will said gently, 'we can be friends, can we not? I knew Madrilene in France—in the court at Versailles. She is a strange girl: very passionate, very impulsive, but most of all spoiled. What Madrilene wants she can see no reason why she should not have.'

'You think she wants Harry?'

Her candour both surprised and delighted him. 'Gossip says that. But 'twill depend on him, would you not say?'

'I don't know what to say, what to think.' Speaking thus to Will, she realised that she was taking the matter of Madrilene seriously; it was a disturbing thought.

'You can say on our return to the palace that you want Harry to take you back to Maiden Court, back to your family and so remove him from the arena. Even Madrilene would not have the presumption to follow him there.'

'I could do that and maybe he would agree, but you know in the end, Will, people must do what their heart and will dictates. I was never one for keeping free things in cages.' She had not commented on his discarding the use of her title and addressing her in intimate terms, so he did not react to her doing the same. But he noted it and thought it an indication of how their relationship had progressed. He sighed, 'You are a nice girl, Bess, but perhaps being nice will not answer this case. Do you not have any other weapons?'

She turned to him. 'Only the love we have between us — Harry and I. 'Tis enough for me, but for him — I don't know.'

What she said brought him back to his senses. He said, 'Listen. . .'

'Yes? To what?'

'To nothing. The rain has stopped and I must take you back. Back to Richmond and to Harry.'

It was late afternoon when they returned. Bess climbed the stairs to her chamber and, finding it empty, began to strip off her wet clothes. She sent a maid running for hot water and when it arrived began to sponge her body. She did not turn when the door opened and closed again, thinking it the maid returning to help her dress.

'Where have you been?' Harry demanded from the doorway. She turned startled eyes on him.

'Why, Harry, I was caught in the rain and sheltered. I hope you were not concerned.'

'Of course I was concerned! I was told you had left the palace with Christowe, the hours elapsed and still you did not return. I repeat: where have you been?'

'We went to Maiden Court. I renewed my acquaintance with our children and my mother. Then on the way back we were caught in a thunderstorm and sheltered——'

'Where?'

A smile lit her face briefly. 'In a church—what could be more respectable?'

He did not smile in return. Was he angry? she wondered. But, no, why should he be? Mildly annoyed perhaps that she had not waited patiently for him to find the time to notice her. He said, 'You took him to our home? Why?'

'Why not? He wanted to see it again, and I. . .I was anxious to see my twins.'

'After a day's absence? I wonder why you left them in the first place.'

'I wonder why myself.' She gave him a challenging look which he returned with a shrug of his shoulders.

'And did he enjoy his tour of his old home?'

'I don't think he did. I think it made him sad, and

in consequence I was sad too.' She returned to her toilette. A watery sun had survived the storm and now entered the room, illuminating her gleaming skin, playing over her loose hair.

'Does he mean anything to you, Bess?' Harry asked quietly. 'Will Christowe?'

'Does the Lady Madrilene mean anything to you?' she countered.

'Do not answer a question with another — you are always saying that to me. Tell me — I need to know.'

She began to dry herself. Honesty was inherent in Bess; she had built the foundations of her marriage upon it. She looked directly at him. 'I like him,' she said simply, 'and feel in some strange way that I owe him something. Is that so wrong?'

'That depends on what it is you feel you owe. If you feel 'tis bricks and mortar, I would dispute it. If you had in mind some other commodity, then I would say our relationship — yours and mine — had reached some sort of crossroads.'

She looked at him carefully. She noticed he had not answered her question regarding Madrilene, but also that he was very serious. At some point in this quiet room they had become antagonists, each with territory to defend, each with deadly weapons. Of the two she thought his the heavier artillery, for her life would be meaningless if he were to turn away from her. With this in mind, she said in an attempt to defuse the situation, 'You were friendly with Will once; at least he speaks very kindly of you. You cannot surely object to a friend taking your wife for a ride.'

It was not what he had wanted her to reply. He had wanted her to laugh and assure him of her love. . . He turned the jewel in his left ear. It was not the first time they had had bitter words about another woman, but it was the first time he had felt like having them about another man, and he did not like it. He began to pace the room, an indication of his state of mind as he was usually indolently disposed, when not indulging in some active sport.

The ladies had changed recently for the supper hour. Madrilene had discarded her day gown; it was a vibrant splash of colour on the dark floor beside her bed. Harry looked at it thoughtfully. Bess began to climb into her gown. It was a rose-pink satin, very full in the skirts and sleeves, and trimmed in Flemish lace. It had always been one of Harry's favourites, but tonight he did not notice it; he was staring out of the window and Bess thought, There, he has already lost interest in our dispute.

'Are you ready to go down to the meal now?' he asked abruptly.

Bess looked in her trunk for her shoes. 'It is obvious I am not. I have not yet dressed my hair and have no idea where Mary is. I imagine she is finding the palace routine confusing.'

'I have told you before—you are too lenient with the servants. They are obliged to do your bidding; it is not your place to fall in with their arrangements.'

'Why, what do you mean by that? Our servants

MAIDEN COURT 81

are loyal and hardworking. If I am understanding, that is no more than their due.' Where were the little satin shoes which went with this dress?

'What is *my* due? I would expect to come first with you, whatever the confusion of others.'

She stared at him, outraged. 'Harry, don't be foolish. You know you are first with me—even before our children.'

'I have seen no evidence of that this day. Was I first while you were riding the countryside with your admirer, and entertaining him in our home as he viewed our children? Or after, when you were in some secluded place with a little rain as an excuse?'

Bess returned in silence to her search for the slippers she knew she had ordered packed. Really, she could have laughed out loud! It was allowed in his reasoning that he might romance a pretty girl in the moonlight with his wife not a few hundred yards away, but not for that wife to take an entirely innocent excursion. And his criticism of her way with their servants! She had always been proud to have received such loyalty from those who attended her—he was merely attempting to make her more conscious of the difference in their ranks. Harry had been raised not to consider those who served him needful of any attention.

Bess, usually so perceptive about others' needs, and in particular Harry's, failed on this occasion to see that he was watching her closely, was waiting for reassurance from her. She turned the contents of her trunk out on to the floor and sorted through the resultant tangle. 'You are apparently in the kind of mood which refuses to see reason—please go down without me, then I may dress in peace.'

'If that is what you wish,' he said politely, and then she was alone.

CHAPTER FOUR

EVEN feeling she was not looking her best, Bess received attentive glances when she entered the hall. Seeing Harry seated with the king, she made her way to a table in the centre of the hall and sat among the chattering courtiers. Whatever had ailed the king earlier, he was apparently recovered sufficiently now to enjoy his meal, and his booming laugh could be heard at intervals. Having missed her midday meal Bess was hungry and, intent on her food, did not notice Will Christowe join her on the long bench until he spoke. She looked up, and smiled a little hesitantly. What he had said to her in the church must be considered now whenever he was with her, also Harry's unreasonable reaction to their budding friendship.

Will kept the conversation in neutral channels. He was content to be near her, to be able to enjoy her beauty in a way he had never enjoyed any woman before. He had discovered that her personality was as intriguing as her dazzling looks, and had the sensation of finding a vague dream suddenly reality in each hour he spent with her. As a boy he had been idealistic, as a young man frequently disappointed that others did not live up to the ideal he created for them. His spell abroad had disillusioned him further—the French court was a breeding ground for the less attractive aspects of human nature, particularly female nature, and a certain cynicism had taken root in the young English knight. Beneath this still ran a strong romantic thread, and he knew now he had been looking, unconsciously, for someone like Bess Latimar for a long time.

What could come of this knowledge, he was not sure. He constantly reminded himself that she was a young wife and mother, obviously loyal and devoted to her husband. It was the fact that Harry Latimar was the husband which gave Will hope. When he had known Harry in the past there had been so many women; they had come and gone with amazing regularity, each new conquest apparently no more important than the last. Will had actually seen Harry dance at a number of the weddings of women who had previously been his paramours, unaffected that those women were now the property of other men. Will was almost able to convince himself that, should Bess become similarly disinfranchised, Latimar would raise no real objection....

He would have been considerably surprised, therefore, had he been able to read Harry's mind at that moment. Harry had seen Bess enter the hall, had seen Will Christowe join her. Only his duty to his king had prevented him from rising at once and contesting Will's right to be with Bess. That duty was not of an official or obligatory kind, but rather based on love. Henry had spent an agonising morning. The sores on his leg were painful, were dangerous to his well-being, but—more than that for a man with the kind of pride he possessed—they were disgusting to behold. In the last days they had healed over, but underneath the poison was still working and his physicians had that morning decided they must be drained. The process involved a cutting and drawing of the most primitive sort, and it was for this operation that Harry had been summoned from his breakfast with Bess.

Henry Tudor was a physically brave man but, growing older now, disliked having his suffering witnessed by any but his old and trusted friends. Harry, entering the stuffy and malodorous bedchamber, had wondered irritably why Henry always chose the gentlemen for his intimate service from his young and attractive courtiers. They had no history with their king, no fondness bred by close association over the years, and were therefore dutiful but largely unsympathetic. Accordingly, Harry had brusquely dismissed young Paston and Culpeper and attended Henry himself, holding the clutching hand, mopping the sweating brow with muttered encouragement and a little ribald humour. At last it was done and the king lay pale and exhausted on the pillows, but eager as always to see his young queen.

Harry, surreptitiously opening a window to let out some of the stink, had watched sceptically while Catherine wept large tears over her husband but could not prevent her eyes sliding to the windows where sunlight spilled into the thick rug, no doubt wondering how soon she might be rid of these conjugal duties and free to pursue her own interests. Harry never voiced such an opinion, but he had little time for Catherine Howard. During Henry's whirlwind courtship of Norfolk's latest protégé — the former being the disgraced Anne Boleyn — Latimar had troubled to enquire into her past a little, and been appalled by what he found.

She had been raised by the ancient Dowager Duchess of Norfolk, who, although autocratic, had not had the least idea how to deal with the bevy of nubile girls who had been thrust into her home by neglectful parents or relatives in order to keep them safe. Her method of ensuring this safety had been to lock them for long hours in their chamber — a room conveniently provided with a large window a mere two-foot jump from freedom. Catherine had, at a shockingly young age, been seduced by several unscrupulous young men and developed a taste for sexual promiscuity. Since her spectacular marriage she had shown scant respect for her new status: within a month of her coronation one of her lovers had been installed as her secretary and recently her sensual roving eye had alighted upon one of her husband's gentlemen, Thomas Culpeper. Their affair, which would have caused a scandal had the lady been the lowliest of England's maids, was for the queen of England a positively dangerous escapade.

Harry Latimar, still bitter that Catherine's cousin, Anne, had been extinguished for innocence of the crime the queen now blithely committed, watched and waited for the inevitable outcome. Sooner or later the scales would fall from Henry's infatuated eyes and another pretty Howard girl would take her last journey to the block on Tower Hill...

'Harry!' Now the king nudged him.

'I am sorry, sir,' Harry said, removing his eyes from his wife's face where they had been fixed for the last ten minutes. 'I fear I did not hear what you said.'

'I said, in a few days we repair to Hampton and I am planning to ride out. My stewards advise me there is wild boar to be hunted in the forest there, and I would join the party.'

'I think you should rest a little,' Harry said mildly.

'I am tired of resting!' Henry said with force. 'I am for some activity — can I count upon you to attend me?'

'You know the answer to that without enquiry,' Harry said. He saw that Bess had risen now and was leaving the hall on Will Christowe's arm.

Henry followed his eyes and said tetchily, 'I wonder if you realise, Latimar, that whenever your wife is about, your eyes seldom leave her?'

Harry smiled his charming smile. 'Is it so? Then I am guilty of the worst of crimes — that of a man in love with his wife.' He said the words lightly, but there was an edge to his voice which Henry heard and understood.

'Is aught amiss between you?' he asked quietly.

'Bess has discovered I won our home from that young man — and reacted badly to the knowledge.'

Henry smiled affectionately. 'Ah, yes, I can appreciate what you say. Bess was ever a champion for the underdog.'

'He is not the underdog!' Harry protested. ''Twas a fair and legal affair — Christowe lost Maiden Court in a card game. I picked up the deeds and now — now he comes back to England whining that I have relieved him of his family seat!'

'Whining,' repeated Henry thoughtfully. 'Not a word I would use in connection with that young man.'

Harry drained his cup of wine. 'Would you not? Last night he complained to Bess that I had taken from him his home; this morning he took her riding and returned to that home, viewed it, and came back to Richmond apparently distraught anew over the loss! Bess has a tender heart and was very moved by events.'

Henry savoured his own wine. It was unusual for Latimar to discuss his personal life, even with so old a friend as himself — Henry thought it a measure of the man's distress. It was also unusual for the experienced Harry not to be able to deal effortlessly with a female's attack on him. Still — Bess was Harry's weak spot — all men had them, Henry mused. His own had been a black-haired, brilliant-eyed woman who had kept him in thrall for a great many wasted years. . . He thrust that disquieting thought away hurriedly, and said bluntly, 'Do you wish me to get rid of young Christowe?'

'Order him shot from behind a hedge?' enquired Harry, with a wry smile.

'No, indeed,' Henry exclaimed. 'I am fond of the boy. You know he is my ward?'

'I didn't know that — the first, or the last.'

'His father was with me in France when I met Francis during the tournament of the Cloth of Gold.' Henry turned his silver goblet, remembering. 'Ralph Christowe was a supreme competitor — 'twas largely due to his efforts that we won that day. . . However, he fell in love with a French lady and stayed behind to marry her. I missed him greatly, and when he was dying and sent me a message asking me to interest myself in his son, I invited William to the English court. He has been extremely useful to me in many ways and I have a great affection for him. Actually, he has always put me in mind of another who fought that day — and won — Robert de Cheyne, who was your father-in-law.'

Harry raised his eyebrows. 'In my short acquaintance with Robert I never heard him complain about the cards fate had dealt him, and one might say that if any had cause for such complaint, he did.'

'No, that was not Robert's way. . . But one must allow for young Will's mixed heritage, see you. His mother was a great beauty, but emotional as is the French way. However, I was thinking more of Will's adaptability to circumstance. He was bred to be wealthy, but most of his inheritance was forfeit to his father's casual ways before his death, then Will mishandled what was left — but of course you know that. He has for some time been without funds but nevertheless kept his pride and fulfilled his obligations to me cheerfully and with great loyalty. In other words, he has adapted.'

Harry brushed an imaginary speck off his gleaming doublet. 'Is that a crack at me, Hal?'

'Why should it be?'

'You frequently rebuke me for continuing my irresponsible ways while growing the grey hairs of maturity.'

'Do I?' Henry looked thoughtfully at Harry's black head, which showed no silver at all. 'Perhaps I am jealous.'

Harry laughed. He said fondly, 'Why are we bickering? I can answer that: 'tis over that damned interloper. First he has caused me to fall out with Bess; now you and I are arguing on the same subject. Let us stop immediately.'

The two men talked of other things then, but Harry, acutely sensitive to anything those he cared for said, thought the king had been trying to make some point. Bess had made the same point often enough... But what did they expect from him? Harry asked himself resentfully. What he was, he freely admitted—a man who liked the easy path in life: good food, comfortable surroundings, fine clothes, spectacular jewellery, the woman of his choice to bed with, and the freedom to indulge his passion: gambling. He had never made a secret of his shortcomings, never asked others to admire him for them, had in fact religiously laid out his failings for Bess to take or leave as she chose. She had chosen to throw in her lot with his, and had been trying to change him ever since. Harry turned the jewel in his left ear and brooded upon why others could not be as tolerant as he was.

Bess had been taken on to the dance floor by Will Christowe. She had hung back a little at the start, not knowing the latest steps, but had found her partner so expert that her incompetence passed unnoticed.

'You are very graceful,' Will commented as they completed a measure and paused while the musicians contemplated their next effort. 'But I expected that to be so. No one made the way you are could be anything less.'

'Thank you,' Bess smiled. Actually she was a little breathless from her exertions; she believed she would never again recover the lightness of movement she remembered from the time before she had borne her twins. Upon that thought, her heart missed a beat. How sweet her babes had been that afternoon! How much she had desired to stay at Maiden Court to be with them. Perhaps if she had known how their father would receive her return to Richmond, she would have stayed. The musicians began to play.

'Shall we try again?' Will enquired. 'Or seek a little fresh air? It is uncommonly close tonight.'

'I believe we are in for another storm,' she murmured. 'The little shower of this afternoon promised a great deal more to come.'

'Indeed,' Will replied. 'A great deal more to come,' he repeated softly. 'Your words could well describe our own situation.'

His tone, what he said, sent a shiver down her spine. Of what? she wondered. Apprehension? Excitement? She no longer could deny to herself she found him attractive. A strange thought, when she had so lately been in despair to see Harry holding another woman intimately. Was she no better than he? A wave of fear washed over her. What was happening here? There was no other man for her but the one she had chosen, was married to for better or worse. Glancing over her shoulder she saw Harry come into the room. He stood, his dark eyes surveying the room. They passed over her and her companion, then he moved with his distinctive step to a lady on the fringe of the spectators. The Lady Madrilene rose as he bowed before her, and they joined the line of courtiers.

'I believe we might attempt this one,' Bess said coolly, and Will took her hand possessively.

It was a new dance from Italy, very intricate, very exuberant. As it gathered momentum, Bess wished she had accepted the offer of a quiet stroll in the night air. Several times she missed her step, each time Will caught her and set her on the right course again. Eventually, in the pattern, she was opposite Harry. He bowed, took her hand and executed the steps demanded. 'You are enjoying yourself?' he enquired politely.

She rose from her curtsy. 'I am. And you?'

'What else? I especially find pleasure in my wife being lifted and touched by other men.'

She stopped. 'What do you mean?'

'I am sorry. I should have said one man.'

Bess's blue eyes turned to icy grey. 'Are you trying to pick an argument in the middle of all this? I am finding it difficult enough, Harry, without something else to think on.'

Harry had the immediate desire to laugh. What a typical comment from his beloved Bess! How lovely she looked, her white brow crinkled with concentration, her mouth pursed a little in the effort not to disgrace herself. Several strands of her silver hair had escaped her careful hairdressing and floated like tinsel around her head. If I could but pick her up now, he thought, and carry her from the floor, set her up on Troubador and ride through the night to Maiden Court! There I would lift her gently on to the wide bed we share, so carefully remove the finery she has decked herself in and kiss and caress away all trace of this artificial and meaningless life we are leading in this fairy-tale palace.

Their pause had broken the formation of the measure; a man on Harry's right said laughingly, 'Move along, Latimar, lest we all arrive in an indignified heap!' Harry bowed again to Bess and moved on up the line.

Later he found himself as Madrilene's partner.

They had not spoken since he had escorted her somewhat forcibly from the gardens the previous night and handed her over to one of the palace matrons with the ambiguous words, 'The Lady Madrilene is overcome by the unseasonable heat and should be put to bed with a soothing cordial.' Madrilene had allowed herself to be led away, with a few choice curses whispered to Harry, and had spent a restless night in the dowager's apartments after an unwelcome dose of warm milk and cinnamon. Now she gave Harry a radiant smile.

'I have not seen you all day, my lord. What have you been doing?'

'Studying my Spanish, my dear,' he said blandly. 'I was unfamiliar with your parting comments yester-evening. I fear I am none the wiser now after perusal of my Castilian papers.'

'I should hope not. Such phrases—learned in Catalonian regions, are unsuitable for one with such high principles as yourself,' she retaliated.

He laughed. 'I have never been called high-principled before—I believe I shall take it as a compliment, and, although I am sure you did not mean it so, let us call a truce—it is really too warm for sparring.'

'I will strike my colours if you will take me for refreshment.' Without waiting for him to agree, she took his arm and they left the floor for the ante-chamber where Harry gave her a glass of wine. She sipped it.

'Did you truly not understand what I said last night?'

'No. I lied, for my Spanish is excellent—both classical and—er—idiomatic. I believe you likened me to one of those gentlemen who prefer partners of their own sex for love. Something else I have never been accused of before.'

'Yes, well, I was angry. . .' She finished her wine. 'Can you forgive me?'

This was a gentler Madrilene whom he had not seen before, and he wondered what new game she was playing. He said amiably, 'There is nothing to forgive.'

'I wonder what it would take to make you truly angry, Harry? You have more patience than any man I have met.'

'I have always felt life far too short for disputing every point.'

'That is not quite what I asked, is it? I am curious as to what would make you show sincere emotion. For instance: there is gossip abroad in the palace tonight about your wife and William Christowe. They were riding together for most of the day— indeed they were gone so long they missed the midday meal. This evening they supped together and now are dancing merrily in each other's arms. Yet you are cool and unconcerned, while your peers whisper and chuckle behind their hands.'

'Where there is a beautiful and interesting woman there is always gossip,' Harry said equably.

Madrilene sighed. 'You turn all I say into a compliment for her. 'Tis most annoying, you know.'

'Once again, I am sorry. But I find Bess so fascinating myself that I cannot blame another for finding her the same. Short of chaining her to one of the chairs in my hall at Maiden Court, I cannot prevent other men from admiring her. Such attentions are the right of any as lovely as my wife — in short, as her husband I must put up with it. It goes with the territory.'

'How much of that territory would you concede, I wonder?'

None, he thought passionately. Not one inch, and I am guilty of the most outrageous dishonesty in what I have just said.

'Are you not going to answer me?' Madrilene asked as the pause between them lengthened.

Before he could do so, the queen, on the arm of Thomas Culpeper, joined them. She had drunk a little too well that night and, in the absence of her royal consort who had taken to an early bed, was flirting freely with Thomas. Harry put down his glass.

'May I take you back to the dance, Madrilene?' he asked abruptly.

'Oh, do not leave us, Harry,' Catherine said. She gave him a provocative glance. 'Thomas has promised I may sit in on one of your card games tonight. You must advise me of the rules lest I make a complete fool of myself.'

Harry looked down his shapely nose. 'Surely that would be quite impossible, madam.'

Thomas looked sideways at him. He had grown close to Latimar during the progress of the northern counties, and admired him very much. That admiration had become even more personal when Harry, towards the end of the tour, had taken him aside and told him bluntly that his conduct with the queen — common knowledge in the king's intimate circle — could have only one result.

'You're a fool, Tom,' Harry had said flatly. 'Henry may be besotted with his new wife, but eventually all will come out and there will be but one end for you. The block.'

'But, Harry,' Thomas had said desperately, 'I am in love with Catherine.'

'Love is a movable feast,' Latimar had said cynically. 'You are — what? Twenty? Twenty-one? Do you wish to die for this love?'

'If I must.'

Culpeper had then seen the side of Latimar few did: Harry had walked him around the gloomy castle they were currently housed in, and spoken to him like a brother. 'Tom,' he had said gently, 'Catherine's own kinswoman died for the offence you have led her to. Do you wish that for her?'

'Anne Boleyn was a witch — and promiscuous with many,' Tom had replied sullenly. 'With Kate it is only me now. Why can't you understand?'

'I do understand, but six years ago I lost a friend

in much the same circumstances that you are creating now. I would not have it happen again.'

'Catherine should never have married him!'

'Maybe not. But 'twas her choice, she made the solemn vows, and must abide by them. Also—before we left Whitehall there were whispers about that evidence was being prepared against her. They have enquired into her past and found things there that can be used to discredit her. How much stronger will be their case if you do not behave in sensible fashion now?'

'I have tried. *We* have tried...but the Lady Rochford makes occasion for us—she is our Cupid in this, Harry.'

Harry had looked out of the narrow stone window which overlooked a grey lake shrouded in mist. 'A grim Cupid,' he had said gravely. 'You know, of course, that she was Anne's sister-in-law, married to George Boleyn, and gave testimony that brought both brother and sister to their deaths? Very well. In that affair, for reasons of her own, she lied most grievously. Should it come to the telling point again she would only have to tell the truth, and will do so to save her own skin. She *cannot* be trusted, Tom.'

That conversation had been held in June, and it was now September, but Thomas remembered what Latimar had said and was uneasy. Catherine had been ever more importunate in the week since their return, and young Culpeper was aware of the stormclouds gathering about him. The king had declared himself too tired to complete this evening's revelries and retired to his apartments, but shortly afterwards he had received Thomas Cranmer... Thomas was nervous, frightened.

'Shall we find our places in the gaming room?' Catherine asked. 'Harry—you will take us there?'

'I will,' Harry agreed courteously, 'as soon as I advise my wife.'

Bess was still dancing when Harry came into the room. The musicians, country-bred, had resorted to a lively, bawdy tune for a harvest dance. Harry cut through the stumbling, laughing crowd and stood before Bess.

'Bess—I am invited to cards with the queen and some of her friends. Will you wish to join me?'

Bess righted herself. 'You wish me to?' She still held Will's hand; the dance was rough and she had felt in need of support.

'I do,' Harry said politely. 'But perhaps you are otherwise engaged.'

'Not at all.' Bess released Will's hand hastily. 'I would like to.'

Will said, 'May I impose also, Harry?'

'If you wish,' Harry said dismissively, putting an arm around Bess and taking her through the crowd.

No serious gamblers that St Martin's summer night met in Lord Wiltshire's apartments. Glancing round the table, Harry thought there would be no large sums laid down and therefore nothing to upset his wife. He found her a seat and poured wine for them both. Will dropped into a chair on Bess's left and helped himself to wine. He wondered if Latimar remembered it had been in these very rooms that they had played out the drama which had resulted in Will losing his ancestral home. There would be no such drama tonight, he determined, for since then he had made it his business to acquire some skill.

At midnight the first hand of cards was dealt. Bess, who had not played for some time, fanned out her cards and examined them. Harry, on her right, extracted a number of silver coins from his purse and placed them before her. She turned one of the round, cold coins in her left hand. Money had never been important to her. On her home farm, while she grew up, actual coinage had been rarely exchanged, but she and her mother had — as was their traditional right — kept 'egg money', the profit from their tending of the chickens and sorting and handling of the eggs, for personal use. The amount had been pathetically small and Bess had always saved hers to buy the few pretty ribbons or trinkets she had then possessed.

Since becoming a part of a more wealthy life she had therefore been in two minds about squandering currency in any enterprise which brought no return. At the back of her mind during every gambling session had been the thought that each coin could be used in so much more profitable a way at Maiden Court. To build up the animal stock, to renew the silken tapestries adorning her hall, to pay the extra labour needed to plough the outlying fields so long neglected. Tonight she thought again such things as the cards went round.

She glanced at Harry. No such thoughts interfered with his intent concentration, she would swear. Had he been angry when he had made those hurtful comments earlier? Surely not, for he had spoken in a neutral tone, the same tone as he had used when enquiring if Will Christowe meant aught to her. . . He was a hard man to be close to, had always been. She knew now she had never, ever been sure of him; never in their five-year marriage had they settled into the comfortable state most married couples achieved, once the first shining splendour faded. But that, she thought, sorting her cards automatically, was because that splendour had not diminished — at least for her: she was as much in love with Harry this day as she had been the day she married him.

'Bess,' Will murmured, 'play has begun.' Bess hurriedly laid a card and the game progressed.

It was very close in the room; during an interval Will rose and pushed open the windows to let in some fresh air. Looking up, he could see a sickle moon riding high in a clear sky, its silvery colour an exact match for Bess Latimar's hair. He rested one hip on the window-seat and watched her face as she accepted a glass of wine and smiled at the tired boy serving it. It was an expressive face, Will thought, declaring her weariness at the lateness of the hour, her concern that various members of the party were losing money they could ill afford — many of Catherine's close friends were not from the wealthy section of society. Now and again her eyes rested on the queen and were both sympathetic and disapproving. All these expressions revealed the true Bess: the woman who cared for those around her.

He now turned his gaze to the legal possessor of his love. Harry was slouched gracefully in his chair, his heavy-lidded eyes blank of expression, one long finger caressing the ruby in his ear, the other hand riffling through the deck of cards before him. As Madrilene had done earlier, Will pondered on what would make Latimar declare himself in terms of commitment.

It was the moment for puzzling over the secrets of others, for Madrilene too was studying the face of her love and his wife. There was some discord between them, she had divined; about what — after Harry's disclaimer that Christowe's attentions to Bess concerned him — Madrilene could not decide. It pleased her, though, as did the fact that Will was obviously now hopelessly in love with Lady Bess. She and Will had known each other quite well in France; he had a reputation for pursuing what he wanted relentlessly. How convenient it would be if he was successful in this venture!

Two hours later the party began to break up. Wiltshire had long since given up trying to stay awake and was snoring in a chair by the fire, others drifted away one by one to their beds. Six were left — the queen and her lover, Bess and Harry, Will and Madrilene.

Bess, yawning behind her hand, wished she could leave too. It had been a strange sort of day, not one she had enjoyed, and she wished to end it.

Will was absent-mindedly arranging his winnings into orderly piles. Catherine said from across the table, "Tis unlucky to count your money while still in the game, my lord. Isn't that so, Harry?'

'Mmm? Yes, that is what they say.' Harry glanced at the neat ranks of silver. 'But perhaps a little bad luck is due — Will has been extraordinarily fortunate so far this night.'

'I have learned a few tricks since last we sat down together, my friend.'

'Indeed you have, and do not display them all at the card table.' Harry, apparently intent only on the game, had not missed one of the little attentions Will had shown to Bess. Several times he had touched her arm to make some whispered comment, twice he had familiarly leaned close to help her decide which card to lay.

Thomas Culpeper said nervously, 'Come gentlemen, ladies, it is time to call it a night.'

'Nonsense,' Harry said casually. 'We all still have the wherewithal — let us carry on. Call for more wine, Tom.'

Reluctantly Thomas did so and resumed his seat. Catherine lolled against his shoulder and Bess, as if in disapproval of this, sat very upright. Madrilene's quick, bright gaze flashed over the others, enjoying the tense atmosphere.

The cards went round again, the players bid or not as they decided, but the contest was between Christowe and Latimar — and it was Christowe's lucky night. When Harry's silver was exhausted, he began to deal a new round, saying easily, 'All will accept my marker, I assume?'

'Not I,' Will cut in over the murmured assent of the others. Both he and Harry had drunk a considerable amount throughout the evening; Harry showed no sign of being affected, Will was obviously beyond his capacity.

'Not?' Harry paused, the brightly painted plaques vivid in his white hands.

'Without security, no,' Will said deliberately.

Thomas stretched his arms above his head and yawned widely. 'I really think we have all had enough this night — in fact it is no longer night, the dawn is here.' Through the narrow windows a grey light, tinged with rose, spread over the room. With it came a colder feeling to the weather.

'What security do you desire?' Harry enquired, as if Tom had not spoken.

'Whatever you have.'

Bess lifted her little jewelled purse on to the table. 'There is no need for that,' she said calmly. 'I have still some money, Harry.' She tipped a small pile of silver on to the surface, now dulled by fingermarks and the red circles left by wine cups, and pushed it over to him. Harry pushed it back.

'I have no need of your little cache, my dear. I repeat: what security do you desire, Christowe?'

'Maiden Court,' Will said, lifting heavy grey eyes to the other man's face.

'Maiden Court?' Harry looked Will over, then said gently, "Tis a property of considerable value, my boy, and it will take some hours to relieve me of it. I doubt you would stay the course.'

Will flushed dark red. 'Let it be hours, then! Were it days I can match you for endurance, Latimar.'

There was another silence, then Catherine laughed and said, 'Maiden Court? That is your home, is it not, Latimar? Best ask your lady wife before you decide to make free with it.'

Harry turned his dark blue eyes on Bess, who pulled at a strand of her hair in a nervous gesture she had retained from childhood. It sprang back against her forehead as she released it. 'Well, Bess?' Harry enquired politely.

'Maiden Court is yours, Harry,' she said composedly, 'to do with what you will.'

'As you say,' Harry agreed. He continued to deal. Thomas pushed back his chair abruptly.

'Harry—let us give this up. If Lady Bess will see madam to her quarters——'

Catherine tugged at his sleeve. 'Really, Tom, you are such a killjoy! I have no wish to leave so exciting a bout!'

Thomas bowed. 'Then I must beg leave to retire—I want no part in this. Madrilene—may I escort you to the ladies' dorter?'

'I think I will also stay,' Madrilene said softly. 'Goodnight, Tom.' When Culpeper had gone, she added, 'I believe there are only two players in this game—Harry, exclude the rest of us and commence battle.'

Harry collected the cards again. He said, 'What

would be your estimate of the property in question, Christowe? I think——' he named a figure '—do you agree?'

Will nodded and picked up his cards.

Bess folded her hands on her lap. Maiden Court rose before her—its rosy bricks, its green lawns and thick sheltering woods. She always carried each beloved detail of her home in her mind wherever she went; it was a part of her heart and soul now. My home, she thought, tears pricking at her eyelids, and that of my two children! They at least had the right to grow up there, happy and free, but no, their father must risk such contentment in a mad hour or two at the card table. Whatever happened now, *whatever*, she would find it hard to forgive Harry for this.

She rose and, going to the sinking fire, lit a taper. Finding fresh candles, she replaced the smouldering stubs in the silver holders. It was a new day outside, but gloomy; true autumn was staking its claim on the countryside now. The seemingly endless game went on.

Harry lost at first. Madrilene had produced parchment and charcoal and kept account religiously. Win or lose, she had seen Bess's eyes in the moment she had allowed her husband to risk their home, and had recognised the anger in them. How much could a man care for his wife when he was willing to gamble with the roof over her head? Madrilene thought pleasurably that, whatever the outcome of this strange bout, the Latimars would not repair the damage done easily.

Bess did not take her seat between Harry and Will, but sat apart in a chair by the fire. She had told Harry that Maiden Court was his to dispose of as he would, and she had meant it. If he was prepared to lay their happiness on the fall of a card, she would not voice an objection. But, looking into the orange and grey ash of the dying fire, she felt a kind of despair. Harry, not unaware of these thoughts, rearranged the smooth cards in his hands. If he could have spoken now to Bess he would have told her there was no risk.

A thousand times he had been in this situation; never once had he lost anything he truly valued. Will Christowe's luck might be in tonight, but Latimar had been challenging fate for more than a decade. Will might have learned the mechanical skills of gambling; he would never lay hold of the essence.

The courtiers at Richmond Palace were progressing down the staircase for their midday meal before the contest was decided. Before the four disparate people, each with a stake in the outcome of what had gone before, rose from their chairs in Wiltshire's apartments and took their separate ways. Harry Latimar was absolute winner. Once again he and Will had disputed the ownership of Maiden Court, once again Will had lost.

Will sat stunned for some time, then rose unsteadily. 'You will excuse me, madam?' he said to

Catherine. 'Ladies?' His heavy eyes flickered over Bess and Madrilene. He rested one hand on the table for support. 'Harry, I thank you for an instructive morning.'

Harry had begun to build a castle of cards. He placed another in position before looking up. 'Goodnight, or rather good day, Christowe.' Will's steps to the door were uneven and Catherine stood up, shaking her silken skirts.

'Come, Lady Madrilene, let us assist this young man along the passage lest he come to grief.' Madrilene followed without speaking and Harry and Bess were left alone. She came to the table and stared down at him.

'I suppose you are pleased with yourself.'

'Should I not be?'

'Risking our home and our well-being? How *could* you, Harry? What if you had lost?'

'But I did not, did I? Lose?'

'But presumably were prepared to—can I expect the rest of our lives together to be conducted on these terms?'

'I did not suggest the terms this night.'

'And did not refuse them either!'

'I couldn't do that. . .' Actually Harry was feeling pangs of conscience now: the reverse side of a nature which craved the excitement of chancing all, but often regretted that others must be hurt in the process. He had known as surely as if he could see into the future that he would win; Bess could not have been so sanguine and must have spent an agonising few hours. Resenting this compassion, he said, 'But perhaps you are disappointed. Perhaps you feel that if Christowe had regained Maiden Court, he would also have been in a strong position to take other valuables belonging to me.'

Confused by lack of sleep, she did not at first know what he meant, then she did. She gasped. 'You should be ashamed to think that of him, let alone of me! But if you did, is that the way a gentleman settles such matters?'

'One uses the weapons at one's disposal, Bess. You no doubt would have preferred me to engage in some boyish brawling, or even a formal exchange of blood in a field at dawn light?'

'How can you say that? You know—you should know that I would never wish you in harm's way. . .' The hot tears threatened again and she turned away. At the door she stopped, and said quietly, 'Do you wish me to go home, Harry?'

He was adding another turret to his castle. 'Tired of me already?' She marvelled that his hands could be so steady.

She gripped the door-handle. 'Why can you not give me a straight answer, ever? I ask you if you wish me to go home.'

Yes, he thought, I want you to go home. Home where it is safe and no man may have your company, especially not a young half-Frenchman for whom you care more than you would admit to me, or to yourself. . . 'Not unless that is what you want,' he said mildly. He heard the door open and close.

Miraculously the draught of air did not disturb his house of cards. He sat back staring at it, then abruptly flicked one long finger under the edifice and it collapsed with a soft shushing noise in the quiet room.

CHAPTER FIVE

TEN days later the court removed to Hampton, and the day after their arrival the king felt able to undertake his day's hunting. Physically much improved, there was beneath his return to health a darkness of spirit not even lightened by the visit his son, Edward, was making from his home in Havering-atte-Bowe where he kept his own establishment. The little boy was now four years old, precociously advanced as were all the Tudor children, plump, imperious, but with a charming sweetness of nature which endeared him to all allowed in his presence.

Little Edward was the apple of his father's eye; he had waited so long for a son, wasted the lives of two women before attaining him, and knew the greatest joy in being with him as much as was possible. Henry displayed his affection in an unusually free way for a royal father, frequently hastening through his regal duties in order that he might enjoy many hours in the royal nursery playing and talking with his son.

But it was not Edward who preoccupied Henry's mind this crisp autumn morning, but his young queen, Catherine. For some weeks now he had had to listen to accounts of her wantonness before she became his wife; yesterday his ministers had laid before him incontrovertible evidence of her infidelity since being elevated to consort of England. Henry's one desire today was to put away the whole miserable business for a few hours.

The hunting party was to be a small one — only Henry's most intimate circle were to take part and Harry Latimar would be one of them. He rose early and dressed quietly so as not to wake his roommate, Thomas Culpeper. In spite of his care, Tom opened his eyes and turned over. He sat up.

'Harry? Why are you about so early?'

'I am to chase the red deer this morning, Tom. Or the wild boar, or any other creature foolish enough to show its hide. In other words, Henry is celebrating his return to health with a little exercise.'

'The king hunts today? I was not invited.' Tom rubbed the sleep from his eyes. 'I wonder why.'

Harry selected a cloak from his trunk, dark grey velvet lined with wolverine fur. He swung it on to his shoulders over the metallic grey silk doublet and breeches, slashed to reveal a paler grey beneath, and considered his reflection in the long glass.

Thomas, distracted from his musings on his exclusion from today's events, asked, 'Why do you always wear grey, Harry? I have always meant to ask you.'

Harry sat down to lace up his riding boots. 'For no particular reason. The choice of colour came about quite by chance. When I was seven, the lord I was to serve sent a message to my aunt — who had taken the responsibility for me when my mother died at my birth — that I must be equipped in green and gold as these were his colours. She had bought the materials, but they were not yet cut when my father died quite suddenly.' Harry paused and stood up. He went to the window and surveyed the sun climbing by inches up into the watery sky, remembering his father with sadness and regret.

'Go on,' Tom said from the bed.

'It seems my father had been less than careful in his financial dealings — when he was taken so abruptly he left vast debts and my aunt, who was a very honourable woman, declared they must be paid at all costs. So she set about selling everything that could be sold: the furniture and silver and wall-hangings from our hall, the land surrounding our home, and eventually the house itself. Among the items she found a buyer for the splendid silk and satin which was to made up into my page's uniform. She then found hearthspace for the rest of her days with a distant cousin, but there was still the problem of what I was to wear to enter upon my new career.

'Eventually she cut up one of her two remaining gowns — it was of a particularly depressing shade of funereal grey. So — I arrived at court dressed so, and the other boys made mock of me. Why do you wear that gloomy garb? they asked me. Why that colour? they enquired, snickering behind their hands. Because I like it! I declared, red-faced and humiliated; 'tis my favourite colour and I will never wear anything else!

'Later, when I was better established and had been transformed from page to squire and the king showed interest in me, when the merchants would come to the palace with their rolls of silk and velvet and satin, any material of a grey hue would be directed to me. Oh, you must show that to Latimar, he does so like that shade! And, do you know, Tom, I *do* like it! Over the years I have truly come to regard it as the only colour I can be seen in.'

Tom smiled. What an odd story, and how typical of Harry! He swung his long straight legs out of the bed and felt for the chamber pot. That done, he said again, 'I wonder why Henry did not invite me for the hunting.'

Harry fitted on his doeskin gloves, softened and perfumed and embroidered at the cuffs by Bess. Was Thomas really so ignorant of the rumours sweeping the palace? he wondered. Francis Dereham was already taken and housed in the Tower, Norfolk and Gardiner, who had promoted the marriage of Catherine to the king, had now abandoned the girl and declared her openly as wanton. Soon would come Culpeper's arrest, then the queen's. . .

Harry picked up his feathered cap. A deadly feeling of being transported back in time came over him. He had travelled this road before when his best and dearest friends had been accused in the fall of another queen. Then he had been more intimately involved, those accused a part of his life. But, although he cared nothing for Catherine or her secretary, Dereham, Culpeper was a different matter. He said suddenly, 'Tom—if you had to, could you leave here at short notice? Could you find a...hiding place, or perhaps leave England altogether?'

Tom was washing at the dressing-table. He turned, drops of water falling from his handsome face. 'What is it you are saying to me, Harry?' Harry came to his side.

'What we spoke of before has come about, my friend,' he said softly. 'There is still time to save yourself—I would help you in any way I can.'

Thomas dried his hands carefully. 'But that would mean I must desert her, Harry, when she needs me most.' He turned his candid eyes on the man beside him, and Harry saw that Thomas knew all there was to know about the situation. He put his arm about his shoulders.

'You're a damned fool, Tom,' he sighed.

'I know that—but aren't we all fools for love? I know what you think of her, Harry, what others think of her. But—for me she is the one. I like to imagine that if fate had not intervened we would have come together anyway and been happy. Happy...' He straightened his shoulders. 'However, it was not to be and now I must pay for the small piece of paradise I have stolen. Go you now and chase the red deer and I will take what is coming to me.' When Harry still hesitated, he added, 'You're lucky—not in the way you are famous for, but in the important way. You have lovely Bess;

don't lose her, and—I thank you for the friendship you have shown me.'

Harry took part in the hunting, scarcely aware of his automatic actions. Tom's words about Bess had struck a chord within him—he too had believed himself the luckiest of men to have her by his side, her loyalty and attention to him absolute. Strangely, when he had always relied so much on chance and appeared to enjoy the insecurity of such a life, it was her constancy that he had loved most. Now he found he questioned that constancy, and the doubt confused him.

This confusion did not produce outward aggression; that was not Harry's way—the indolent tolerance he was renowned for was not, as most believed, apathy, but the result of long years of watchfulness. Early in his life Harry had discovered a rage within him which he guarded fanatically. On the few occasions in his adult life he had permitted this rage to erupt into violence, there had been more danger to the man who provoked it than from another of the hot-tempered gallants who might display ferocity at any fancied slight. But that rage was working in him now and directed both at Bess and the man she showed a great preference for now.

Bess had not gone home on the day of the card game, indeed had not mentioned again that she would. Instead she had, without applying for permission from her husband, respectfully asked the king to allow her to come to Hampton. Before leaving Richmond she had not sought Harry's quarters once, and they could have been passing acquaintances at the meal table, and at the plays and on the dance floor. How this state of affairs had come about, Harry could not have said. He had been prepared to let Bess sulk for a few days, perhaps she was entitled to that — after all, she had thought him capable of losing their home for her. But she had not sulked; instead she appeared to be enjoying herself immensely, enthusiastically a part of the court again. And Will Christowe was ever at her elbow.

Lately the horrible thought had come creeping to Harry in the dark nights that Bess had washed her hands of him, tired of his obsession at the gaming tables. So today he could take no pleasure in the proceedings; indeed, if he should lose Bess, he doubted if he would ever take pleasure in anything again.

As the dull afternoon gave way to dusk, and with several sleek deer slung on poles carried by the foot servants, the royal party turned for home. Where the forest thinned a little the dogs set up a great barking and the king, riding abreast with Latimar, said, 'They have the scent of something — come, Harry, let us end the day on a high note.' He spurred his mount and the two men left the other riders behind. They chased the dogs for some miles, then the hounds lost the scent of whatever they had been so eager to pursue and slowed down in disarray, noses down among the drifting leaves.

'They've lost it,' Henry said, disappointed.

'No matter — it has been a good day's hunting. Let us turn back; 'twill be true dark before we see Hampton.'

'Where are we?' the king asked, looking around. 'Do you know?'

'We have left the main bridle path but, yes, I know the way. There is a still pond up ahead — if we skirt it and go west we shall soon be right again.' He called to the dogs and they left the sheltering trees and were soon in an open space surrounding the lake.

Henry drew up at the water's edge and looked out over the stagnant expanse where insects swarmed. Here and there the dying light caught the darting magic of a dragonfly. He let his horse lower its head and crop the sparse grass growing amongst the reeds. He said thoughtfully, 'Once, Harry, you offered me advice on my marriage. Do you remember?' Harry had in an impulsive moment tried to persuade the king to reverse his decision to execute Queen Anne; in fact they had quarrelled bitterly on the subject.

'I do indeed. You didn't take it, I recall.'

'No. . . I believe, though, it is easier for an onlooker to see more clearly what is happening between two people than those closely involved.'

Harry gripped his reins. 'It is near dark now, sir. We should ride on lest we miss the others along the path home.'

'Stay awhile, Harry. Days like this, when I am able to mount a horse and spend a pleasant few hours in the company of my friends, are few and far between.'

'The rest of your friends will probably be hallooing through the forest for you at the moment.'

'Let 'em. Most did not want me to come abroad and have been nagging at me all day to "rest now, sir. Do not tax yourself, sir"—I swear they look at me as if I were already a corpse!'

'They love you,' Harry said mildly, 'and I sympathise with them in that.'

'Hmm.' Henry turned in the saddle to survey his companion. 'I am indeed glad to hear that. I have sometimes thought you had never really forgiven me for Rochford.' Harry said nothing and the king returned his reflective gaze to the water. He sighed. 'Those times, sad times—I think of them with regret, if that is any pleasure to you.'

'Regret will not bring the dead back to life. George Boleyn was my friend, I loved him and his passing leaves a large gap in my life.'

'Feeling as you do, it seems strange you are now about to allow another such gap to develop.'

Harry half smiled. Henry had always been an acute observer of others' affairs. The division between the Latimars had not escaped his attention. 'Bess and I have our problems at the moment, but 'twill pass. I hope you will not mind my saying that I know my own business best.'

'If your business is to drive the girl into young Christowe's arms, then I believe you,' Henry said with asperity.

Harry's face hardened. Again he did not speak.

'Perhaps you feel I am the last person to offer advice on the subject of marriage,' the king persisted. 'But Bess is too unusual a woman to let slip.'

'As you say.'

'You won't speak of it? Well, I suppose I must not press you. However, I will say I speak not just out of concern for you and the lady, but also on Will's account. I should not be doing my duty by him if I did not attempt to keep him out of harm's way.'

'He is not in harm's way—unless you suggest Bess to be dangerous.'

'I am speaking of you, Harry,' Henry said irritably. 'And you well know it.'

'Me?' Harry raised an eyebrow. 'I am sure I am the least warlike of your gentlemen.'

'I wonder. I wonder. I once had the disagreeable task of explaining to Lord Spalding's aged sister why her brother was being despatched home from my court scarcely breathing.'

'Ah, yes, Tom Spalding...' Lord Thomas Spalding had been an unwelcome suitor for Bess de Cheyne's hand and had made himself a nuisance to her while she was first at court six years ago. When Bess had gone home to Devon, Spalding had, in Harry's hearing, made an extremely offensive remark about her. That remark had come back to haunt Tom in the following years, for he had never truly recovered from the assault Latimar had made upon him...

'Yes indeed,' the king said severely. 'Tom Spalding.'

'I am older now.'

'But no wiser — at least as regards that young woman. She is your Achilles' heel, my boy, the only human being I believe you would attack for — and you are wild when out of control. Pray do not give me that pained look; I have loved you too long not to know you as well. You would do well to admit I am right and mend the rift between yourself and Bess before young Will finds himself in similar case to Spalding.'

'I cannot put it right, one, two, three,' Harry said sulkily. 'She does not accuse me and therefore I have no case to answer. In all truth, Hal, I cannot imagine why she is behaving the way she is.'

'Can you not?' Henry asked incredulously. 'I have heard you risked her home — and that of your children — in some game of chance not a fortnight since. And your conduct lately with the little girl from Spain. . .'

Goaded, Harry said bitterly, 'I would have thought you had enough marital problems of your own without interfering in mine.' Immediately he spoke he regretted it. Henry's face changed, his body sagged in the saddle and he turned a ravaged face to his friend.

'Yes, that is so, but it ill becomes you to taunt me with it.'

'Yes, well. . .' Harry muttered. 'I must ask your pardon for so doing.'

Henry eased his sore leg — a day in the saddle had been the greatest delight to him, but he was paying for it now. 'It seems I am unlucky once more with my queen. She is wanton, they tell me — not only before I took her for my wife, but since and with a man I counted a friend.'

Harry shifted uncomfortably in the saddle. His horse, sensing his master's unease, threw up his head and danced on the marshy ground. Harry shortened the rein and glanced at the sky. 'We really should ride on now, sir. I know these woods well, but darkness changes even the most familiar path.'

'Darkness,' repeated Henry slowly. 'Yes, it is dark — and not only around me in the forest of Hampton, but here —' he laid a hand on his breast ' — here within me. My rose without a thorn — that is what I have called her! Sweet-smelling and beautiful, but treacherous. But do you know, Harry, I have the weakest notion that I would forgive her grievous sin — treason, my ministers insist?'

Harry remained silent.

'You will not tell me I must? Once you pleaded for one of my queens. Once you begged me to overlook evidence presented to me. Will you not do so again?'

'I cannot do so,' Harry said. ''Tis not my place, after all.'

'No.' Henry smiled in the darkness. 'Sometimes I believe that to be your greatest strength, Harry — knowing when to remain silent. Certainly those of my friends who could not do so have met untimely ends. However, on this occasion I suspect you would rather plead for...Tom Culpeper than for Catherine.'

'He is young, sir, and romantic in ways you and I may have forgotten.'

'He cannot escape,' Henry said grimly. 'We speak now of Catherine. Come — there is no other able to overhear our conversation. Beg for her life and I will listen.'

Beg for Catherine, who had been a harlot before she ever came into her king's life? Before she could tempt and destroy a young man whose only real crime had been to fall desperately in love? No, thought Harry, I will not do that. Would not do that for any treacherous woman. All his sexual life he had avoided any liaison with a lady already married, despised a man who would set the cuckold's horns on the head of a brother. Perhaps he himself was wearing those horns now — if so, Bess would be as dead to him as Catherine would shortly be to the king. Once again he resorted to silence. He lifted his eyes to the black sky.

'I see,' Henry sighed. He too looked up into the clouded sky where only a handful of stars seeded the darkness. 'Well, let us take the way home.'

Harry reached out a swift hand to grasp the king's reins. 'And Tom Culpeper?'

'Dead already,' Henry said, his mouth cruel. 'And after his actual end on Tower Green, his good-looking head impaled on the teeth of London Bridge so that all may understand that Henry Tudor may be old, but is not yet done.' He snatched back his reins, clamped his thighs to his horse and administered a sharp cut with his whip to the glossy flanks.

Thomas Culpeper, gentleman of the king's bedchamber, lover to the king's wife, was arrested during the meal that evening. The king, who had not wished to be present while his instructions were carried out, had not tarried after finishing his meal. Catherine had not appeared to sup at all. Bess was there to witness it, seated some way from table where Thomas was sharing his last hours of freedom with Harry Latimar.

Harry, who had been expecting the interruption all evening, watched with a neutral expression his young friend escorted under armed guard from the hall. The hubbub in the vast chamber, which had died down to a deadly silence during the arrest, began again with whispers which built to the normal crescendo. Bess got up and went to Harry's side. He looked up, saw her and got to his feet.

'I may sit with you?' she asked.

'Do you need to ask?' They took their seats.

'I notice you have eaten nothing tonight, and drunk a good deal,' she said, looking at his untouched plate. 'It is not good for you, Harry.' She asked a page for hot food and when it arrived arranged it on a fresh plate. She looked at him expectantly, and he gave her an ironic smile.

'Don't you want to cut it up and feed it to me?'

'I will if it will encourage you to eat.'

'I find I have no appetite tonight.' When he had helped her sit down, the touch of her hand, her hair brushing his face, had set his blood pulsing. Even Tom's unhappy situation could not prevent him from wanting to take Bess from the hall and demand she be a wife to him again. But was she still his wife? Or did she now belong to another man?

'And no wonder,' Bess said. 'But 'twill help nothing for you to go hungry. Come — to please me.'

He speared a small piece of meat and ate it, then raised his wine glass again. Putting it down empty, he said, 'My tutor used to tell me that a man's life is divided into portions, each portion lasting seven years. Seven years old: the age of reason, fourteen: young manhood, twenty-one: maturity, and so on. It is almost seven years since we witnessed similar events as now. Had you thought of that?'

'No. When I think of that time, I remember mostly that I was painfully falling in love with you.'

'Painfully? I suppose nothing has really changed there, then.'

'Why do you say that? We have had so much that is good.'

'Your use of the past tense is quite revealing.' Harry refilled his glass.

'You are determined to be gloomy tonight,' she said lightly, but a faint flush rose in her face. The sensation of falling down a steep slope which had gripped her in the last week was heightened tonight. She had meant only to teach Harry a lesson by ignoring him a little after his disgraceful conduct at the card table, had expected him to restrain her forcibly from spending all her time with Will Christowe. When he had not behaved in that way, she had at first been dismayed, then angry. Now she was frightened, not only that she had ruined her marriage, but also because Will had lately become so possessive and proprietorial. Last night he had kissed her in the shadow of the palace wall and she had been dismally aware of feeling nothing. Nothing. Without turning her head she knew that his eyes were on them at this very moment. She had crossed the hall not only to persuade Harry to eat, but seeking protection herself..

It was obvious from Harry's casual manner that he did not care enough about her to do so; Bess struggled with the sensation of speaking with a stranger. In an effort to restore ordinary, intimate conversation between them she said, 'It will soon be the Christmas season. Do you intend keeping Yuletide at Maiden Court?'

'No.' Some days ago he had asked Henry for leave and received the curtest refusal. 'You will go, of course?'

'Yes. . . But I had expected you would be there too.'

'Had you?'

'Harry —' impulsively she touched his hand '— I wish to talk to you.'

'Do so.'

'Not here — may we not seek a more private place?

Come — you have drunk enough tonight; let me take you to your bed.'

His eyes wandered over her. 'I would like that,' he said politely, 'but had thought you would have a prior engagement in that respect.'

She drew back. 'You can say that! To *me*! Harry, what is happening with us?'

Over her shoulder he saw Will Christowe making his way towards them. The heat from the mountainous fires built against the cold night was overwhelming. He felt suffocated. Rage like a tidal wave engulfed him as he got up to face Will. Bess too jumped up, and the three looked at each other.

Will, sober and alert, thought: At last, now the man is willing to come to grips! Bess, confused and upset by Harry's acid words thought: Oh, no, not here! Not in front of all these people, so that no later retraction will be possible. Harry, unable to think at all in the grip of a killing rage, said, 'Yes? What is it you want, Christowe?'

'The lady Bess had promised I may escort her to the play tonight. I have come to collect her.'

'To collect her,' Harry repeated heavily. 'I do not think I wish her to be. . .collected.'

'That is surely for her to decide,' Will said confidently. Both men looked at Bess.

'I am a little weary tonight,' Bess said faintly. 'Perhaps another time.'

'There will be no other time,' Harry said deliberately.

Those around them had ceased eating, talking,

their upturned faces showing a lively interest in this new drama following so soon upon the last.

'I do not accept that,' Will said, 'and scarcely know how you dare to lay down the law in such a way. After all, sir, if one values something, one does not leave it around for others to. . .collect.'

Harry struck him. It was a blow designed not to injure, but to show contempt — the back of his left hand merely grazed Will's cheek. There was a united gasp from the onlookers.

Will, deathly pale, said, 'We must not take this quarrel any further in this place, Latimar. But I will ask you to account for what you have just done at a later date. My seconds will visit your quarters tonight that a suitable time may be arranged.'

A duel, thought Bess desperately. And I am the cause of it! If anything happened to Will she would never forgive herself, but if Harry sustained even the slightest hurt. . .

Will turned on his heel and walked away. Several gentlemen rose and offered their services to Harry, who had eyes for no one but Bess. He took her arm and led her away. Outside the hall she said breathlessly, 'Harry, please go straight away to him and make it right between you. You cannot go through with this.'

'You doubt my ability?'

'I doubt your motive! For what does any of it amount to? I was angry with you — at first for not telling me how you came by Maiden Court, then for being prepared to chance it away. So I have behaved foolishly and this is the result.'

'In what way have you behaved foolishly?'

Bess leaned against the cold stone wall. His insulting question asked only one thing, the thing that all men cared for most. He should have known she would never give that willingly to any man but him. . .and even if she had, no incident could touch the heart of her. Irrational sophistry, she rebuked herself, for hadn't she been in misery ever since she had seen him caress Madrilene?

'Harry,' she said determinedly, 'you know very well I have no feeling for Will other than a sympathetic friendship. Would you allow this small feeling to endanger both your lives?'

She does not realise, he thought mistakenly, that that small feeling is the seed for a greater passion. He regretted not one of the minutes in the great hall, only that he had not dealt with Christowe there and then. Harry had no taste for drawn-out rituals.

'Harry!' Bess said urgently. 'You are not listening to me!'

'I have listened, but what you say cannot change what must happen. The thing is done.'

''Tis not done! Not until you meet. Please, Harry, I beg of you to put it right.'

'I did not issue the challenge.'

'You forced it!'

Harry abruptly and completely lost his temper. 'Be silent,' he said between set teeth. It was Christowe she was begging for.

Bess burst into tears.

'Do not cry, madam. Or if you must do so, take yourself away to your private chamber, where you cannot embarrass me further. This coil is of your making and having begun it the least you can do is support me now.'

'I do support you,' Bess wept. 'Always, and in everything, but——'

'Then go to your room!' Harry thundered. 'I have had enough of your company this night.' Bess turned away, scarcely able to find her path. At the foot of the stairs Thomas Seymour stood politely aside to let her pass. He raised his eyebrows at Harry who gave him a black look before pushing open the door into the gardens. He gulped at the sharp night air.

'I should have thought,' observed Seymour, coming out after him, 'that there was enough trouble in this place without your adding to it.'

'I do not care what you think.' Harry pulled at the sparkling white lace on his high-standing collar. Bess in tears — before him, who had sworn when he married her that she would never cry again. It was freezing outside, but he was sweating.

Thomas hugged his rich furs about him. 'I know Christowe quite well — have been a friend to him since he was a boy. If you wish I will go to him and try to calm matters.'

'*I* am the one who needs calming,' Harry said furiously. 'He insulted me, after all.'

'You will be calm soon enough — it is not your style to bear a grudge, Harry.'

'That is what you think, is it, Seymour?' Years of bearing just such a grudge against the Seymour brothers made Harry feel able to take Thomas by his fancy, miniver-clad shoulders and toss him on to the frosty ground. Thomas, intrigued and amused by this show of temper from the usually indolent Latimar, wished only to administer oil to the troubled waters a man he admired was struggling in. From the hall came the wistful sound of a woman singing. Hardly aware he did so, Harry registered that it was Madrilene's voice and the song from her homeland of Spain haunting and romantic.

'He is not a soft courtier, Will,' Seymour said consideringly, 'but a trained soldier who has, in the past, earned his bread from carrying arms. He has in mind no polite exchange of formalities, I am sure.'

Harry, his temper receding, shrugged.

'Harry,' Thomas said gently, 'you and I are of an age—it is assistance I am offering now, for one whom I would like to call a friend. You and I have often been at daggers drawn in the past, but we are a certain breed. Christowe is not of that breed—he can be an unscrupulous young devil, as you will find out in due course.'

'I feel dead already,' Harry remarked.

Thomas laughed. 'Well, I pray that will not be so in reality. . . Take my advice — as challenger he must offer you choice of weapons. You would do well to decide upon the courtly rapier — an art in which you excel and he does not. Goodnight to you, Latimar.'

Seymour turned inside again and closed the door against the wind.

Harry sat on the low stone boundary wall, already crisp with ice. Tom Seymour's words made the situation suddenly real to him: he had provoked a man and been called out! He had never before been entangled in such an enterprise. Always in the past he had been able to find the words to avoid such foolishness. The affair with Spalding had been a thing of the moment and, although hard fought, neither participant in danger of death. Also, he had been an odious man and well deserving of the beating he got. Will Christowe was just a young fool who fancied himself in love with another man's wife. The cold was making itself felt now; Harry got up and went inside.

In his rooms he found Richard de Vere waiting for him. The young squire was folding and packing Culpeper's gear into a battered trunk. He said, 'I thought to send these on to the Tower, sir. No one has asked me to do this, but I thought. . .'

'Yes, please carry on,' Harry said. He took off his clothes and, in linen shirt and hose, got on to his bed, linking his hands behind his head. It was a waste of time, of course, Tom would need none of his apparel in that dire place, nor in the future.

Richard completed his task and remade the fire. He came to the bed. 'Two gentlemen came earlier, sir. They were Lord Christowe's friends and asked who they might apply to to arrange the question of time and place for the — er —— I was not sure how to answer them.'

'No more am I.'

'It is true, though? You are to meet him?'

'Apparently. I must confess, however, I have had little experience of these matters. What should you advise, Richard?'

'I?' Richard looked astounded. 'Since you ask, I should favour going to Lord Will and attempting to patch the matter up. I have seen him in the lists, and the practice yard — he will be a dangerous opponent to engage with.'

'Everyone seems agreed on that,' Harry said wryly. 'I wonder how I am regarded, so insistent are all that I should withdraw.'

'I can only answer that question on my own behalf,' Richard said quietly. 'As far as I am concerned, you are the best master I have ever had. Your kindness and care for me is probably more than any father would have shown. I do not question your bravery, my lord, or your prowess in the knightly arts but — if you will forgive me for commenting personally, it seems to me a pointless exercise to engage in battle for that which is already won. Lady Bess is yours, loves you in a way I have seldom witnessed among the couples I have observed.'

Harry regarded the blushing boy with a mixture of amusement and interest. 'You are a noticing sort of boy, Richard. But,' he sighed, 'I have brought this trouble on my head, and have no alternative but to see it through. As to practical advice? I believe I am to choose weapons.'

'Then let it be rapiers,' Richard said without hesitation. 'Lord Will is not practised in the more. . .delicate tools of strife.'

So had Seymour said, thought Harry, puzzled about why two such different males of his acquaintance should have his welfare so much at heart. 'You will act as my second?' he asked Richard.

'I? But, sir, you should choose from one of your own friends — a gentleman, and a knight of your own standing.'

'I prefer you,' Harry said. 'What is the next step?'

'Gravely is to be Christowe's supporter. He suggested tomorrow at dawn in the fields adjoining the apple orchard. An acceptance from yourself would confirm it.'

'Then go to Gravely and tell him I agree the terms.' Harry sat up and reached for the jug of wine on his table. 'You have obviously been this way before — what else can you tell me?'

'I have — if you will recall, I served Lord Silas Marchmont before you.'

Harry looked around for a glass. 'Ah, yes. . . Silas. He was killed, was he not, last year? In a duel at Nonsuch?'

'He was.'

'But I'll not hold that against you. As I asked — what else can you tell me?'

'Only that you should sleep now, and——' Richard took the wine from his master's hands ' — have a clear head on the morrow.'

CHAPTER SIX

BESS had reached her chamber in a state bordering on panic. She could not remember any occasion when Harry had been so angry with her, had shouted at her, and she was in despair. All my fault, she wept, all my fault! Her room was empty at the moment, for it was still early by palace standards, and she was grateful that the other ladies sharing her room were not present to see her tears.

She removed her hood and jewellery and sat down by the fire. She longed to be in her home, with Harry accessible to talk with and solve this problem. She had always deplored the court etiquette which insisted that husbands and wives sleep apart, unless both were permanent members of the assembly. She never felt closer to Harry than when, at Maiden Court, they retired to their handsome bedchamber with its welcoming fire and broad comfortable bed where they could talk over events of the day. Here, lying in the dim light from one candle, he had been able to reveal himself. His hopes, his fears, the personality which dwelt beneath the handsome charming exterior he chose to present to others. In the early months Bess had been greatly saddened by the confidences they shared.

For Harry had never felt secure. His father had

died when he was seven years old, his mother at his birth. His aunt Julia had been worthy enough, and determined to do her best for her nephew, but had cast him away into a competitive and confusing world at a time when he was very vulnerable from losing his best-beloved parent. Harry's father, Stephen, had been an unusual man. Vague and unworldly certainly, under the thumb of his domineering sister without doubt, but a brilliant musician, a talented poet, a free thinker in a world uncompromisingly narrow if you were bred among the first families of the English aristocracy. He and his only son had been the greatest of friends and, when Stephen died, Harry was lost.

Thrust into the service of a great nobleman, Harry had struggled for a place among boys who had not been raised to care for others, to regard the weak as the responsibility of the strong; here wealth and ambition were all and Harry had neither.

By the time he had been promoted to squire he had learned to deal with these disadvantages. Naturally athletic, he excelled in the games the boys at court must take part in, and his comrades admired him accordingly. Acutely intelligent, he soon acquired a slick tongue to avoid the kind of confrontations all young males were subject to and which, aware of his wild temper, he did not trust himself to engage in. Sexually precocious, he found that a powerful supportive woman could be more valuable than gold to a young man living on his wits. Along the way he also discovered in himself an ability to predict with an almost uncanny accuracy the outcome of any contest of chance.

But underneath, where it counted, Harry had retained a sensitive soul, around which he had erected a durable shell to hide the complicated and insecure self that Bess de Cheyne discovered and fell in love with. She perceived immediately that whatever image Latimar projected, there was within a man worth cherishing...

'My lady.' The timid serving maid touched Lady Latimar's arm for a second time.

Bess started. 'Yes?'

'His Grace is asking for you. The Prince Edward is unwell, and the king wishes you to come to the nurseries.'

Inside the stuffy apartments the little prince tossed and turned on the overstuffed bed. Henry, an unlikely member of any scene involving the sick, came across the floor and took Bess's hand.

'Lady Bess — my son is sick and the doctors are telling me some fantastic tale.'

Bess dropped her neat curtsy and smiled encouragingly. 'Do you sit down, sire, and I will look at the little lad now.' She approached the bed. Edward's doctors were hovering over the boy, their faces gloomy.

'What appears to be wrong?' Bess whispered. The court physicians, Doctors Owens and Butts, looked at her with relief. They were both eminent men, well respected for their knowledge, but the responsibility of tending the heir to the throne was a grave one, especially when the incumbent of that throne refused to accept their carefully considered opinions.

'We feel—we are almost sure 'tis the quartan fever, my lady,' Dr Owens said.

'The quartan fever?' Bess took the hand of the child and sat down beside the bed, noting the dry and burning hot fingers which gripped hers convulsively. She looked into the boy's face, seeing it was the colour of a tallow candle, the eyes glassy and staring. Edward's night-rail and bed-linen were damp with sweat. At first sight she was inclined to agree with the diagnosis.

The quartan fever, commonly known as the sweating sickness, was dreaded by nobleman and peasant alike—there were survivors, but their survival always mysterious. This particular plague was capricious regarding its victims: a sickly child would recover, a strong man die within a few days. Bess had been one of the former. When she was ten years old, delicate and frail, she had contracted a form of it, but, nursed devotedly by Joan for five days, had survived. Harry was another survivor—he had been nursed equally devotedly by his friend, George Boleyn.

'He must take liquid,' Bess said, standing and holding out her hand to the water jug. 'As much as he can, as often as he can.'

Dr Butts frowned. 'The sweating is severe, my lady—to give him water would only feed the malaise.'

'Water', repeated Bess firmly. 'Sweetened with a

little honey for sustenance. I will assist with the nursing and all will be well.'

Henry, at the door, grasped like a man drowning at the straw that was Bess Latimar. 'Everything shall be as my lady says,' he ordered. 'Shall I. . .?'

'You will go and take your rest,' Bess said, smiling her sweet smile. 'There is nothing that you can do for your son except leave him in my fond hands. Also — you must not risk any infection to yourself.'

Glad enough to retire, Henry repeated his instruction that Lady Bess's orders must be carried out to the last detail, and took himself away.

Bess rolled up her sleeves and prepared for battle. Her wishes, gently but determinedly expressed, were fulfilled. Fresh sweet water was brought regularly from the well, vinegar-soaked sheets were hung in the doorways to prevent any spread of the disease, Edward's clothes and bed-linen were changed frequently that he might lie more comfortably. Often Bess rose from her chair by the bed and opened the window briefly to let in air to replace that which was stale. She constantly pressed soft linen to the little boy's damp forehead and murmured tender words of encouragement. It was a very long night, but Edward survived it and at dawn fell into a more natural sleep.

Shortly afterwards there was a commotion in the ante-chamber and Bess rose again, stiff and cramped, to admonish whoever was foolish enough to be noisy while their little prince was enjoying his first real sleep in two days. Harry was just beyond the door. When he saw Bess he shook himself free from the restraining hands of the guards and came swiftly to her side.

'Bess, what is happening here? I have been refused admission for several hours.'

'Hush, Harry. The little boy is sick, but sleeping normally at last. What is amiss?'

'What is amiss? I was told my wife attended the royal nursery. As I come here to have words with her, these oafs——' he indicated the stolid guards '—tell me on the king's instructions no one may enter.'

'Ssh! Come in then and say what you must.' Bess went composedly before him into the dim room. Harry stood at the foot of Edward's bed and surveyed the child.

'While waiting I overheard one of the doctors declare he cannot live long. The man insists the prince is too fat and weakly to survive.'

'Nonsense!' Bess said sharply. 'I believe he will. I am sure he will.' Harry looked at her. Even a night of watching and waiting over a sick child had not dulled her shining beauty; Bess was as dainty and fresh as after a full ten hours' rest. His heart contracted. My sweet love, he thought. What was wrong between them? No more than a series of misunderstandings, which he had resolved during the dark hours to put right without delay.

'What is it you wished to say, Harry?' she asked. She had also been thinking during the night.

Recovering from his attack on her, she had suffered a reversal of opinion, and now was on the defensive.

'I am not sure,' Harry said slowly. 'Only that I much regret what happened earlier.'

'How much earlier?' she asked crisply. 'In the garden with the Spanish demoiselle, or in the great hall with Will Christowe?'

'You know I mean the affair with Christowe, and what I said to you afterwards. The other was nothing, and I cannot believe you think otherwise.'

Bess carefully folded the square of linen she held. She glanced at the bed where Edward still slept peacefully, one plump hand beneath his flushed cheek. It was not over yet, she thought; the disease, once present, had lulls and storms before it left the body altogether. She said, 'It hurt me, Harry. I witnessed your hands upon her, your lips on hers.'

'Sweetheart,' he said helplessly, 'both hands and lips belong only to you. I have never, never. . .' He stumbled over the resented denial, and resorted to attack. 'Can you declare the same?'

She gave him a straight blue look. 'Since that time in the gardens at Richmond, she has been constantly at your side! The girl is infatuated with you — am I to believe this came about with no encouragement from you?'

'Christowe is infatuated with *you*!' he protested. 'Has that happened without *your* encouragement?'

'Yes. It has. For Will told me he fell in love with me at the moment of meeting.' There, let him know that she too was desirable, and had to fight her own battles in this arena.

'Damn him, then!' Harry exploded. 'What made him believe you were available for his lovesick fancies?'

'Past association with you,' Bess said coolly. 'And recent observations of a husband who appears to care little for what is his. A complaisant husband, I believe is the term used.'

Harry's eyes narrowed. He had come here prepared to apologise for his hasty words, for distressing her. Prepared to. . . Now she taunted him with these insulting remarks. Some said it was impossible to love greatly without also hating the object of that love; at this moment he could believe it. 'Then a lady would have indicated what you describe is not the case,' he said coldly.

There was a bitter silence, broken only by the constricted breathing of the child on the bed. Beyond the windows the dim November sun climbed higher into a leaden sky. It was day.

Bess said, swallowing, 'You will not ever forget my humble beginnings, will you?'

'I have never thought of them!' he returned furiously. ''Tis you who can never forget my reputation. You persist in thinking I can prefer another woman—indeed you hold yourself cheap, my dear.'

'I do not! But every time I am with you there is some woman hovering, and I am tired of it! Why should I have to compete for you, Harry? It is. . .it is. . .humiliating.' Both their voices had been raised in the quiet room: Edward moved his head on the pillow and half opened his eyes. Bess said tearfully, 'I think you should go now. I have undertaken the task of nursing the prince back to health and do not wish to fail in this as I have apparently failed in my marriage.' Tears stung her eyes; she hardly knew what she was saying now.

'You have not failed,' Harry said desperately. 'Please Bess, never say that.'

'What does it matter if I say it?' she replied drearily. 'I never expected security when I married you, Harry, and have not been disappointed.'

This time the silence was overpowering. Security. The one thing Harry Latimar craved above all others, and which had been so generously offered by the girl twisting her hands before him now. He had accepted that most valuable gift and tried to return it in full measure. Now she stood before him in this evil-smelling sick-room and denied his efforts. Denied them with a look of despair in her eyes.

'I must prepare the physic for when he wakes,' Bess said. 'Have you nothing you should be about?'

He looked at the shaft of sun slanting over the embroidered bedspread, his mind blank. If he could only find the words, words which came so easily with any other person, not one tenth as dear to him as Bess. . . But he could think of nothing to say which would take that look from her eyes. He turned to the door. 'You have pressing duties,' he said dully. 'When you choose to take a break from them, seek me out and we will speak again.' He opened the door, lifted aside the bitter-smelling sheets and went out.

Bess sat again beside the bed. She concentrated her mind on the sick boy, ignoring the turmoil within her. Gently she replaced the covers Edward had tossed back in his delirium, and leaned back in her chair and closed her eyes.

Harry descended the stairs to his apartments. There he found Richard de Vere waiting for him. Harry leaned over his bowl of washing water and splashed a little on his face.

'Sir,' Richard said tentatively.

'What is it, Richard?' Harry turned, drops beading his thick black lashes.

'Lord Christowe's seconds have been looking for you. I hardly knew what to tell them.'

Harry rubbed linen over his face. My God, he thought, the duel—I have forgotten all about it! He said, 'Is Christowe waiting for me?'

'Yes, sir. Out beyond the orchards. Shall I tell him you are indisposed and unable to meet him?'

'No,' Harry said. 'I will go there now. What did we decide now? Rapiers? Has he them with him?'

'Yes, sir. But——'

'Then let us get on with it, my boy. This day can scarcely get any worse. . .'

Will was pacing the meadow when they arrived. He did not know what to make of Latimar's late arrival, and Harry's face told him nothing of the reason for it. He handed over the corresponding foil to his own without speaking.

Richard said nervously, 'Let us wait, Lord Will, for your supporters to arrive.'

'For what reason?' Harry said easily. 'I think we three can be relied upon to see there is fair play.' He removed his doublet and gave it to his squire; at leisure he took off his arm bracelets and the emerald pendant at his throat.

Richard retired to a space a dozen feet away, his boy's face anxious in the feeble light. Harry contemplated the weapon in his hand, its length of steel more brilliant than the light. In his youth he had excelled in this sport. He had had a special friend from the French court who had coached him in the art. What had been his name? François. He could recall him now—slim, dark and witty. He had been killed in the slaughter of Henry's first invasion of Calais... He glanced at Richard, who said awkwardly, 'Then begin, gentlemen.'

Harry raised the foil and lowered it in salute. '*En garde*,' he said casually.

The two men engaged. Young squires were required to learn the skill of fencing as part of their preparation for knighthood, and both men had been well trained, although under different masters. Harry's, Richard recalled, had been a dour old man, more concerned with style than victory, Will's his successor—who held that to win was more important than style.

Knighthood attained, the gentlemen with aptitude

passed on to mock warfare with lance and short sword in the tournaments. In the early days, before he discovered gambling as an easier way of supplementing his poor stipend, Harry had often travelled to tourneys held both in England and abroad where the prizes were in cash rather than in glory. At Maiden Court the hall cupboard held a glittering array of silver cups which Harry, having spent their useful content of coinage, had bundled into hopsacks and forgotten. On their marriage, Bess had resurrected this evidence of her new husband's skill and proudly displayed them, regularly supervising their burnishing with wood ash and soft cloth.

In spite of moving on to more dangerous sport, Harry had, over the years, kept up his fencing practice mainly because the graceful, stylised movements pleased him; the ritual stances so precise, the concentration — a necessary tool of his present source of income — invaluable. But he had never fought an opponent in this exercise intent on deliberate injury. Now he found he did.

Will Christowe, he suspected, would not be content with the traditional strike on either side to decide the winner. He was prepared to pursue the matter to the limit. Harry knew this instinctively as the opening moves were made, and prepared to decide what he must do to prevent, or counter, such determination. While assembling this thought, he came across another: Will must be very sure that if he took Bess's husband out of the game, she would turn to him, be his. This knowledge did not bring a return of the anger against Will he had felt last night in the hall, but a furious resentment against Bess for allowing her admirer to believe this. In the first minutes of the engagement Harry knew he could best this young man, kill him if necessary, but had no wish to. He felt, perhaps irrationally, that Will was less at fault in this than his wife. The bout continued.

Richard, near enough to observe both men closely, relaxed a little. Seymour's advice, spoken to Harry in the gardens, and later to his squire, had been sound. Will Christowe was an experienced soldier, but he did not have the expertise in this particular field to take Latimar. His master, Richard decided with relief, would allow the bout to go on for some time then make his move, draw blood, and insist that honour had been satisfied.

This decision pleased the boy. If Harry had made it clear he would go another route, Richard would have supported him, but it would have destroyed the romantic hero-worship he had for the man. Latimar was an integral part of the English court, and therefore, presumably, as unscrupulous as the rest of the courtiers who jockeyed for position in that unhealthy atmosphere, but Richard had never observed him in a shabby act, never witnessed the casual cruelty his peers displayed. He had seen Harry strip a man at the tables, then press a large gift of money on the same man a day later, seen him rail at a young courtier for a breach of etiquette, then in private gently advise him of more seemly conduct.

As to personal matters—Latimar did not disappoint him there either. Richard de Vere had served his pageship in the household of a relative and observed the activities of those considered to be the highest in the land. Promiscuity was accepted and the norm, but Lord Harry had no part in this. In the absence of his wife, he escorted the ladies to the various entertainments, danced with them, was charmingly evasive to their open invitations, but he slept alone.

Half an hour into the contest Harry decided it. He parried one of Will's wild assaults, stepped back and delicately inserted the tip of his blade into Will's shoulder. The blood spouted freely, but the wound was superficial and would cause no lasting harm. He lowered his rapier. Richard hurried forward.

'It is over, gentlemen, I think.'

'Not so,' Will declared. 'I am not bad hurt; we will continue.' Who, he thought, would have suspected Latimar of being so formidable an opponent?

'Come, Christowe,' Harry said. 'You and I have better things to do this morning.'

'I have nothing better to do,' Will said aggressively. He had clapped a hand to his shoulder, but the bright blood seeped through his fingers and sullied his white shirt.

Before Harry could reply a big man came through the apple trees and across the cropped grass towards them. It was the king, and Harry tossed down his weapon and bowed.

'What are you about here?' Henry demanded, his bloodshot eyes passing over the three standing still before him.

'A little early morning exercise,' Harry said genially. 'You protest that your gentlemen grow flabby; Christowe and I were attempting to remedy that.'

'I have heard gossip of a duel,' Henry said, turning his gaze on Will, who flushed darkly.

'Nonsense!' Harry said. 'Such is forbidden in your court. 'Twas only a friendly exchange — Richard, if you please, escort Will back to the palace and bind up his wound.' He gave his charming smile. 'I am out of practice and a little careless, sir. I know you will excuse Lord Will to the ministrations of my squire.'

Richard, recovered from the sudden advent of royalty, stepped forward and grasped Will's uninjured arm. 'Come, sir, and I will attend to that for you.' He used a little force to propel the other man across the damp grass.

Henry retrieved Harry's foil and looked at it thoughtfully. He said, 'What was really happening, Harry?'

'Nothing.' Harry picked up his doublet which Richard had laid on the dew-soaked field, and examined the dark stains, frowning. 'Best Canterbury silk,' he said regretfully.

''Twas over Bess, I suppose,' Henry sighed. 'I warned you, Harry. Now you have hurt the boy.'

''Tis only a scratch, Hal.' Harry shrugged into his

doublet and felt in the purse attached for his jewellery. 'You are abroad early this day.'

'I have been wakeful all night,' Henry said gloomily. 'My son is sick.'

'Bess will see to him. I spoke with her not an hour ago and already the boy is improved.'

Henry's face lightened, then fell again. 'I have just signed Culpeper's death warrant,' he said quietly. 'Dereham's also — although I will not grieve over that. Catherine is to be arrested before noon. Truly, Harry, this is a dismal day for me.'

Harry looked over the land stretching out under the dull sky. He felt an inexplicable longing for his own land — Maiden Court, so peaceful, so beautiful, so far removed from the dark atmosphere of this place. ''Twill be a sad Christmas for you, sir. Why do you not allow me to entertain you in my home? Quit this place with its bitter memories and ride for Kew with me.'

'It is impossible,' Henry said shortly. 'I cannot leave Edward until I know him better, and many pressing duties await me during the next weeks.' Both men were silent then; above them a rigid formation of wild ducks flew, uttering their harsh cries.

'I truly loved her, you know,' Henry said painfully. 'I would have given her anything, *anything*. She betrayed me, and since knowing that I have felt. . .old. . .finished.'

'Ah, don't say that, my friend. 'Tis not over, you know, until the last card is laid. You have many happy years ahead, I am sure. And in those years there will be another lady to love you.'

'Years without my Catherine—she is to be executed in the New Year. My ministers left me little choice in the matter.' The king turned the weapon he held in his hands. 'I will not ask for sympathy for her—I know you will not regret her passing.'

'I regret the passing of any so young and beautiful,' Harry said sincerely.

'Which presumably explains why Christowe has walked from this place today, and was not carried,' Henry said drily.

'I have told you it was nothing,' Harry insisted. 'Now, let us eat—I am not used to prancing about in a field before fortifying myself first.' As they walked back he wondered what, if anything, had been resolved with Will Christowe after their ridiculous posturing that morning. Would it be easier if he accepted the king's offer to find an occupation for the young man away from the English court? That way he would be removed both from Bess and himself. Harry had seen enough feuds between courtiers over the years to know how uncomfortable they were at best; how potentially explosive they were at worst. Today he had governed himself to let Will off with a prick, in the future—under constant provocation—maybe things would be different. The difference would depend on Bess, and after their conversation this morning he was unsure how she would act. He sighed as they turned into the courtyard and passed through the stables. Bess, Bess, he thought, why did you not stay safe at home?

The king went ahead into the palace and Harry heard his name called and turned to find Madrilene, mounted on a tall chestnut, coming towards him. He looked up.

'What do you think of him?' she asked. 'A new acquisition of mine—is he not beautiful?' She was simply dressed that day in velvet skirt and short jacket which moulded her pretty figure seductively. Her hair was unconfined and streamed over her shoulders. After Bess's cruel words that morning, Madrilene's adoring glance soothed his injured pride.

'Very fine.' Harry moved as the animal flung up his head and showed his teeth. 'Perhaps not the best-tempered creature, though.'

Madrilene soothed her mount with tender words. 'He has a mind of his own, certainly, but what male worthy of the name does not? I like a challenge, as you know.'

'And costly, I imagine,' Harry went on, ignoring her provocative words.

'Probably—I did not enquire. I was shown him yesterday, and immediately knew I must possess him.'

'How very pleasant it must be not to have to ask the price of what you want.'

'He has a beautiful brother—say the word and he is yours. A gift.'

'Kind, but impossible.'

'Why? You know I would do anything for you,

Harry.' She leaned down and brushed her gloved hand over his bare head. He moved away as he had from the strong teeth of her horse.

'If you wish to do something for me, my dear,' he said mildly, 'do not make matters worse with Bess.'

Madrilene's slim fingers plaited the glossy mane. Since the night at Richmond when Harry had played fast and loose with his wife's home, she had seen no contact between the Latimars. Constantly with Harry, he was still totally resistant to her advances. Now, this morning, in spite of his words, she sensed a change. She gathered her reins. 'Perhaps I should have said — almost anything.' She chirruped to the great animal and manoeuvred away. Harry went into the hall alone.

Yuletide came to Hampton with sleet and strong winds. This year the pervading atmosphere, despite the usual revels, was one of gloom. Culpeper and Dereham had already answered for their crimes — the king, true to his words by the still pond, had ordered his former friend's remains paraded on the Tower gates for all to see. Catherine had been transported under heavy guard to Syon House to spend the days in contemplation of her own death. The date for her execution was irrevocably set for early in the coming year.

On the day of her arrest Harry had been a horrified witness to the young queen's last words to her husband. Seated in the little chapel gallery with Henry, he had heard a commotion in the passage outside, then the pathetic sound of small hands beating on the wooden door. Catherine had slipped the guards at the door of her apartments and run screaming to plead with the king to protect her. 'Save me, Henry,' she had cried three times before being dragged away. All those in the gallery had had to endure this wretched scene, as Henry sat with rigid limbs and face of stone. It was hardly surprising that the court Catherine was now exiled from found it difficult to abandon themselves to pleasure.

They were cheered as the year drew to a close by the news that their little prince, after an anxious time, was now fully recovered from his illness and even the king's face lost some of its misery.

Bess, released at last from her duties in the sickroom, was able to return to the round of gaiety. In truth she could have left her charge some days before, but shrank from it. Although Harry had not communicated with her, Will Christowe had written regular letters which had grown more passionate as the days passed. She dreaded having to hear those fervent words from him in the flesh. She knew nothing of his confrontation with Harry — few did. Most believed that the incident in the hall had been resolved by a little of the Latimar diplomacy and had come to nothing. Bess was one of those who believed this.

Howsoever, as she dressed in the apartments adjoining the nursery, she knew her brief retreat was over. She had amused herself in the night vigils by adding a few fashionable items to her wardrobe. The king, relieved of the responsibility of worrying over his son's health by the obvious competence of his nurse, had been generosity itself, pressing costly materials on her, instructing her to make use of the needlewomen housed within his palace. The result of their combined efforts was several gowns and kirtles and a half-dozen examples of the charming and fashionable French hood. These delightful little stiffened caps, worn far back on the head to expose the wearer's hair and ornamented with jewels in the shape of a halo, were very flattering to Bess, with her distinctive hair and perfect, cameo-pure face. She put one on now—her favourite with its silk ruched border and ring of pearls—and thought how well it became her.

As she dabbed a little distilled rosewater on her wrists the door opened and Edward stood there. He advanced into the room and made his little bow. 'Good morning, my lady Latimar.'

She smiled. Edward had lost flesh during his illness and she believed she detected a resemblance now to his half-sister, Elizabeth, whom Bess seldom saw now but remembered fondly. 'Twas the pallor, she decided, the thin intelligent features and bright eyes. She dropped a respectful curtsy.

'Good day, sir. You are looking very well today.'

'As are you.' Edward's eyes roved appreciatively over her. Towards the end of his convalescence he had begun to love Bess. She was so calm, he thought, that was what he loved most about her. In the early days of his illness his room had been a furore of doctors and nurses wringing their hands and lamenting. Then Lady Bess had come, soft-spoken and gentle-handed. She had sung to him that first night, he remembered vaguely, not the popular ballads of the court, but lilting country songs—lullabies to send him into healing sleep. Now she would pass out of his life again and leave a space not adequately filled by the fawning men and women he spent his time with. He said wistfully, 'I am to leave Hampton today, lady.'

'So soon? I thought 'twas to be next week.'

Edward glanced out at the heavy sky. 'Those who know such things predict snow—I must not be on the roads when it begins to fall. I have come to say goodbye.' He extended his hand.

Bess took it and curtsied again, but the child flung his arms around her waist and hugged her. 'How I wish you could come home with me,' he said, his voice stifled against the fur which lined her full sleeves.

'Nay, little boy,' Bess said gently, touching the stiff fair hair which had grown long in the weeks he had lain abed. 'I have babes of my own, you know; they need me.' Joan had been a good correspondent—or rather her steward had, at her dictation—and Bess knew all was well with George and Anne, but how she missed them. . .

'I need you more,' Edward cried. 'See how you have cared for me when I was sick enough to die.'

'That would never have happened, with prayers

said in every church in your land—and your father, willing your recovery with all his strong will.'

'Yes. . .' Edward went to the window and climbed on to the seat to look out. 'My stepmother is to die, did you know? After the Yuletide.'

'No, I didn't know.' Bess put an arm about his thin shoulders. 'But you must not think on that—or any sad thing. Only eat your food and be strong again and learn to laugh a little. Life is not so serious, you know, Edward.'

'It is for me. When I go home my education begins in earnest. I have to learn to govern England when my father is gone.'

'That is so, of course,' Bess said absently. This window overlooked the little courtyard where the ladies took their exercise in poor weather. A group of three, huddled in long cloaks, laughed together in the wind. The hood fell back from one animated face and Bess saw it was Madrilene, her long black hair lifted in shining ebony strands. I could go home now, Bess thought. All danger of contamination is past. Why not go home and be with my babes for Christmas?

'Lady?' Edward looked up. 'I am sorry for acting the baby—I know, really, I must face my duty. We all, if we are worthy, must do that.'

'That is true, Edward,' Bess sighed. 'Go now and find your nurse, my prince. And God speed to Havering-atte-Bowe.'

* * *

As soon as Bess entered the great hall three people ceased concentrating on their meal to watch her. Harry, beside the king, suffered a constriction of the heart which almost stunned him. Will Christowe, reaching for the ale jug, experienced as intense a jolt. Madrilene tore apart a piece of white bread with her long pointed fingers and thought, Pity indeed she did not contract the disease of her royal charge and so make my task easier!

Harry touched the king's arm and indicated his wife. Henry nodded and Harry rose and went to her. They stared at each other across the room heavy with the smell of savoury dishes and thick with smoke from the fires, as if seeing each other for the first time. Will Christowe, Bess thought, or any man was less than nothing in her eyes when considered against Latimar. My darling, thought Harry, a little pale from her close confinement, but more beautiful and desirable than any other lady on earth. He said, 'The king would like words with you, Bess. Come to him now.' He drew out a chair beside Henry and put her into it, glad to have annexed her from any other attention. Across the room Will subsided back on the bench, his eyes hot in his tanned face.

Henry nodded and smiled as they discussed Edward for a while. When Henry was called away by one of his ministers, Bess turned to Harry.

'The danger being past of my taking infection home, I see no reason why I may not return to Maiden Court without delay.'

Her first words to him a demand to leave! Looking

into her calm face, he could see no sign of her having suffered from their separation. 'I suppose not.'

'But you cannot come also?'

'No,' he agreed. 'The king asks most particularly that I be here.'

'I see.' Henry had poured her a cup of his own sweet wine and she drank a little.

'You are wearing a new gown,' Harry said with an effort. 'It becomes you very well. I like you in that pale blue.'

'Indeed? I have heard you favour a brighter colour on a lady these days.'

Harry appeared to consider her words carefully. Then, 'On a lady of more definite colouring, yes — red, emerald are flattering.'

Bess looked pointedly out over the assembly. Madrilene wore vivid green this morning. 'What became of the challenge from Lord Christowe? Did you manage to avoid anything as vulgar as a direct confrontation?'

'We met the morning you were summoned to the royal nursery. We indulged in a little schoolboy sparring then went our separate ways.'

She looked at him. 'There was no hurt to either side?'

'I am sorry to disappoint you if you wished for a more dramatic outcome but — no — Christowe suffered a small prick to both his body and his pride, other than that. . . But surely you must know this — I have heard a messenger has been in regular employment carrying his missives to you.'

'He wrote to me, yes,' Bess admitted.

'And you wrote back? Tender letters from the heart?'

She did not reply. He settled more comfortably in his chair, turning his silver goblet in his hands. The desire to punish her for her composure formed his next words. 'Now you are about again,' he said calmly, 'perhaps we should continue the conversation we began regarding the fact that you and I may have come to a parting of the ways.'

'I remember no such conversation,' she said indistinctly. 'If you wish to be rid of me, Harry, you will get no help from me in the enterprise.' What had happened in her absence? Had Madrilene made such headway that he talked now of ridding himself of his wife?

'Please explain,' Harry said politely.

She turned various answers over in her mind. I cannot live without you—please, whatever is amiss between us, let us talk and resolve it... Whatever feeling you have for Madrilene, whatever feeling you think I have for Will, it *cannot* stand against what we have...or at least on my side. Finally she said stiffly, 'I do not wish our children to grow up knowing their parents were so at odds they must part.'

Harry refilled her cup. 'I am not sure I can rearrange my life to accommodate the future speculations of two babes even now only nine months old.'

'Eleven,' she choked. 'They are eleven months.'

'I am rebuked,' Harry said placidly. 'However, they are not yet a year old and when they grow to reason I am sure they will understand.'

But I do not understand, thought Bess. However did we reach such a pass? She stole a glance at him, noticing things only a wife would: that he was dressed in a new costume of fine grey velvet, cut in a more severe style than he usually favoured, that he had a half-healed cut upon one hand, probably due to his habit of reaching into the cock-pit to rescue the losing bird made snappish by the pain. That he had not lately bowed to the king's rule that his gentlemen wear their hair very short — his now curled over his high lace collar.

After a moment he returned her scrutiny, seeing that if he had wanted revenge for the sleepless nights imagining the content of the letters exchanged between her and Christowe, he had with that remark gained it. Wild when out of control, Henry had said. True words. But she gave him no opening to retract the words. After that fleeting expression of pain, she said coolly, 'We cannot decide anything suddenly. Do I have your permission to leave Hampton for Maiden Court?'

'The weather is uncertain,' he said slowly. 'Unless you plan to leave immediately. I do not wish you to travel in snow, even so short a distance.'

'Is that yes or no?'

'It is. . . Wait and see what the next days bring. Now, Henry is anxious to play a new game he has devised with a set of cards presented to him. Will you come with me?'

'I have not eaten yet.'

'Ah.' Harry rose as the king beckoned from the door.

'Let me not detain you,' Bess said, helping herself to food she knew she would not eat.

'Perhaps you will join us later?'

'I think not after the last occasion. No, you go on, Harry, I will find amusement elsewhere.'

Harry still hesitated until Henry called, 'Latimar, we are waiting.'

Still Harry hesitated, reluctant to leave Bess after his treatment of her. But — how much did she really care for what he had said? She was like a stranger to him now, almost she appeared to belong to the man sitting a few yards away, watching them... He bowed and left her.

Harry was kept at the king's side all day. At dusk he excused himself and presented himself at the door of Bess's chamber intending to take her down to the supper table. For a time he disbelieved the maid who told him that my lady Latimar had left the palace at midday. It was impossible that Bess had left without a word to him! But, thinking back on their conversation that morning, he recalled that he had only denied her permission to leave unless she go immediately.

Had she taken this to mean he wished that? He did not know. Actually, he thought, going down to the meal with no appetite at all, he found it hard now to understand anything she said or did. He admitted his share of the blame for this — he had, as usual, hidden the fact that she had hurt him beneath a show of indifference. But Bess knew this was how he dealt with emotional pain. She knew.

As he sat over his meal he saw Will Christowe come in and their eyes met over the heads of the others. Harry wondered if Bess had found time to bid him farewell. If he asked, he would get an honest answer, he knew, but pride kept him from doing so. Pride, thought Harry bitterly, was about all he would have left if Bess had truly deserted him. Why had he said what he had about their parting? When nothing could be more horrible to him? Harry spent a miserable supper, and left the table early.

Bess had indeed said goodbye to Will, not because she had sought him out especially, but because he had been in the stable yard when she had gone there in haste that morning. She and Mary had packed their trunks swiftly and Walter had been summoned to prepare their mounts. The dismal day reflected her own bleak mood. Sitting alone on the dais that morning, she had thought, Now I know. Harry not only cares little if I stay in this place near him, or go back home, but he cares nothing if I be dismissed from his life completely.

A desperate thought, but one which must be faced. This moment, she decided, had been creeping up on them over years, not weeks. Her husband was not to be domesticated—not by a loving wife, a comfortable home, or by the advent of two charming dependants. He must be free. Free to pursue his own interests. A pretty wife was an asset to him as long as she knew and kept to her place; but one who questioned his wasteful ways, his addiction to the gaming tables, who reminded him of his responsibilities and reacted aggressively to his pleasure in another pretty face—that he would not tolerate. Today had been a dire warning and if she did not heed it, it would become fact.

Will came to her side as she prepared to mount. 'Bess?'

'Good day, Will, you are riding today?'

'I have been seeing for my destrier—he is failing now and past his best, but I am fond of him.'

Bess drew on her gloves. 'Is he sick? I am sorry.'

'Not sick. Just old. I fear I must give him the grace of a swift end any day now, but keep putting off the moment. I am a coward when it comes to doing my duty.'

'Aren't we all?' Bess smiled ruefully.

'But I am free now—if you ride out I shall be glad to accompany you.'

'I am going home, Will. Back to my duty—if my sweet babes can be thus described.' *And to do my duty by my husband, allowing him a freedom I wish he did not desire. . .*

'Home?' Will looked amazed. 'But surely you are to keep the Yuletide at Hampton?'

'No... I stayed this long only to ensure the little prince was truly recovered. Now I must go.'

Will watched the dull light caress her bright hair and rest on the translucent skin of her face. How beautiful she was, how perfect. 'I am surprised your husband can bear to be parted from you—even to nurture his children.'

'I think Harry will not be sorry that I go,' she said quietly.

'Did you receive my letters?' he asked abruptly. 'You replied not once.'

'I received them, and read them. But you should not have written them, Will.'

'Should I not? How many such letters did you receive from Harry, Bess? Not a one, I would swear, for he has spent the time of your seclusion——' He stopped, flushing.

'Yes?' asked Bess challengingly.

'I should not say what is in my mind.'

'But since you have begun—pray go on.'

'Do you think he cares for you now, Bess?' Will asked awkwardly. 'Indeed—do you care for him?'

'I am not sure, is the answer to your first question. Yes, and yes, and yes, the proper reply to the second,' Bess said softly. She turned to Walter and he assisted her into the saddle.

''Tis goodbye then, Will, I wish you luck in the future.'

He caught her bridle. 'He met me on the field of honour, you know. But mocked me. In mocking me he mocked the reason for our meeting. You know that, do you not?' Bess said nothing. He retained his hold on her reins. 'He would not even fight for you, Bess. Can you still care for a man who will not meet such an obligation?'

'Yes again, Will,' she answered, half smiling.

'May I call upon you at Maiden Court?'

She considered, then said, 'As a friend, yes, you may. In any other capacity you will not be welcome.' She raised her leather crop in salute, turned her mount's head and clattered out of the yard.

CHAPTER SEVEN

BESS kept Christmas at Maiden Court, and the spring of 1542. As early summer began to show itself in the woods and fields around her home, she looked for Harry each day. But no temperamental black horse set its hooves on the grassy lawns before the house, no tall figure strode into its stone porch, flung open its stout oak door, and called out in musical voice, 'Bess? My darling — I am home.'

Her mother watched her anxiously. Joan had been displeased when her daughter had abandoned her children in favour of her husband last autumn, and delighted when she returned. But that return had not been of Bess's free will, she was sure. Bess had arrived on the last day of November as sleet swirled over the smoking chimneys. Exhausted and numbed with cold, the mistress of Maiden Court had almost fallen from her saddle and had subsequently been abed for two days.

Rising on the third, apparently recovered, she had greeted her twins ecstatically. But the girl who had ridden away had not come back, and Joan, knowing that however much Bess adored her babies their father was the mainspring of her life, was fearful.

Christmas Day had been merry enough — George and Anne were almost a year old now and able to

167

take joyful part in the proceedings, and their laughter did a little to ease Bess's longing for Harry. It had begun to snow the eve before, but shortly after the splendid goose had been consumed at midday, two strong messengers from Hampton Court Palace braved the glittering drifts and delivered gifts to all at Maiden Court.

Harry had sent luxurious and expensive toys to both his children, magnificent jewellery to his wife and mother-in-law. Joan de Cheyne had never seen such wonderfully matched and perfectly coloured pearls as she received. She held them in her slim work-worn hands and in an unaccustomed flight of fancy imagined them being raised from the depths of an alien ocean by dark men whose features she could not envisage.

Bess's gift was a ruby. In the shape of a heart, it resembled one half of her engagement ring which was in the unusual design of two great stones — one a heart-shaped ruby, one a diamond — linked by pale gold. She seldom wore the magnificent trinket; even at court it was as ostentatious an ornament as could be imagined. But she treasured it deeply, often took it from its little velvet pouch and looked at it, cleaned it frequently with loving hands.

Now, holding the new and shining jewel, she relived the evening she had agreed to marry Latimar. Heard again the pounding of the surf on the Devon beach, felt again the sharp tang of salt against her lips, a preparatory sensation only to the insistent taste of Harry's mouth on hers.

She reached for the little note in the tissue packaging, and unfolded it. 'You have the more vulnerable original,' Harry had written in his distinctive upright script. What did it mean? she wondered.

When two tired and excited children had been cajoled into bed, and the blue twilight had become night, Joan and Bess were able to rest a little beside the blazing fire. Joan fingered the necklace.

'It is so beautiful,' she said, running the smooth beads through her fingers. 'I have never been given such a thing in all my life! Show me your lovely gift again.' She examined the ruby, touched the slim gold chain reverently. 'It is very valuable,' she whispered. 'Are you pleased with it?'

'Who would not be?' Bess asked crisply. 'But you know Father would have dressed you from head to foot in such baubles had he the means.'

'Of course. . .I know that,' Joan said, taken aback by her daughter's tone.

'His gold was spent keeping food on our table and earned working fourteen hours a day at hard manual tasks. Harry probably spent an arduous evening at the gaming tables to provide all this.' Bess's bright blue gaze included the gems and the toys which Anne and George had left reluctantly behind them when they went to bed.

'Well. . .yes,' Joan answered doubtfully. It was a small thing; chit-chat by the fireside, but she felt it to be significant. Bess had never criticised, or allowed others to criticise, her husband before. . .

As the new year began with a spell of bitter weather,

Joan looked anxiously towards the spring. Surely then Harry would come home. . .

When the June buds in Bess's rose garden began to bloom a visitor did come to Maiden Court. Will Christowe, mounted on a handsome bay, sprang down before the house and raised the brass knocker. Bess received him in the hall. She curtsied.

'Will, I am happy to see you.'

'I remembered your instructions,' Will said with difficulty, as the sight of her had affected him so greatly. 'I come in friendship only.' The two sat and Mary Weeks brought wine and small cakes.

'How is it with you, Will?' Bess asked politely, taking up one of the spiced cakes she had made herself that morning.

'Well — or as well as can be expected. I have come here today to ask you blessing on my head before I go to war.'

'War?' Bess laid down her tasty morsel.

'You might not be aware of the latest developments,' Will said slowly, 'but our king is about to declare war on France.'

'But how can this be?' Bess demanded.

'Very easily. The Emperor Charles is at odds once more with his kinsman Francis, and Henry sees it as an opportunity to join with him and regain his kingdom in the northern provinces.' He laughed. 'Don't try to understand the intricacies of it all, dear Bess; I am sure I don't. . . In any event, that is what the king and his ministers are set upon, but before we attack France we must first ensure that Scotland will not be in a position to support our enemy. Hence — I ride shortly for the border.'

'You are for Scotland?'

'I am. In Norfolk's train.'

'Norfolk?' Bess asked coldly. She had as little regard for that ambitious and unscrupulous man as her husband did. After all, he had forced two of his pretty nieces upon his king, and abandoned them both...

'Indeed.'

Bess rose and opened one of the windows. It overlooked her rose garden — a sweet scent now invaded the room. 'So,' she said, 'you are leaving — when?'

'Within the month. But no doubt Harry will advise you of the details next time he visits.'

Bess kept her eyes on a honey bee vigorously exploring the heart of one of her roses.

'Harry will have told you, of course, of his own plans to march north?' Will went on. Bess turned, astonished.

'I think I have misheard you, Will! Harry is to take part in this? *Harry*?'

So she doesn't know, Will thought. It came as no real surprise to him. All at court were convinced now that the Latimars' marriage was over; now he felt he had the proof. This would be the moment to press his advantage. But how pale she was! And that stricken look —— He was half ashamed to have broken the news to her. But how could Latimar have thought he could keep it from her? What else had that irresponsible man chosen not to disclose? He said, 'I beg your pardon if I have told you something Harry intended for some reason keeping secret. However, now I have done so, please don't worry. Harry is as accomplished as any other in the skills needed——'

'But Harry is no soldier!' Bess broke in, too distraught to consider her words.

'He perhaps feels strongly about the cause involved. The king has long wished to reclaim his empire in France——'

'Harry cares nothing for politics!' Bess interrupted again. 'And has often said that all war is an abomination—to kill unless in defence of one's own home and family an insult to humanity.' She stopped, tears springing to her eyes. 'Why, he is a pacifist, who cannot understand why men cannot live in peace.'

Then I think less of him than I did before I came here this day, Will thought scornfully. To be great, a country must display its might, and gather countries and subjects into its empire as a squirrel gathers nuts. What he felt showed on his face, and Bess said challengingly, 'Is all this not a dilemma for you, Will? You would, after all, be taking arms against your maternal country.'

Will coloured, but replied calmly, 'My father was English, and my loyalty to the English throne.' Her cool attack forced him to disclose the real reason for his visit—which he had until now managed to persuade himself was purely based on friendship. 'If

Harry has not seen fit to advise you of his plans in respect of his immediate future, has he made mention of those affecting yours?'

'What do you mean?'

'I have heard that Maiden Court has been offered to the money-lenders for auction to recoup money lent to Latimar to cover his staggering gambling debts,' Will said bluntly.

There was a taut silence broken by footsteps on the stairs. Will looked up and saw Joan coming down, a child by either hand. Bess turned away a moment to try to recover from the shock Will's words had brought her. She ran her fingertips under her eyes to remove the tears and turned with a smile.

'George, Anne — come and join us.'

Will watched the two children toddling across the shining floor. If Bess had not changed in the past eight months, her babes had — they had grown in beauty and strength. They were eighteen months old now and there could be no mistake as to which was the male. George Latimar was a full head taller than his sister, bold-eyed and with an arrogant set to his handsome head. The twins were dressed alike in lace smocks; he kicked his skirts aside aggressively as he came to his mother's side. Anne hung back, her lashes long and tangled on her flushed cheeks, her chubby hand firmly in her grandmother's.

'My mother,' George said, holding on to Bess's skirts and looking up into her face. 'Why are you sad? Has this man made you sad?' While both children were forward in their growth, George was extraordinarily articulate in his speech.

'No, dear. This is your Uncle Will Christowe. You won't remember him, I think.'

'No, I do not,' George said dismissively. He gave Will a penetrating glance—his father's glance, thought Will uncomfortably; from crown to foot, then straight into the eyes.

'Good day, George.'

Joan led Anne forward to make her little curtsy. Will smiled on her—any man would be delighted with that flower-like face and rich, curling black hair. Will put out his hand and the child took it shyly.

'Did my father send his love?' she whispered.

'Had he known I was coming, I am sure he would have.'

'When will he come?' Anne had no memory at all of her father, no real picture to conjure up and love, but her mother spoke so often of him that Anne felt strongly that she would like him, should he ever come home again.

'Soon,' Will said awkwardly.

'You will eat with us, Lord Christowe?' Joan said. 'We have freshly killed meat, and an early crop of strawberries.'

'I would like to, if Lady Bess invites me.'

'What? Oh, yes, Will, you are most welcome.'

It was rather an uneasy meal. Bess, usually the most attentive and amusing of hostesses, was preoccupied and disinclined to talk. Indeed, she could think of nothing but what Will had told her. She had tried so hard to understand why Harry had not come to see her — or written — in all these long weeks. She had tried to convince herself that she wished him to have this time to reflect on their problems without her there to press him. She had fought the mounting depression and despair in being without his warm and vital presence, telling herself that it would be worth all the desperate days and lonely nights if it all came right. Now she had to accept that he had used this time to continue his wild ways, to lose them their home, and to plan a move which was the ultimate betrayal.

However casual Harry had been over the way their life went, any really important decisions had always been made jointly. With much discussion and, occasionally, heated argument. But now he had committed himself to a major enterprise which must seriously affect them both, and had not consulted her! Why? Why had he taken this step, which was such a reversal of his ideals? As to the other thing Will had told her — his obsessive gambling and its resultant effect on their finances, it was an all too familiar story——

'Bess,' Joan said sharply, 'I asked you if you thought the children should not be put down for their rest.'

'I am sorry, Mother. I was thinking of something else.' Bess rose and lifted Anne from her little chair. 'Yes, I do think they must go to their beds now. If I take this little one, perhaps you will bring George. Excuse us, if you please, Will.'

The twins were removed, George protesting, Anne eager to go. Bess tucked them both up. As she bent over George's crib he grasped a strand of her hair to hold her face close to his.

'Does the man go back to where he came from now?'

'Yes, dear, he does.'

'Is Father there?'

'I think so, dear.'

'Then you had better go with the man and bring Father back here.'

How had her son known what she was thinking? Bess marvelled. How had he detected her immediate desire to go to Harry? She said, 'Go to sleep now, sweeting.'

'Not 'til you tell me you will go.' George's eyelids fluttered. It had been a busy day for him. At first light he had jumped from his cot and trotted down the stairs to eat sweet white bread and frizzled bacon, then out into the glorious day and into the barn where a new foal had been born, stumbling and bloody from its mother's womb. So much excitement, George had to admit, was very tiring. He was ready to rest now, but first, first, he must get the answer he wanted. 'Say it please, Mother.'

'Very well, George,' Bess sighed. 'I will go.'

In the passage she found her mother waiting for her.

'Well?' Joan demanded. 'Did you mean what you promised him?'

'I don't know, Mother. I must think on it. 'Tis not a simple matter of going and getting George's father for him!'

The afternoon sun was full on the back of the house now; it poured in through the narrow gallery window, flooding the passage with light and turning Bess's hair to a sheet of silver. Joan waited hopefully for Bess to add to what she had just said—to confide in her. She had been such an open child, such a straightforward maiden, but when Joan had lost her to Anne Boleyn's court those years ago, and eventually to her husband, her daughter had shown herself capable of keeping her secrets well.

All the same, thought Joan, surely I have the right to know something! Nearly eight months without word from Harry! Then the arrival of that extremely handsome young man downstairs in the hall, whose grey eyes followed his hostess wherever she went. . .

She said bravely, 'Is there anything you would want to tell me, Bess? Anything I may help you with?'

Bess hesitated. She knew she ought to tell her mother something of her trials, prepare her for the knowledge that the marriage she had finally begun to accept could be over, but putting the whole affair into words would give it a reality she shrank away from. It was foolish to tell herself that if the problem were not spoken of, then it would not exist: the facts were impossible to dispute. She and Harry had quarrelled; she had come home expecting him to come after her eventually and make it right. He had not; instead he had ignored her all this time and had now made plans not only to deprive her of her home, but also to embark on a hazardous course of action he must know she would never approve. She said bleakly, 'I have been been remiss in not advising you of events, Mother. The truth is Harry and I have. . .had a serious dispute, and I believe he no longer wants me for his wife. Indeed, I believe he no longer loves me.'

'Nonsense!' Joan did not know what she had expected to hear, but this made no sense at all. Truly, she had been wary of the man her daughter had chosen, definitely she thought him not the stuff that good husbands were made of, but no one could be in his company for an hour without knowing how he felt for Bess! He wore his love for her like a banner. She had spoken so vehemently that Bess had to smile.

'Really, Mother, you cannot say that; you do not know the facts.'

'But can guess them,' Joan replied with asperity. 'Some woman, I suppose, and you have allowed the little hussy to drive you home! I'm ashamed of you!'

Bess frowned. 'I was not driven home, and it was not only that. . .' But it had been, mostly, she was honest enough to admit. Since coming back to Maiden Court, she had spent so many nights reliving the scene she had come upon in the gardens of Richmond. Priding herself on her reasonable and gentle nature, Bess had been astonished sometimes by the raw emotion contemplation of that scene aroused in her. Over and over again she had regretted not striding down the path and tearing Madrilene literally from Harry's arms... She went on coolly, 'You may not say "nonsense" when I tell you that Harry risked—in my presence—this house. Your home and mine—on the turn of a card. If he had lost, we, and the children, would have been out on the public highway!'

'How dramatic you are. But he didn't lose, did he? He never loses when the stake is something he values—really, Bess, even I know that about Harry.'

Bess stared at her. This from her mother, who had so often raged about the Latimar fortunes being balanced on Harry's peccadilloes at the card table! She should tell of the latest news—that Maiden Court was definitely in jeopardy now—but some misplaced loyalty within her would not allow those words to be spoken without confirmation. Instead she said angrily, 'It is not a question of winning or losing, but the fact that he was willing to risk it! Can't you see that?'

'Of course I can, but can't you see that you are condemning the man for what he is? For what he was when you married him? I do think, my dear, that you should have managed better.'

'You have often said that Harry gambles too much, that he flirts too much...'

'So I have,' Joan agreed placidly. 'But that is the way he is. After all, women chase him, do they not? Where Harry is there will always be some woman—

in the same way that where there is a hive there will be bees.' With this country homily Joan rested her case.

Frustrated, Bess said miserably, 'Then what am I supposed to do?'

'You are supposed to go and make it up with him. Don't you think you can do that?'

'I am not sure I want to,' Bess said coldly. 'It would not be every woman who could spend her life in such a state of confusion, Mother.'

'Not every woman, no,' Joan agreed gently. 'But for you there is no other way. Am I not right?'

Bess left two hours later with Will, their destination Greenwich Palace. Everything had been arranged in the greatest hurry, made easier by the fact that Bess found her trunk had been packed and ready for several weeks and all she needed to do was to add a few of her personal things. When she accused her mother of interference, Joan had admitted it.

'I knew that sooner or later you would go—if he did not come—so I gave you a head start,' she said brazenly.

Will had made little comment when she had asked him to escort her. 'If that is what you wish, Bess,' he said gravely.

George, lifted from his sleep to bid her farewell, had kissed her a dozen times, saying, 'Remember now—bring my father back with you. Tell him I said he was to come.'

Little Anne, sobbing, for she hated goodbyes and

especially to her adored mother, said, 'Don't stay away long, *please*.'

Joan patted her daughter's cheek, and said, 'Remember what I said: the man loves you. You told me once that is all that matters.' Thus armed with the support of her family, Bess set off with a lighter heart.

The road to Greenwich had improved with the onset of fine dry weather and, although traffic was heavy towards the capital, Bess and Will had the advantage of good mounts and little luggage. They spoke seldom on the journey. Bess was too apprehensive and Will, sensitive to her mood and reluctant to prolong the ride with unnecessary conversation, set a fast pace.

When true dark was only a short while away Greenwich Palace was in view. As always when she took this road, Bess remembered her first sight of the imposing T-shaped building. Then, she had been sent from a loving home to take her place in a society she knew little of. It had been a raw January day and rain had been falling in icy torrents. Her escort on that occasion had been a pedlar called Master Soames, dour and uncommunicative, despite the fair payment in advance Robert de Cheyne had granted him for his services.

Bess had been left in the main courtyard of the palace while Soames sought entrance for her, and it had been there that she had first seen her future husband. Pausing now in this same cobbled area, Bess remembered she had lost control of her horse that day and Harry Latimar had come to her rescue. He had tamed the unruly beast and introduced himself, looking her over with an interested dark blue gaze.

How handsome she had thought him, how sophisticated and beyond her understanding. Now he was her husband, still enigmatic but indescribably dear to her. Her heart hammered as it had six years ago, her senses strained towards him.

Will helped her down from her palfrey. 'Should I send word to Harry that you are here?'

'If you would be so kind. I think I will wait for him in the chapel.' Bess smoothed her skirts and hair with trembling fingers. 'I do thank you for bringing me, Will.'

'It was a pleasure.' Will watched her disappear into the south door. With a sigh he arranged for her trunk to be taken into the palace, called a page and gave him the message for Latimar, to be delivered without delay. Then he took both horses into the stables and used some of his frustrated energy in rubbing the animals down and seeing them safe in stalls for the night. As he worked, he wondered if he had been wise to bring her to this place, to put her in the way of more blows on top of those he had already struck. Still, he could have said more. . .

'Should I send word of your arrival to Harry?' he had asked her. He could have added, Should he care one way or the other. For Latimar showed no signs of being lovelorn these days, and Madrilene de Santos was still his constant companion. Many of the court thought them lovers, but Will did not. He knew Madrilene too well to mistake the barely restrained excitement she showed for satisfied lust. Rather 'twas frustration, Will decided. Blanketing both mounts and turning out into the twilight, Will could almost wish the rumours true. Presumably even loyal Bess would not forgive such blatant infidelity.

Bess walked timidly through the cloisters. This time she had not brought a maid. Mary had been blushingly married in the little chapel at Maiden Court at Christmas and already whispered that Walter would be a father within the year. Bess had not wished to ask her to undertake the journey in her delicate condition and had fancied bringing no other of her servants. Now she wished she had a little moral support from someone who loved her. Straightening her back, she walked up the aisle in the silent chapel and sat in the front pew facing the plain altar. She had chosen this place because, being so near the supper hour, she and Harry could be private. On the journey she had tried to rehearse what she must say, but no words had come for she had no idea what she would feel — or he would feel — when they met.

It was cold here; the afternoon heat had given way to a chilly night, more apparent in this place where sunlight could only shine through small high windows. The silence, too, unnerved Bess; she had a foolish desire to run away. If Harry had wished to see her, he could have come to Maiden Court. . . Thinking of her home conjured up George's handsome little face, and also the words he had spoken which had prompted her coming. There, she told herself, George has said I must come, so. . . She half smiled at this foolish thought, then rose with a start as a splash of colour in the side doorway caught her eye. Madrilene de Santos closed the door behind her with a thump and advanced on her.

CHAPTER EIGHT

MADRILENE had been outside Harry's rooms when the page had arrived with Will's message. She had been waiting there an hour in the hope that Harry would take her down to supper, and fretting that he did not come, for she was beginning at last to have hopes that their relationship would progress in the way she wished.

He had behaved very strangely for some weeks after his wife's abrupt departure, indeed had been most shamefully drunk for most of the time, and inclined to irrational conversation when he spoke at all.

His friends had borne this unusual behaviour on Latimar's part with indulgent affection — it was Yuletide after all, and the season of excess. The king had been far less sympathetic. He disliked seeing the debonair Harry in turns reeling and noisily tipsy, or soddenly, sarcastically maudlin. He was also worried about his friend's health — his own being much on his mind lately, as the pain in his legs was often so excruciating it all but consumed him. . . He had known Harry too long not to be aware that his capacity for liquor was phenomenal, proof that the amount he was taking in these days must be great indeed to produce outward signs of drunkenness. If he did not show some temperance he would surely damage his superb constitution—or so Henry reasoned. He had sent for Harry one February morning and brusquely ordered him to curb his appetite for both wine and provocative conversation. The last was a reference to Latimar's baiting in public of young Christowe, which the boy had turned a deaf ear to thus far, but which would sooner or later result in an episode like the one last year.

'In what way am I provocative?' Harry enquired. He had been expecting to break his fast with Henry and indulge in a little cheerful talk—he had no desire for a lecture. He threw himself down in a chair and lifted his long legs on to a stool. He was half-drunk already, and the hour scarcely past dawn.

'We did not give you leave to sit,' Henry said coldly. Harry rose immediately, looking in the pale dawn light oddly young and defenceless.

'Yes, well,' the king said irritably, 'sit by all means. Before you fall—you obviously had a jug for breakfast instead of solid food.'

Harry lowered himself back into the chair. ''Tis the season for such behaviour,' he remarked.

'The festive season came to an end a week ago.'

'Did it?' Harry looked surprised. 'I had not noticed.'

'You notice nothing these days but your own personal trials, and boring indeed they are becoming.'

'Sorry—I was not aware I had ever bored anyone with them.'

'Do you think I don't know why you are behaving so? Of course I do! But—my boy—we have all suffered at some time or other in this way. I have myself, and well you know it.'

'I don't believe you could have,' Harry said. 'Or you would not be still above the ground. I myself don't expect to be shortly: at least, I cannot live with this pain much longer.'

Henry heaved himself out of his chair. He limped to the table, lifted the wine flask, then lowered it again. 'Harry,' he said testily, very moved by such dire words, delivered in such a casual tone, 'it is in your own hands, surely, to end the pain! If you were to go to Bess——'

'I cannot!' Harry leaped up and began to pace the room. 'She doesn't want me, Hal, or she would have come to me—or not left in the first place. She has sent no word during the time of our estrangement. I truly believe she no longer wants me, and I am in despair knowing it!' Sudden movement had made his head spin alarmingly; he sat down abruptly in a chair opposite the window from where he could see the bleak snow-laden branches of the tall trees overlooking the winding river.

It had snowed relentlessly for days now, the endless white curtain no more suffocating than his own thoughts. The court had been confined to the palace by the hard weather for some weeks and Harry had had too much time to think. Round and round he reviewed the last days Bess had been at Hampton, seeing too late where he should have acted differently, what words he could have used instead of those he had. Before they had left Hampton for Greenwich, he had resolved to beg leave that he might visit Maiden Court, but when the day arrived he had been too drunk to sit his horse and had been transported to the palace two days later in one of the king's litters.

Henry imposed his solid bulk between Harry and the dismal view. Damned women, he thought compassionately, how they could make minced meat of even the best of men! He said gently, 'Very well, you feel your marriage to be over. But your life is not, and if you think your wife does not need you, there are others who do. *I* do.'

Harry recalled himself with an effort. He said quickly, 'God, yes, Henry, I know that.' A wry smile crossed his face. 'I have been poor company lately. I should not, myself, have wished to be cooped up with me these past weeks.'

'No, no, you are never poor company. . . But let me help you make a belated resolution for the new year: no more drinking to such excess — that can all too soon become a hard habit to break. And leave young Christowe alone. The pair of you are like a powder-keg awaiting a spark.'

Harry grimaced. He knew he had behaved without grace over Will Christowe. He almost admired the boy for refusing to react to the frequent insults. He said, 'I will try, Hal — on both counts.'

'Good. And in the more clement weather, perhaps

there will be a change of heart for Bess. Who knows?'

Who knew indeed? thought Harry. What Bess felt, far away across the snowy fields within the warm heart of Maiden Court, he had no idea. Nor could he believe he would have the courage to find out — in fair weather or foul.

But he had tried after that day to follow Henry's advice. He stopped drinking so heavily, surprised at first how much he had come to rely on the dubious comfort of spending his days and most of his nights in a haze. He also kept his tongue off Will Christowe, knowing with cynical amusement that Will thought he had lost interest in baiting his wife's admirer, as he had apparently lost interest in his wife.

He was gentler company altogether in February and March, and the first person to notice this was Madrilene, waiting to slip into Bess's place. She felt she had been patient indeed while Harry grieved a little over his wife's defection, and now thought she saw signs of his coming back to life. She increased her pursuit by being forever in his sight, shunning all other hopeful suitors, waiting eagerly for propinquity to take its course.

Nothing happened. Harry had had a great deal of practice in eluding a female intent on seduction. A hundred times Madrilene thought him on the brink; as many times she was left gazing at the space he had vacated. When spring came at last to Greenwich, she had decided to force his hand.

Harry had retired early. The king was unwell again and had not left his apartments for some days, so his friends were free to amuse themselves as they wished. Harry had had such a continuing run of bad luck at the card tables and other gambling pursuits that he had, this evening, chosen to take to his bed.

In the light of one candle he was reading. He turned the pages slowly. He was actually a more intellectual man than most gave him credit for, and lately had found some solace in occupying his mind with some of the wealth of books in Henry's library. When the door opened and closed, he thought, Richard, come to make up the fire before he finds his own bed for the night.

'So this is where you are hiding yourself!' Madrilene was beside the bed, staring down at him. He sat up.

'Good God, Madrilene, you will have no rag of reputation left coming here at this hour!'

She smiled scornfully. She had brought a jug of wine and two glasses and now set the glasses on the table and filled them. She put one into his hands and, taking up the other, sat on the edge of the bed. She had never seen a man in a state of undress before; she was convinced none could look more attractive than Harry Latimar, his thin velvet robe open to the waist to reveal a milk-white muscled chest, black hair disordered and glossy on the linen pillow.

Harry looked at her, half amused, half annoyed.

He said sternly, 'What will you do next, you silly girl?'

'That,' she said deliberately, 'is up to you, is it not?'

He drank his wine, set the empty glass on the table, leaned back and linked his hands behind his head. 'The wine is good — not, I think, from the palace cellars?'

'No.' She wrinkled her nose. 'What is served here in this great palace is horrible. I have my own, shipped from Madrid especially for me. We both appreciate fine wine, Harry, in fact we both like exactly the same things.' She refilled his glass, but left it on the table. She put her own beside it untouched and looked at him in the flickering light.

'Aren't you going to drink it?' he asked. He should order her out of his rooms immediately, he knew, but was suddenly curious to know what she would do next and what would be his reaction.

She leaned forward, letting her hair fall either side of his face as she kissed him. He made no move to take her in his arms, but let his lips respond to the pressure of hers. Then he took her wrists in his hands and sat up, holding her at arm's length.

'You kissed me,' she said breathlessly.

'Yes,' he agreed, 'but that is all. Now I think you should leave, unless you wish me to dress again and escort you personally to where you belong.'

'Here is where I belong!' She had taken no wine that night, but was intoxicated. Her warm Spanish blood ran through her veins like fire.

'No, Madrilene.'

'I don't believe you want me to go! You want me as much as I want you. Now, here.'

'No,' he said again. 'I don't want you.'

'You are unnatural!'

'Yes,' he agreed, 'and I am as distressed to discover that fact as you appear to be. But that is the way it is.'

'You are still thinking of that cold woman. . .that disloyal wife who has abandoned you!'

'I am afraid that is also true,' he admitted, as much to himself as to her.

'Then — this is what you have brought me to!' She got up so suddenly that the setting of one of the rings she wore cut into the palm of his hand as she wrenched hers away. A bright bead of blood appeared on his white skin and with an exclamation he raised the hand to examine it. Madrilene flew across the room and fumbled with the window-catch.

'I will throw myself from your window! I will be dashed on the stone below and you may live on, knowing your cruel treatment caused my death.' She had succeeded in opening the window and had one knee on the window-seat although hampered by her full skirts. She was a vivid figure framed in the black darkness beyond.

'Jesu!' Harry sprang off the bed and, covering the space between them in a couple of steps, put an arm around her waist and swung her back. He put up a hand and closed the window with a resounding crash and turned her about to face him.

'You are demented!' he said furiously, shock at her desperate action translated into hot anger.

'Yes, demented! With love for you!'

'I don't want your love! I am being driven insane by it — understand me once and for all, lady, nothing you can say or do will induce me to love you, to bed you, or — after this night — even to like you!' He released her and stepped back. 'Now leave me in peace. Go and throw yourself from another's window if you must: I care not one way or the other.'

Expecting a return of hostile words, he was unprepared for her response to his outburst. She sank on to the window seat and began to cry — deep, wrenching sobs. Tears spilled out of her brilliant eyes and fell on to her velvet gown.

'Good God,' Harry murmured uncomfortably. 'Please forgive me for what I have just said — I scarcely know what I am saying or doing these days. . . There — don't cry so.' He put an arm about her. She took the loose sleeve of his gown and began to dab at her eyes.

'It is I who should ask forgiveness. Of you and of God. Suicide! The sin never forgiven.' She let go of his sleeve and rocked to and fro, sobbing harder. But in her mind a bright light flowered: he had not been able to let her die! Surely, this meant he cared for her. . .

Harry patted her back awkwardly, then looked up as the door opened and Richard de Vere came in carrying a basket of logs. He blushed crimson when he saw the two at the window.

'The fire, sir,' he said. 'But, perhaps later. . .?'

Harry said, relieved, 'No, mend the fire now, Richard. Or — at least, shall you wish de Vere to take you back to the ladies' dorter, Madrilene?'

Madrilene sniffed and stood up unsteadily. 'He need not trouble himself, nor you, Harry. I will go now.' Harry took her to the door.

'Madrilene. . . You are feeling more yourself now? Not — not. . .?'

She managed to smile. 'Not intending to try my hand at mortal sin again? No, Harry, I shall not do that.' She slipped through the door and disappeared down the corridor. Before she had reached her rooms she had almost managed to convince herself that she had been the victor of the skirmish.

'Have you a message for Sir Harry?' Madrilene asked the breathless page four months later.

'Yes, my lady, 'tis that his lady wife is within the palace walls and would see him in the chapel at his earliest convenience.'

Madrilene turned to face him. The boy — a brave boy normally — felt a thrill of fear along his spine. That very morning he had, during the tedious business of book-learning that all pages must endure on the road to knighthood, been taught of a mysterious nation of ancient kings who had been prone to execute the bearers of any message they disliked. It had seemed to Wat Blandford a very irrational course of action, for how could the messenger be held responsible for the message? Now little Wat thought it probable that the foreign kings might have looked exactly as the Lady Madrilene de Santos looked just before they struck... Wat backed away and trotted off along the passageway in case his perceptions were true.

Madrilene remained motionless a moment. The enemy was here, then, she thought. The woman who had her icy hand so firmly about Latimar's heart! Here at Greenwich. For what reason? None other than to try to reclaim her lost territory, Madrilene decided. But not if I have a hand in it, she thought. Not when, at last, he seems to be turning to me.

For there had come a change in Harry's attitude towards her since that terrible night when she had been prepared to leave a world where the man she loved scorned her. He no longer either teased or ignored her, but treated her with gentle consideration and, she believed, a growing affection.

She had been very unwise, she decided, to try to make him take a step no knight of this court could contemplate. She was the king's ward, after all, and Harry the king's friend. That was why he had resisted her. But he had saved her life and sought her company since. It all fitted, or so Madrilene, very young in spite of her adult feelings, was able to persuade herself.

When Harry had begun to speak of joining Norfolk's force and marching on Scotland, Madrilene had supported him. She came from a family of soldiers — her father and grandfather had been warriors, her maternal ancestors too. Let Harry go to war briefly, she reasoned, let him earn the fabulous sum Norfolk offered his commanders. He needed the money, obviously, so that their estates would not be so unequal. And when he came back...

But all this planning would come to nothing if Bess Latimar became a part of his life again. Madrilene might be able to convince herself that her fantasies were almost truth, but she had seen the frozen look which would invade his eyes if Bess's name were mentioned, the tenseness in his body, the rigid misery in his pale face... Madrilene hurried along the maze of passages to see what she could do to prevent any kind of reconciliation.

On the way she paused in her chamber to examine herself in her glass; it would not do to be seen looking less than her best before her rival. She opened her jewel-box and slid on the ring she had won from Harry in a game some weeks ago. She had meant to return it, but now it might serve a purpose. It was one of his favourite jewels, a huge table-cut diamond etched with his initials and instantly recognisable.

Bess watched the girl make her way between the wooden pews. She wore scarlet: silk and lace trimmed with the delicate summer fur of the silver fox. As she drew nearer Bess saw the sparkling flash of the diamond on her left hand. Harry's diamond ring! Presented by the king upon his return from Devon with his new bride. Now this girl wore it, Bess thought bitterly, the prized gift that marked Latimar's love match! Bess re-seated herself and Madrilene sat beside her.

'Lady Bess,' Madrilene said, smoothing her silken skirts, the light from the candles catching fire in the magnificent ring. 'How very delightful to see you again.'

'I was expecting my husband to attend me here,' Bess replied distantly.

'Oh, Harry is somewhere about,' Madrilene said lightly. 'But I heard of your arrival and felt I must greet you.' She looked sideways at the other girl, disappointed to see that while Harry bore the scars of his enforced separation from the woman he thought he loved in loss of weight and fine lines about mouth and eyes, Bess showed no such thing. Instead, she was as delicately beautiful as ever. She doesn't care for him, Madrilene concluded, not really.

'May I expect Harry soon?' Bess enquired.

'I'm sure he will see you very soon. Meanwhile. . .' Madrilene took a breath. Her eyes slid to the altar. She was Catholic; in her childhood she had been quite devout as all young Spanish girls were — she hesitated to lie in the house of God. And yet, she assured herself, God is not truly here in this Protestant place.

'Meanwhile?' Bess asked.

Madrilene turned to her. 'Lady Bess, in truth

Harry does not yet know you are here. I received your message and have sought this interview with you before you see your husband for one reason only — to spare you pain.' She hesitated, looking for some sign on Bess's face that her words affected the still figure at her side, but no emotion disturbed the cameo-pure face. She hastened on. 'I do not know why you have come here but feel it may be because you have had word that Harry is bound for Scotland. 'Tis true he intends to take that road and for a special purpose: Harry needs money, he has been very unlucky at cards recently and he needs it because. . .you see. . .I am so very rich and in order to feel my equal he must bring to our. . .liaison some comparable wealth.' She stopped.

'Your liaison?' Bess enquired politely.

'We are in love, Harry and I,' Madrilene said swiftly. 'We plan to make our life together. For myself, I have loved him from the moment I set my eyes on him. For him. . .'

'Yes? For him?'

'It is more lately.' Angry at the lack of response she was receiving, Madrilene allowed her temper to flare. 'You left him, lady! A man like that! Left him and took your own course. Small wonder he would look elsewhere for consolation.'

'Small wonder,' Bess repeated dully. None of this was real, surely? She could hardly take in the words she was hearing.

Madrilene's exotic eyes slanted again to the altar. 'Also — now I fear I must say the thing which will displease you most of all, and hardly know how to phrase it, so I shall simply say that I have been a visitor to Harry's bedchamber. . .at night.'

Now she had the reaction she had expected, for Bess turned paper-white and for a moment Madrilene thought she would fall from her seat on to the stone floor. In the deathly quiet could be heard the sound of faint ringing bells from the adjoining palace advising the courtiers that the supper hour was near.

White-lipped, Bess said, 'I thank you for your candour, *demoiselle*. Also for your courage in coming here to talk with me.'

Madrilene stood up. She had told the great lie, but could feel no satisfaction that it was believed. If Harry ever knew of her perfidy he would probably throw her bodily from some convenient window. . . But he would never know — Madrilene had lived at close quarters with all sorts of women all her life and knew that Lady Bess would be too proud ever to reveal what had passed between them tonight. Even so, she faltered, 'I hope I have not distressed you too much; that there is no ill feeling between us. . .'

An ironic thought crossed Bess's mind. No ill feeling? Her fragile looks of silver and alabaster belied a strong spirit beneath the skin. She was a fighter; her father had been a knight of a young and virile court before his injuries drove him away, her mother from a line of sturdy yeomen used to wrestling daily with harsh elements for their very existence. No ill feeling! For two pins she would have engaged this wealthy, spoiled girl in physical combat. In a moment she could have torn the black hair out by its roots and marked the rich cream skin. Could have, were it not for the facts: Harry had apparently made his choice and he was a man who knew his own mind. I am not one for keeping that in a cage which wishes to be free, she had said to Will Christowe... The moment of hot fury passed, leaving behind a kind of numb desolation. She said woodenly, 'No, indeed. 'Twas as you suspected—I am here because I have heard rumour of Harry's intention to take up arms for the king. Also, word is about that my home is in jeopardy. Obviously I had to come in order to protect myself and...my children.'

'Oh, naturally,' Madrilene agreed. 'Well, I will leave you now.' She moved away, paused before the plain cross on the altar, then hurried to the door she had entered by, opened it, and disappeared into the black night.

Bess sat on, her mind a blank, until she grew so cold she felt little different from the vast stone pillars supporting the vaulted roof of the chapel. It might have been minutes or hours before she rose to leave. She was quite calm; very well, she had lost her husband, but she must still fight for her children's home. Her soul turned painfully to meet this new challenge.

In the cloisters she thought, I will not stay in this place. Will not see Harry, but leave immediately for home. What I need to say can be said in written message. A young man was coming towards her. She would have passed him without a word, but he stepped out in front of her and bowed.

'My lady Latimar.' When she did not reply, he said, 'I am Richard de Vere, my lady.'

'Of course, forgive me. I did not for the moment recognise you.'

'You are seeking Sir Harry? May I take you to him?' What was wrong with her? he wondered. She was like a sleepwalker.

'Come, my lord is with the king in his apartments.'

She walked with him, but said, 'I do not need to see Harry. I think I will just leave him a letter.'

'Lady Bess,' Richard said gently, 'you have not come all this way from Kew to write a letter.'

'I think it would be best.'

'No, no,' Richard persisted. 'My master would be very displeased with me if I let you leave without seeing him. Besides, night has already fallen — you cannot go anywhere in the dark.' He put a firm hand beneath her elbow and did not release her until they were standing outside the royal apartments. Then he put her into a chair in the ante-chamber. 'Wait, if you please, while I send word you are here.'

Bess came momentarily back to life. 'No, Richard, I will just wait here quietly for Harry to come out — do you go down to your supper.'

She sat, under the eyes of the impassive guards, her mind still refusing to function properly. As the moments passed she suddenly could not remember why she sat there, could not think why she was trembling so in this warm room. The great doors opened at last, the guards stood back, and the king came out. Bess got to her feet. Henry held out a hand and she curtsied mechanically.

'Bess, you here?' the king said jovially. 'Well, well, we are pleased to welcome you to Greenwich.' As Richard had been, Henry was struck by her appearance. No change in her beauty, he noted, but she appeared quite lifeless. 'I am going to my meal now, but Harry is in my rooms—please feel free to treat them as your own.' He left her, and the guards looked at her expectantly. She went past them still in a trance and looked into the chamber beyond. It was empty. A liveried servant sprang forward to open the inner door and she passed into the bedchamber.

Harry was seated in a chair by the window staring out into the dark night. He turned his head and leaped up. Bess, at least, was in some way prepared for the meeting, Harry was not. He had been imagining her for so long in one particular place that to see her materialise here stunned him. He could no more have crossed the floor and greeted her at this moment than he could have grown wings and soared out of the open window and up into the star-studded sky.

One part of Bess's paralysed mind registered the thought: not even a greeting! After all this time, not even a word! and the expression on his face! Disbelief! Displeasure?

For a time they stared at each other, suspended in

time, then Bess looked vaguely around the sumptuously appointed room. Her eyes alighted on a flask of wine. Moving slowly, she went and poured herself a beaker.

Harry found his breath. 'Bess, what are you doing here?' He was still standing by the window; the light from the candle-sconce on the wall to the left of the glittering panes chose the dark red depths in his hair to illuminate.

Bess finished her wine, poured more. She downed half the contents and miraculously her mind cleared. She helped herself to more then took a seat at the foot of the massive bed. 'I think you can imagine why I have come, Harry,' she said coolly.

'I know why I hope you have come,' he said quietly. 'But from your expression fear it to be another reason entirely. I suppose you have heard of my run of misfortune, that Maiden Court may be forfeit to the money-lenders, and so have come hotfoot to remonstrate.' It was not what he wished to say, nor in that dismissive tone, but how cold she was. And not even a word of greeting—after all this time! He raised the armour he had worn all his sensitive life into position to protect himself from the emotions he felt now.

'Not entirely,' Bess said. 'Although I have heard such rumours. They, however, did not surprise me. I am used to your putting your family at risk to satisfy your...appetites.'

Harry moved at last. Casually he came to the table and poured himself wine. He was closer to her now, and Bess found it harder to maintain her cool composure. With the recovery of her senses had come the familiar susceptibility to Harry's physical presence. Also—he was so thin, so pale. He had always had the look of a creature never exposed to sun or wind or rough weather, but now he was almost ghostlike. All that was tender and caring in her rose up to defend him. She wanted to cry, Have you not been eating properly? Have you not been sleeping enough? She subdued these irrelevant questions and said, 'You apparently have no answer to the charge. However, 'tis another matter which has brought me to Greenwich. I am told you go north in the king's army to engage Scottish troops, and thereafter to France to fight.'

'Ah.' Harry refilled his glass. 'Yes, that is so. Do you mislike the idea?'

'You know I do! Have you so reversed your opinions since last we were together?' Let him say he had; let him declare that he felt for the cause Henry Tudor had so rashly thrust upon his subjects, and was to take part to please his old friend, and——

Harry smiled grimly. 'No, I still believe war to be a waste of time and a waste of life. Young life usually. . .' He seemed reluctant to settle in any chair, to cease pouring and drinking the red wine.

'Then why are you going?'

'For the money, my dear. Norfolk offers a sack of gold and I need it.' Harry tossed off the full glass and set his beaker down with a sharp click. 'Especially now.'

'Why especially now? We have been in low financial water before. Why is now so different?' Foolish, foolish, she chided herself. You know the answer to that question, and need not hear it from his lips.

'This time I am afraid I have been particularly profligate. I know it will displease you to hear it, but my resources—our resources—are truly exhausted at this time. Good housewife that you are, you will appreciate the need to secure the wherewithal for the next loaf of bread.'

Good housewife! A sly reference to her pride in the management of her home, to its smooth and comfortable running—and to her humble origins in taking that pride. 'On laying your hands on this bounty, can I expect you to hand some of it over to me for the purchase of this loaf of bread?' she asked bitterly.

'Certainly. What else?' He had the audacity to look surprised by her question.

What else indeed? For the securing of a new life with his mistress, Bess thought. 'So the money is to make safe Maiden Court?' she asked deliberately.

'As I have said—what else?'

Bess was tired. She had had a tiring journey and at the end of it the cataclysmic meeting with Madrilene de Santos. Her newly acquired strength was waning. Also—even what the Spanish girl had told her did not seem to prevent her from loving the man who had betrayed her. Oh, she was a weak thing! Bess was both furious and despairing with herself.

Harry came to her and rested one hand on the low back of her chair. His greatest beauty was the delicate construction of his bones, clearly visible beneath his flesh, his hands the most exquisite example. George had inherited those long loose joints; his childish fingers were an exact replica of those of the man who had begotten him. Bess sat more upright in her chair. 'I don't believe you.'

Harry did not reply immediately, but his hand tensed on the rich brocade of the chair. Then he came around and took her gently by the shoulders.

'I don't think I heard you correctly, Bess.' He spoke softly but, impossibly, had turned even paler. She pushed him away and rose.

'Oh, *why* must you pretend? Why not be straightforward at this time?'

He looked bewildered. 'Straightforward? I am that, I think. But what is it you wish me to say? What is it you want?'

'I don't know,' she said tiredly. 'I don't know anything any more. Except that you have betrayed me!'

He was facing her. 'I know I have! But I can make it right with this new enterprise. Do you think I would let you and our children have less than your due because I am a fool?'

'Less than our *due*? You have already decided, have you not, what our—*my*—due is to be?' She had not meant to raise the main issue in her mind, had only meant to take arms for the future of the children, but...how could he look her in the eyes and continue to pretend this was about *money*?

He said quietly, 'Why don't you simply tell me what you are really talking about? No more riddles, no more half-accusations. Say what you have to, and I will answer you with the truth.'

'At last!' She was practically hysterical now — she, who was usually so calm! 'Then tell me the truth about your affair with the Lady Madrilene!'

'Madrilene?' The turn in her attack caught him unawares. Had she been brooding all these months on that old bone? He said slowly, 'What is it you wish to know of Madrilene?'

'You want the money from your prospective employment, not to save Maiden Court, as you would have me think, but to leave me and run off with this rich girl!'

Harry was thunderstruck. 'Bess...what can have given you that idea?'

'It is not an *idea*, it is fact! She is your lover, is she not? Perhaps it is unseemly for a wife to ask such a question, but I think you know — indeed have frequently pointed out — I am a wife who does not know her place.'

'You do not know your place indeed if your must ask me that question,' he said hotly. 'Your place in my life and in my heart.'

'Can you deny she has been to your room at night?' she asked wildly, ignoring the last part of his answer.

'*One* night.' Who in hell had told her of that? he thought. And she not in Greenwich Palace for more than a few hours!

'One night or a hundred,' she cried. 'One act of infidelity or a hundred! You promised me the truth, Harry, and I am waiting for you to answer what I have just charged you with.'

Harry picked up his glass again. He tipped it so that the ruby liquid swelled from one side of the brim to the other, staring at the reflection of the candle flames in its warm depths. How dared she ask him that? he thought bitterly. The utter lack of desire he had suffered the night of Madrilene's assault had attacked his opinion of himself. Harry Latimar, legendary for his excellence in this field, had failed to appreciate a beautiful and eager woman! He had tried to counter this feeling of being unmanned by telling himself 'twas the measure of his consuming love for Bess that had produced this lack. Now the object of his love, of the affection and respect he had thought mutual, stood accusing before him. He said, 'Then you will have a long wait, Bess, until hell freezes over in fact, before I have such a low opinion of myself that I feel the need to answer such a question. I would despise myself for granting it an answer—as I despise you for asking it of me.'

'You despise me! Then at long last we are in agreement over *something*, for the feeling is entirely mutual, Harry.'

It would have been difficult for any observer to

say who was more wounded by her remark; she for making it, when it was only the result of her loss of control, or he for provoking it, when it was the last thing he wanted to hear. They turned away from each other, breathless and tormented. Bess walked to the tall pier-glass and examined her reflection.

'You will not have eaten since you arrived here?' Harry said eventually. 'I have not myself, and suggest we seek our supper now. If, of course, you feel you have disposed of all your grievances for the present?' His conversational tone grated on Bess's jangled nerves.

'I am not dressed for the banqueting hall,' she said bleakly. Harry was evasive, Harry was clever at moulding the truth to suit himself, she thought, but asked a direct question would scorn to lie. It followed, therefore, that all Madrilene had said was true. . . But life went on. It was the supper hour and they must—even if her life was ashes now—descend to the dining-hall and eat. 'Do you wish me to change?'

'Your clothes? No,' Harry replied ambiguously. He watched her brush a little dust from her skirts and sleeves, retrieve the shining strands which had escaped the jewelled fillet which bound her hair. She turned from the mirror.

'I am ready,' she said.

A great many interested spectators watched the progress of the Latimars into the great hall that night. The two most concerned, Will Christowe and

Madrilene de Santos, drew their own conclusions from the pair's set faces and polite but distant behaviour to each other. Their reunion has gone exactly as I planned, Madrilene thought exultantly, and the lady has not involved me in her confrontation, I would swear. For Harry, running his eyes automatically over the assembly, had caught her eye and nodded briefly. Let me just wait quietly in the wings, as it were, and the glittering prize will be mine at last!

Will saw the situation differently. The two were not reconciled — that was obvious — but the love Bess felt for her husband could not be hidden; at least not from the man who was hoping to step into Harry Latimar's shoes. Will finished his meal quickly and then joined those dancing in the ante-chamber.

At midnight he went for refreshment and found Madrilene at the table. She greeted him cheerfully and the two took their glasses and sat in one of the alcoves overlooking the gardens. Outside the windows there was a tracery of green branches, each with a frosting of fine white ice: the freakish cold weather had produced a frost this night.

'Dear Will,' Madrilene said gaily as she signalled a page and asked for more wine, 'is this not a great night?'

'You certainly look as if you have been celebrating,' Will commented. Madrilene was usually quite abstemious, but tonight she was obviously tipsy.

'Celebrating? Yes, that is so. And with cause, for

I have today rearranged my destiny—and yours too, as it happens.'

'Mine? How have you done that?'

'By the process of. . . Oh, what is that word Harry uses in connection with his card games? Ah yes, bluff! It means—am I right—to pretend you hold higher cards than you actually do? That is what I did this evening—in the chapel with the lady Bess Latimar.'

'In what way did you bluff Bess?' Will asked.

Madrilene leaned conspiratorially towards him. 'I told her that Harry is intent on going a-soldiering to gather funds enough to run away with me!'

'That is not the truth, is it?'

'Of course not! Harry is only joining the expedition so that he may recoup some of his losses at the gaming tables and secure his estate once more. But I did not tell her that! Also——' her eyes brightened '—I strengthened my hand by laying a rather outrageous wild card: I told her. . . No, I let her believe that Harry and I were. . .intimate.'

'And that is not true either, is it?'

'Well, no,' Madrilene admitted unwillingly, 'but that is only because Harry is actually much more conventional than he appears. . . 'Tis true in all but deed, though, for he loves me now. I am sure he loves me.'

'But you allowed Bess to think what you wish were true? Your father would not have approved of such tactics, Madrilene,' Will added slowly. 'He was so honourable.'

'As I am,' she protested, uncomfortable under his grey stare. 'But all is fair in love or war — you should know that, Will!'

In war, yes, Will thought. He had long ago abandoned the knightly ideals he had once held — most men did when faced with a real enemy who felt, in the circumstances of battle, that it were better you died than he. . . But in one's personal dealings? Will felt he had so far retained his honour there.

'I thought you would approve,' Madrilene said sulkily. The amount of wine she had drunk was making itself unpleasantly felt now — she felt quite sick. Or perhaps 'twas the expression on Will's face making her feel so.

'Then you are wrong,' Will said heavily. 'I wanted Bess to decide for herself without duress where her affections lay. I hold no brief for Harry Latimer — he is a reckless and arrogant man who deserves to lose his most precious possession. But I have known him many years, lady; in all those years I never knew him perform a mean or shabby act. God knows, he could not even kill me when he had the chance!' he ended violently.

Madrilene got to her feet. She should obviously not have shared her triumph with this priggish young man. Will looked her over. 'Do you want help getting to your room?'

'From you? No.' Madrilene went uncertainly away and Will frowned after her. The best course for him would be to forget all the Spanish girl had said. To keep his own counsel and await developments. But what if those developments should include Bess breaking her marriage and turning to him? Such a move would only be for all the wrong reasons, and how could he ever be content knowing he had not allowed her to choose her way with all the truth at her disposal? Will sighed in aggravation for the fact that Bess Latimar seemed to bring out the best in others. His best now demanded he take some action.

Bess had spent a miserable evening. She sat beside Harry at the table, hardly touching her food. He ate nothing at all and, although he answered when spoken to by others in the hall, he ignored her and had, Bess knew, gone away to the mysterious place he retreated to when seriously hurt. She could not follow him there and help him, and wished she could harden her heart sufficiently not to want to. Eventually she excused herself and got up. Harry followed her to the door.

'Where do you sleep tonight?' he asked abruptly. She looked so tired, so drained, it took a conscious effort of will not to pick her up in his arms and carry her bodily to some comfortable bed.

'I am not sure. I must beg a corner somewhere.'

'You are free to use my room, if you wish,' he said courteously. 'I do not share at Greenwich, and can make shift in my dressing-room.'

'That is kind,' she replied.

'Please forgive me for not taking you there, but I

have an engagement I cannot break.' He opened the door and she passed through.

The dressing-room was placed through an arch off the main bedchamber. It held a cupboard and numerous trunks filled with Harry's clothes. There was also a narrow cot which Richard de Vere sometimes used if he attended his master into the small hours. Bess surreptitiously felt the mattress, finding it thin and hard. She supposed she would not easily break the habit of worrying about Harry — even that he should take his rest in some soft bed. She moved back into the main chamber.

For an indolent man Harry was fanatically tidy with his personal possessions. Her eyes were drawn to his writing table with its pile of fresh parchment, row of neat sharp quills and the yew box filled with correspondence. With the tip of her finger she opened the lid, then quickly let it drop. On the top lay one of the passionate letters she had written when he had returned from the royal tour last year; what other love message from other women might be under that? But she would not rifle through Harry's private papers, she told herself sternly. She opened the door to allow her trunk to be brought in, and wondered how she was to endure the evening.

The page had to knock twice before receiving an answer. He proffered a note, which with a sinking heart Bess recognised was addressed to her in Will Christowe's hand. Into the fire, was her first thought, then what she had not read, she need not think about or act upon. The page was looking at her with sleepy eyes. She unfolded the paper and read:

> Bess, I must see you immediately. You will not wish me to come to Harry's rooms. I will wait for you in the small library. Will.

'I am to take you there, my lady,' the page said. He set off at a swift pace and Bess had no choice but to follow. Arriving at the door, a little breathless, she opened it and went in. Few courtiers used this little ante-room to the magnificent library Henry had furnished so excellently with every book written or printed in every country he had access to—it was mainly used to store his more personal collection of poetry and music. Will was standing by a table piled with yellow parchment. He said, 'Bess, thank you for coming here.'

'Your message sounded quite imperative.'

'So it is.' He fixed his eyes on her face, his heart contracting when he saw how ill she looked. 'I can order wine, if you would like it.'

'Thank you, no.' She sat down in one of the pair of high-backed oak chairs which flanked the small hearth. Will remained standing.

'I have something to tell you, Bess. It is most difficult for me to say for I think you will accuse me of meddling in your personal business.'

He has heard rumour of Harry's and Madrilene's intended flight, Bess thought instantly. Dear Will— how embarrassed he was to have to say the words, how embarrassed I shall be to hear them. She gripped the arms of her chair and said calmly, 'I think I know what it is you wish to tell me, and there is no need. I am already acquainted with what you will have heard.' She rose, but he prevented her going to the door with a sharp gesture of his hand.

'I don't think you are. Won't you hear me out?'

'Of course.' There was only a small fire in the room, but its soft light behind her made a bright halo of her loose hair, blurred the clearly defined contours of her face.

'You have, I believe, had a conversation with the Lady Madrilene this evening?'

'Indeed. But really, Will, there is no need for you to go on——'

'There is.' In later years Will Christowe would be a famous soldier and statesman — already he had the kind of personality which demanded that when he spoke others must listen. 'She will have said that Harry's objective in going to Scotland — in earning the consequent bounty — is in order that they may make a life together.'

'Yes, she told me that.'

'She lied.'

'She lied. . .' Bess repeated slowly.

'Yes, for reasons of her own, she lied. I dislike speaking so of a lady — and that lady an old friend, but she lied, Bess. Harry has no thoughts of leaving you, or your children, but simply of repairing the damage he has done to his financial affairs through his incessant gambling.' A wry smile lightened his face. 'Blame him for that, if you will, but a greater sin he is not guilty of.'

In the silence Bess could hear the dismal fire fall with a soft sigh into ashes. 'I see,' she said through a closed throat.

'There is something else,' Will said awkwardly. Now he betrayed his youth in the colour which flooded into his face. 'What this same lady has declared to you about a more personal matter — in that too, she lied.' Lord, he thought, this was a horrible conversation to be having with any woman, let alone the girl he cared so much for.

'I know what you are saying,' Bess said bravely. 'But I have spoken with my husband on this matter, and ——'

'I had the truth from her own lips not an hour ago,' Will said forcefully. 'I do pray that you will consider her youth and. . .and the extreme fondness she has for Harry. . .and find it in your heart to forgive such a lie.'

Bess found she was standing rigid — her very bones ached with the effort of remaining upright. 'But I taxed him with it, and he did not deny it, Will.'

'Bess,' he said swiftly, 'you know I love you, don't you? Well, nothing would please me more — for I am human after all — than to be able to confirm what you apparently believe, but I cannot. Harry — in that way — has been the best of husbands to you.'

'He did not deny it!' she repeated.

'Would you have done, had he asked the same question of you?' Will asked bluntly. 'I beg your pardon for commenting so personally, but I have come to believe that you and Harry have the kind of relationship where such matters are. . .are carried on trust. At least—I think that is what Harry feels. . .'

Bess looked at him. She was ashamed to be told something she should know already. If it were so obvious to this man who plainly disapproved of Latimar. . . Her eyes filled with tears. 'I have been such a fool, haven't I?'

Will shrugged. He could hardly bear to know that she cried for joy, not pain. 'I would not, myself, care to speculate on what Latimar's motives are in anything. But as regards you, sweet Bess, they are as honourable as can be possible. That being so, I believe this is the end for you and me. If indeed there was ever truly a beginning. . .'

'I care for you very much as a friend,' Bess said quietly, 'and greatly appreciate your efforts tonight.'

'That is something for me to treasure,' Will said sincerely. 'And I shall choose to believe I have given you back something you thought lost, but which was only in fact mislaid.' He took her hand and kissed it, then went swiftly to the door.

Outside in the cold passageway he took several deep breaths. He had had a dream and pursued it, but the central character in that dream had always been elsewhere committed. Very well, now he must look onwards—to the future and the northern borders.

CHAPTER NINE

HARRY'S engagement that night was a council of war in Edward Seymour's apartments to discuss the king's impending invasion of France to secure what he felt to be part of his rightful kingdom. Before he could begin this, Henry knew he must deal with the Scots—no general wished a second enemy at his back, no army could satisfactorily fight any war on two geographically diverse fronts. When the explosive intransigent neighbour had been taken off the chessboard, England could then march on to glorious battle with their traditional enemy.

The king's plan was to mass troops along the border and present the young Scottish king, James, with a treaty which would make his country a nation under the rule of the Tudor throne. Henry had no real hope that such a document would be agreed to, or signed, even under threat of force—as far as he was concerned his battalions would have to fight, and his officers must be well prepared to do so.

Edward Seymour, the Earl of Hertford, was to be the commander-in-chief of the northern force, Norfolk and Suffolk among his lieutenants. Each lieutenant would have his senior captains in the field. One of Norfolk's captains would be Sir Harry Latimar.

Harry had sat through a number of these meetings lately and always marvelled at how much time could be wasted on discussing trivialities. Tonight the topic under discussion concerned what colours would be worn by each English regiment to distinguish friend from foe in the heat of battle. Personally, Harry believed he would recognise the enemy in the shape of a wild border chieftain quite easily, without first ascertaining the man did not wear the colours to be designated this evening.

He was seated at the vast round table next to Norfolk's eldest son, the Earl of Surrey, an excitable self-opinionated young man who had so much to say for himself that his right-hand neighbour was saved having to contribute anything at all to the proceedings. Which was just as well, for the whole of Harry's concentration was centred on his crumbling personal life. His mind was back on its familiar treadmill.

He should have answered both Bess's forthright questions — however much he resented them. He should have taken her into his arms, denied each charge forcefully and kissed her lips before they could speak the final bitter words. He should have. . . These three words had prefaced so many of his thoughts in the last months. All the dazzling winter weeks when he had been so lonely for her, so hungry for her, all the bright spring mornings when he could not see the miracle of new life around him, and now — as summer blazed through June — he was still doing it. It was hard for him to decide now which was his strongest emotion: desperation that he had probably lost her forever, or anger that she had forced the break.

Where had she got that insane idea that he was set on amassing a little gold to run away with Madrilene? How could she believe it of him? Surely she should know that he was incapable of such dishonourable conduct—even if he desired it. And to ask him point blank if he had taken another woman into his bed! How dared she ask that——?

'Do you agree, Latimar?' Seymour thrust his leonine head across the table.

'Yes, of course, my lord. I do.'

'Good.' Edward collected his papers and rose. 'We are agreed on all then. I will wish you goodnight, gentlemen.'

'Don't you wonder what you have agreed to, Harry?' Surrey asked teasingly, as the chamber cleared and Seymour left to report to the king.

'Please tell me. I do hope it was not to wear palest pink during the forthcoming slaughter.'

Surrey laughed delightedly. He was as surprised as any other that Latimar was to join them in the adventure, but he looked forward to having his amusing company in the weeks to come. He enlightened Harry, 'Tut, we had moved on from that! No, you have been elected to oversee the provisioning of our troops. Wolsey's old job—if I recall my recent history.'

Harry rolled his eyes. He thought himself the most unlikely candidate for such a meticulous and crucial appointment; also he would have trouble enough getting himself organised in this affair, let alone a thousand men.

'We all voted for you,' Surrey added maliciously.

'Thank you.' Harry got up and bowed. 'And now — goodnight.'

'Oh, stay! We will find a game, eh?'

'Not tonight, Surrey.'

'Oh, yes, of course, I have heard your luck is out these days.'

'As you say, and I have never had so many cordial invitations as lately to prove it.'

Surrey chuckled. 'Well, you know what they say, my dear Harry: unlucky in cards, lucky in love.'

Harry wandered around the empty corridors for some time before going to his rooms. He was tempted to find space for himself elsewhere than his dressing-room, but felt this would be more evidence of the weakness Bess had brought him. Eventually sheer weariness drove him up the stairs. He opened the door quietly, hoping Bess would be asleep.

But Bess was not asleep. She had changed into her chamber robe, rebuilt the fire and was sitting on the bed waiting patiently. She glanced quickly at him to see what the evening had brought him after their disagreement, but as usual he looked quite relaxed. He said casually, 'Ah, Bess, not abed yet? I will not disturb you.' He was in his dressing-room before she could speak and she heard the rustle of silk as he shed his doublet, and the creak of the cot as he sat to untie the ribbons of his shoes. She got up and went through the arch and bent to retrieve the garment from the floor.

'You don't have to do that; Richard takes good care of me,' he said. There was no window in here, only a pale light drifting in shed from the few candles she had left burning in the main chamber. She could hear his light breathing in the semi-darkness, but only see the pale oval of his face.

'I wanted to talk to you, Harry,' she said, folding the doublet over her arm, smoothing it with nervous fingers. He took it from her and tossed it on to one of his trunks.

'I think we have probably talked enough.'

'What I said earlier I much regret,' she got out. 'I was wrong.' He looked up. 'Wrong,' she went on in a stronger voice. 'From first to last.'

He brushed past her and went into the bedchamber. He opened a cupboard and helped himself to wine.

'I would like some,' she said, following him. He gave her a beaker.

'What has brought about this change of heart?' he enquired.

'I have been speaking with Will Christowe——'

'Oh, Will Christowe. . .' He turned away. She caught his arm, then flushed at the glance he gave her and let it go. 'When have you spoken to Christowe?' he asked, watching the colour wash over her face.

'Just a short while ago, and what he said has righted me on. . .various things.'

'That seems rather unlikely in the circumstances.'

She could never talk to him when he took up this indifferent stance; it had been a feature of their very early relationship. It had annoyed her then, and annoyed and hurt her now. 'What he told me carried the more weight because of the. . .circumstances.'

He picked up the flask of wine and dropped into a chair. 'Well, what did he say?'

'He said 'twas not true that you were going to Scotland to obtain monies to. . .to abandon me for. . .for. . .'

I told you that, but it seems you prefer to believe him. Very well, what else had he to say?'

Why must he make it so difficult for her? Sitting in his chair, so relaxed, staring at her? She took a breath. 'He said what I accused you of in your friendship with the Lady Madrilene was not true either.'

'How the devil does he know that?'

She sat back down on the bed. 'What does it matter?' she gulped. 'Except that he knows and now I know and. . .and——'

'And now I know what he knows and you know?'

'Please stop tormenting me! Why must you be so cruel? I know I was wrong and ask you to forgive me. It is all quite straight now in my mind.'

He filled his glass again. 'I wish it were in mine. Why did you accuse me in the first place? Why should Christowe choose this night to be advocate?'

She did not want to tell him any of that. She evaded his question by resorting to attack and saying sharply, 'None of this would have come about if you had not spent the last six months frittering away our small finances at your favourite occupation!'

'Don't you think I know that? But have you considered why I have been so careless lately?'

'You have always been like that!'

'Not so. I have never in my life before lost anything I valued. No, Bess, if I must take responsibility for what has happened, then so must you. When you left me in November, you took with you the ballast in my life. You cast me adrift without a backward glance and if I steered my poor leaky vessel into rough waters, then you can take some of the blame for abandoning ship, can you not?'

She was in tears now. 'It was not like that!'

'Oh, but it was. Or am I to doubt what I heard you say on our wedding-day? You promised to love and cherish me — there has been little of that in the year of 1542!'

'I do love and cherish you! Always. But — 'tis the women, Harry. I have never been good at coming to terms with them.' She felt in her sleeve for her handkerchief and dabbed at her eyes. *Why* was he doing this? It was so unlike the careless Harry to wish to prolong any argument.

He appeared to consider her words for a moment, then said judicially, 'Certainly I like women. I cannot deny it. But since you came into my life there has been no other woman who could do more than momentarily take my eye.'

'I know,' she whispered. 'I know that, really.'

'How? Because Will Christowe told you it was so? You did not know before? I had not shown you in the last six years?'

'Yes, yes, you did show me!'

She was overcome by tears now, but he went on relentlessly, 'When you found me, Bess, I was quite lost. I knew that within a month of meeting you. I was just a walking, talking shell of a man with no substance or worth. You changed that. You changed *me*. You gave me the gift of your love, but when the times grew hard last year, you took it back.'

'No, I never took it back! Never. I was just confused——'

'You chose to believe rumour and gossip, instead of what I told you to be true. You chose to believe what you thought you saw with jealous eyes—you chose not to trust me, when I would trust you with my life. Before you left Hampton a half-year since, you spent your time with another man. He showed his regard quite plainly, and you showed your preference for him. But did I believe the worst of you?'

She lifted her head. 'I don't know. Did you?'

He held her eyes. 'No, Bess,' he said gently. 'I did not. Certainly I did not like the situation—I am a jealous man where you are concerned. Perhaps I felt that you cared more for him than you would like to admit—even to yourself. But I knew, I *knew* were you seriously involved you would come to me yourself and advise me of the fact. Whatever base thoughts my jealousy brought me, I discounted. Why could you not do the same?'

The fluency of his prosecution bewildered her, made her feel dishonest—petty, in her actions and words. But it had not been that way! She forgot her prideful wish to leave her meeting with Madrilene out of the proceedings, and said bitterly, 'I could not do the same, Harry, for what I believed was confirmed by the woman involved! Madrilene told me you were to abscond together. Madrilene told me you were in love with her, had made love to her.'

'Madrilene said that?' He was astounded. He was an experienced man and courtier, he had been a vital part of an assembly notorious for its intrigue for twenty-five years. But this——

'And when *she* said that,' Bess went on miserably, 'I believed her.' Bess was silent a moment. One of the new logs she had added to the fire to keep it alive while waiting for Harry to come was too green to burn. It began to smoke and the sweet smell of applewood filled the room.

So that is the way of it, Harry thought, watching her, his heart contracting. My poor darling! Months without proper word from himself, in which to brood on his cruel last words, and at the end of it a sword-thrust to the heart from a scheming young wanton not worthy to clean his Bess's shoes. The tough shell around his heart shivered and cracked. 'For it had been months, Harry,' Bess went on, 'since I had seen you. . .months with no word from you.'

'No word?' His eyes, as if by accident, alighted on the ruby pendant she wore on her breast. Had worn since receiving it.

'I didn't understand the note you sent,' she said slowly.

'Did you not? Then I must explain it.' He got up and came to her side. He sat beside her and his eyes travelled over her for several seconds, then he tapped the ruby lightly with one finger. ''Tis very hard,' he remarked, 'for all its warm colour. This heart is not so impervious to hurt.' He took her hand and slipped it inside his shirt and pressed it against his breast so she could feel the gentle thud against her fingers.

Nothing has really been solved in our discussion, she thought. Harry had, as usual, directed the course of the conversation and there was so much more she wanted to say. But she was distracted by his closeness, by the scent of his skin and hair. She relaxed against him, and he turned up her face and kissed her.

'We have wasted so much time,' he murmured.

Later, much later, Harry turned in her arms to relight the candle. 'We never get to the root of any of our disagreements,' Bess said. 'Because I am so very susceptible to that part of me which desires you so much.'

'Good,' he replied, settling back beside her. 'I would not have you any other way.'

She leaned up on one elbow. 'But there are still problems between us, you know. Shortly, we will all be homeless.'

'Not at all. When I return from Scotland, we will be solvent once more.'

'But you won't go now!' She sat up. 'I will not allow it!'

'Sweetheart——' he reached out a long arm and drew her down again '—that part of your grievance is still valid. I am near destitute; I *must* go north with Norfolk. If I don't we will lose Maiden Court.'

She leaned above him. 'So let us lose it! Better that than you should go against your principles, or be in danger for one instant!'

'No, don't say that. I am one of His Majesty's chosen knights—I should long ago have proved my loyalty. I can do what is required of me.'

She drew decisively away. 'You are not listening to me, Harry. Not taking what I say seriously.'

'Do you expect me to? When you are looking so lovely, and there are still some hours before dawn?'

She evaded his caressing hand. 'If you go, I shall not wait to receive the blood money. I shall go back to Kew and burn Maiden Court to the ground! Then perhaps you will believe me when I say you are the most important thing in my life.'

He both welcomed and resisted such vehemence. He had been only half alive without Bess, but had he not also been . . free? Now the cords binding them together had tightened again, and he was truly glad, but also—— What? He could not have put a word to a feeling so mixed. He sighed. 'Let us not speak of it now. Not spoil this moment of reconciliation with words. Let us not talk at all.'

There was a vast silence in the palace now. It was that time when its courtiers had finally retired to sleep, and a few hours before its army of servants would commence their working day. Bess felt a depression envelop her like a weight of dark cloth. She said wistfully, 'I know I am a trial to you, Harry.'

'Never a trial, but sometimes I believe you *think* too much, sweeting. Can we not just admit to each other that we love each other, that we are in love, and be content with that?'

'I am content, of course,' she said quickly, 'and will try most sincerely not to...think, but——'

'But? There is always a but with you! Love cannot be worked out like the mathematical problems the tutor of my youth inflicted upon me. For them there was but one answer—the right one. In matters of the heart, there may be several, also right.'

'Sophistry, Harry,' she murmured. 'From someone well practised in the games of this court.'

'I no longer play those games,' he said sternly. 'And have not for a long time.'

'No games? Not even with the Lady Madrilene?'

He groaned. 'Especially not with her!'

'I know I must not mention about...about that which I accused you of. I believe you when you say there was nothing, but I will always wonder a little if it is not all out in the open. So...she came to your room?'

'Yes.'

'But you turned her away?'

'I did.' He was giving her no help at all.

'Oh, tell me what were the circumstances! Why did she come? What did she want?'

'I think she came for me,' Harry said blandly. 'I think she wanted me.'

'Harry,' she said warningly. 'Just be straight with me now.'

He sighed again. 'Very well. Madrilene is in the grip of an obsession. I understand that, for I am in similar case over you. I don't enjoy being the object of hers and when she came I fought valiantly for my virtue and——' he smiled wryly '—won.'

'Having done so, why did you continue to allow her to be with you all the time?'

'Because,' he said bluntly, 'I was afeared she might do herself a mischief if I cut her off. During the course of my defending my honour that night she tried to throw herself from my window. That window.' He gestured to the dark window.

'Oh, no!' Bess was horrified. 'That young girl—how could she be so foolish?'

Harry said thoughtfully, 'Tom Culpeper said we are all fools for love. How else explain my peculiar behaviour over the past months? Now——' he pinched out the light '—you know everything; let us get our rest now.' He drew up the covers.

On the edge of sleep Bess thought, It is right between us now—and I am so thankful. But of course I have made it right; had I waited for Harry to do so it might never have happened. . . As he had had doubts to spoil the moment of reunion, so did she, but neither spoke of these disquieting thoughts.

Will Christowe was already in the hall when the Latimars came down to break their fast the next morning. One glance at their faces assured him that his noble action had rewelded the link between them. Madrilene, with banging head and sick stomach from her excesses the previous night, saw the same, with the added knowledge like a knife in the heart that cordial conversation was not all that had been resumed. Bess wore the unmistakable glow of a woman who had been set sensually alight during the long night.

"Tis over for us, Madrilene,' Will had said when he had come to her earlier to tell her what he had told Bess, 'and we must be gracious losers.'

Easy for him, thought Madrilene, trying to eat to pacify her churning stomach, and not to stare across the smoky hall at Harry, so attentive to his smiling wife. For Lord Will lay ahead the distraction of war; for herself nothing but the time to brood on what she had lost.

She had just come from a distressing interview with the Lady Baldwin who had accepted responsibility for the aristocratic girl during her visit to England. Lady Baldwin had advised her charge to make preparations to return to France with all speed. The climate in England would soon become violently anti-Frankish, the kindly dowager assured her. Thus was the nature of a country planning to engage, and both Madrilene's Spanish and French heritage would tell against her in the months to come and her position in the English court would be uncomfortable indeed.

Appearing to accept this advice and curtsying dutifully, Madrilene was not convinced she should go. She would be prepared to renounce her ties with both countries if she had good reason for it. When Bess rose from the table and left the hall, leaving Harry to finish his meal, Madrilene scribbled a note asking him to meet her in the rose gardens and gave it to a page for delivery.

She was first in the leafy beauty of the Greenwich rose garden. It was another perfect June day, the air refreshed by the cold night, and already warm and slumbrous under a blue sky. Brought on by the hot sun of the last week, the mass of blooms had opened and released their potent scent. Madrilene was sitting contemplating their splendour when Harry came down the winding path towards her.

She rearranged her wide skirts to make room for him to sit with her, but he stood before her framed against the bright colours of green and red and white.

'You have been a very naughty girl again,' he remarked, 'and nearly brought my life to ruin. What have you to say for yourself?'

She raised her head to look at him and said meekly, 'I did it for us, Harry, for us.'

'No such thing. You did it to make mischief.' There was no anger in his voice, and this somehow advised her that her case was more hopeless than if he had railed at her. I am truly little to him, she thought, no more than a passing irritation that has affected his love affair with his wife in only the smallest way. Nevertheless, she appealed to him.

'I know you think you love her, but can there be such love when the two concerned are so different? You and I are alike. We are two of a kind with a past and ambition in common. What can *she* know of the sort of life we have led?'

'Very little,' he admitted. 'But that, for me, is perhaps one of her attractions.' He saw the truth of what Madrilene said: they had both been brought up in the rarefied atmosphere of royal courts, they understood and revelled in the constant machinations necessary for survival among courtiers in a different mould to ordinary men and women. Bess had no such history and never pretended it. When she chose she could fit easily into any company, however exalted, and had a strong appeal for the wealthy and well-born. Again and again he had noticed that: George and Anne Boleyn had both loved her in their way; Tom Seymour, even Henry Tudor, showed their regard more and more. Perhaps such spoiled and cynical creatures—and he himself was one of them—naturally reached out for her purity of spirit. He said thoughtfully, 'Love takes no account of suitability, you know. If I could have chosen with a clear head six years ago, I might have decided differently. But there was no such option for me when Bess entered my life, when I finally had to admit I could not happily contemplate the rest of it without her.'

He is not even talking to me, Madrilene thought with a sinking of her already bruised heart. She tried one more time.

'What is there for me now? I have seen the man I would have by my side through the long years. What can I do? Where can I go?'

Her passionate voice penetrated his selfish thoughts. He said gently, 'You must go home. This place will be unfriendly to you soon.'

'So I am told.' She glanced around the the peaceful, fragrant garden. 'Are you angry with me? For lying to her?'

'No, not angry. But in the future you may do well to consider we all must live together somehow. What we do affects others to a greater or lesser degree.'

She hung her head, tears filling her eyes, and twisted the great diamond on her finger. He is speaking to himself again, she thought. With an effort she removed the glittering bauble and held it out. The sun was caught and trapped in its glittering heart. When he made no move to take it she tossed it over the space separating them and he put up an automatic hand and caught it. She said, 'Keep it, Harry. I have no right to it.'

He considered the marvellous jewel in his palm. 'You won it fair and square.'

She got up and doubled his fingers over the ring. 'I have won nothing! Take it back—'tis unlucky, I am sure, for any but its rightful owner. So I believe there is nothing more to say other than to wish you luck, Harry, and—if you won't laugh—a little advice. I did not nearly bring your life to ruin; I, or any other woman, could never be so important. Your dispute with Bess is about you. I could have let you be yourself, but she never will; you must adapt, my friend, or ruin will definitely be the word to use.'

He gave a wry smile. A shrewd thrust, and true, but he did not want to hear it... There were footsteps on the path and Will Christowe came towards them. He was walking with a bent head and did not see them until it was too late to turn aside; he came on, a faint flush showing under his fair skin at finding them together.

'Good day, Christowe,' Harry said easily.

'Latimar—Madrilene.'

Madrilene brushed away her tears and moved swiftly away down the path, without looking at either man, her skirts brushing the warm earth either side.

'When she was a child, I never knew her cry,' Will observed. 'No matter what the provocation.' Harry stroked the jewel in his left ear without answering. 'You never used to have that effect on your women, Harry.' Bess's tears, too, hung between them for a moment.

'It is too fine a day for bickering,' Harry murmured, raising his eyes to the radiant sky. 'Actually I believe I must thank you for saying what you said to Bess last night.'

'I want no thanks,' Will muttered. 'I didn't do it for you.'

'I prefer to think you did it for us both.'

'You may think what you like.' Will took a pace back along the paving, then turned back. 'I imagine you won't be joining me on the border now?'

Harry looked surprised. 'Why should you say that? My reasons for going are unchanged.'

Will stirred the moss growing between the flags with the toe of his boot. 'You disapprove of the whole affair. Frankly, reluctant warriors make poor soldiers.'

'Do they? Never having been one, I couldn't say, but rest assured I shall do my duty by my brothers-in-arms.'

'If you explain it to Henry, he will understand.'

Harry raised one eyebrow. 'Explain it how? Say my wife doesn't want me to go out to play in Scotland and France, so I must retract my promise to him? Really, Christowe, I have said I am grateful for your meddling thus far in my private concerns, but there must be a limit. Excuse me, I have various things to do.' Harry turned on his heel.

Will grimaced at the other man's dismissive tone. He would be quite happy to mind his own business, but he seemed to be in the habit now of involving himself in the Latimars' affairs.

The king sent for Harry as he and Bess were dressing for supper a week later. They had had no serious conversation in the past seven days; they were too afraid of breaking the rather uneasy peace, but they both felt the cloud over their new happiness and Bess, particularly, was growing increasingly frantic at the thought of losing him again — this time to a vastly more dangerous place.

There was to be a masque that night — courtiers were bid to appear in the guise of a mythical character and Bess, having no suitable costume with her, had sacrificed a white dress to be cut about that she might impersonate the Spirit of Spring. Harry had chosen to be Hephaestus, and needed to do little more than dress in his usual grey and add a sparkling jet-studded mask. He was not entirely pleased with his appearance: a week ago he had not cared for the loss of his jewellery over the tables, now he regretted it.

Bess peered doubtfully into the glass. 'I am not sure it suits me, you know.'

'Everything suits you,' Harry said, helping her to fasten the fresh rosebuds in her hair.

''Tis something for a very young girl,' she frowned. 'Spring belongs to the young, or so I feel.'

'You look quite perfect, little grandmother,' Harry assured her. 'Why do you persist in speaking as though you were old and decrepit? It is most discouraging to me, for I am some years older than you, after all. Perhaps I should appear tonight as Old Father Time.'

Bess turned from the mirror to survey him. 'You do not show your age, Harry. In truth, you have changed not at all from the first time I met you.' She bent to put on her white silk slippers. 'It is an unfair advantage men — some men — have over us women. Also — '

'Also?' he enquired, as she straightened up and pushed back her hair which she was wearing loose that night.

'What has happened to me over the last five years shows on my face. The children, and — '

'And the worry over having such a worthless husband? Well, let me see.' He took her face in his two hands. 'I see no evidence of the terrible time I have given you.'

She pushed him away, laughing. 'Don't tease me, Harry. Not tonight, when I want to feel particularly my best.'

He unstoppered his bottle of perfume and tipped a little of the pungent liquid into his palm. Passing his hand over his hair, he asked, 'Why particularly tonight?'

'Oh. . .I don't know. Except I feel I have come through some kind of conflict, and wish to present myself as not only victorious, but also beautiful.'

'You are always beautiful, Bess — to me, and I am sure to all others. As to the conflict you speak of, my own squire said of it: one does not fight for territory already in one's possession. He referred to my case but it could equally well apply to yours.'

Bess put the finishing touches to her toilette. 'Richard de Vere is very acute,' she said thoughtfully.

'He but stated the obvious. Obvious, at least, to me——'

'And me,' she said hastily. But she thought: yes, the territory has been reclaimed, but no lasting treaty spoken of, or decided upon. 'Now, let us go down and see how we compare in ingenuity to all those glamorous others.' She opened the door to find the page with the urgent summons for Harry to go to his king.

Henry was just preparing to join the revelry when Harry was announced. 'Come in, come in,' he said cheerfully. 'Ah, I see you have made little concession to the instructions. Grey as usual—what, or whom, do you represent?'

'Hephaestus,' Harry told him laconically.

'Indeed? Or Vulcan, as the Romans had it. Married to Venus or Aphrodite—very apt. But the man was lame, you know.'

'I will affect a limp as I enter the great hall,' Harry said, hiding a smile. He had been first scholar in his Greek studies. . .

'Hmm. Well, sit down. We will have a little wine.' When their beakers had been filled and the servant had withdrawn, the king said, 'I gather you are now reconciled with Bess. We are pleased to know that. And you will, naturally, wish to take a little time and perhaps escort her back to Maiden Court, and, er. . .'

Harry drank a little of the wine and looked politely enquiring.

'Yes, yes, home to your little son and daughter,

and to. . .' Henry tossed back his own wine and looked about him for inspiration.

'Have you something special you wish to say to me, sir?' Harry asked gently.

'I have, I have. 'Tis this way, Harry: we have been friends for a great many years. During those years I have been to war several times, but you have not accompanied me. I have always understood this.' He looked over the glowing expanse of Turkey rug at Latimar. 'This time you have chosen to do so, but I. . .'

'Doubt my competency to give a good account of myself in your name?' Harry supplied helpfully.

'No, no,' Henry said quickly. 'That is not what I am saying at all! If, when we are abroad in the forest, or on the public highway, an assassin should leap out to assault me, I know there would be no other man in my retinue I could rely on to contest that assault more energetically. I truly believe you would die in my defence, and without a second's hesitation. But—'tis the business of taking sword in hand in cold blood to carry out my ambitions which I feel you do not have the heart for, Harry. So—so I am prepared to release you from your obligation. You do not have to go either to Scotland with Norfolk, or to France later with me.' Henry sat back, having got out what he had found so difficult to say. Difficult because he believed what he said about not doubting Latimar's courage, but—in an age which estimated this quality on performance in events such as the one about to take place—he had no wish to offend. Difficult, too, because he would very much have liked to have Harry along on this his last tilt at encroaching old age. This last thought had been in his mind for several weeks now, for at last Henry Tudor felt *old*. The pain from his disabilities in the days was both maddening and weakening. Worse, oh, much worse, were his disturbed nights. At night, in the still black hours, he was tormented by strange fancies. These visions included a parade of ghostly beings all accusing, all horrible. Men he had wronged, discarded if their opinions differed from his own, rose up now to haunt his rest. Never an imaginative man, despite his ability to create beautiful and romantic verse, Henry was at a loss to explain these aberrations. It could only be, he concluded, an experience of the purgatory to come — and soon. . .

'I wonder, Harry said slowly, 'why everyone seems so anxious to protect me from this enterprise'.

'Not protect!' Henry protested. 'But it is well known you have no taste for such exploits, and are only going on this one for the sake of a little gold.'

Henry's expression changed. 'Who told you I was going just for that reason? Will Christowe?'

Such a direct question was not usual for Harry, and the king was startled into telling the truth. 'He may have mentioned it, yes.'

'He did more than mention it; he told you I wanted the money for Maiden Court, didn't he?'

'Don't cross-examine me in this way!' Henry said testily. He eased the tight breeches he wore which were made from gold tissue, as was his doublet — he portrayed the Sun God tonight. 'It is a foolish reason to change the habit of a lifetime, my boy. If you need money, you only have to ask me. You know that.'

'I don't choose to ask you,' Harry said arrogantly. 'Is it so inconceivable I might like to earn a little of my own for once in my life?' He got up and roved around the luxurious room. 'You are right, I don't want to fight, and as you have said it is not because I fear it, but because war is such a sorry business — especially that conducted on another nation's soil. Why should men wish to cross a sea and kill men they have never met? Men like themselves, probably, just anxious to hold on to their little piece of the world——'

'Treasonable talk, Harry,' the king commented mildly. 'But I will not take you to task for it, although I would scarcely relish it if all my subjects felt as you do. If they did, then England would be only a minor force in the world.'

'That would indeed be terrible,' Harry murmured.

'Yes, well, we have had this conversation every five years or so since we met. . . Help me up now, if you will, and let us get to the entertainment.'

Harry heaved the older man up and held him until he was steady on his feet. He said, 'It was not just for the money, Hal, that I decided to embark on this unlikely new career. I wanted to be with you in this. I feel you need your friends at this time.'

Henry had his balance now; he put a strong arm

about his helper. 'I know that. But, whatever your loyalty to me, I feel a strong protection towards you.'

'Do I still need protection?' Harry asked ruefully. 'At my advanced age?'

'I think so.' The king leaned against him, not in weakness, but in affection. 'Men do not—or should not—speak of fondness—but that is what I feel for you. Please allow me to demonstrate it in this small way. Now——' he rallied '—let us get on with the festivities: there is a special lady I would have you meet.'

Harry laid a detaining hand on his arm. 'Before we go down...what you have said to me—it is in the nature of a request that I think again? About going with Norfolk?'

'No, Harry, it is in the nature of an express order,' the king replied quietly. 'That you do not go.'

'And if I say—I need to go? I *want* to go?'

'Then I would say that I am commander of this enterprise.'

'I see.' Something in Harry's face prevented the king from saying any more on the subject and the two men turned down the stairs, the trumpeters at the foot sounded a triumphant rally, and they entered the hall.

By chance the lady Henry wanted Latimar to meet was at this moment engaged in conversation with Lady Bess. Catherine Parr was in her early thirties in this year, a handsome well-bred woman, already married and widowed twice. She had a reputation for being practical and kindly as well as well-educated. Bets were already being laid within the court that she would be the sixth wife of the monarch.

Henry's puffy eyes scanned the assembly until he found her, then came slowly through the crush to her side. Both women rose and curtsied, chairs were brought speedily for the king and Latimar and all four watched the dancing.

Catherine was dressed in crimson, with an embroidered design of fruit and wheat on the skirts and bodice, and an intricate garland of flowers around her plump neck.

'Ceres?' guessed Harry, in an undertone to Bess. 'Very apt. What do you think of her?'

'She is kind,' Bess returned in a whisper. 'If the marriage does come about, she will be a good wife to Henry and a sympathetic mother to his children. Certainly, all three could do with a little petting.' Bess had got to know, and like, Mary, Henry's oldest daughter over the years, and loved Elizabeth and little Edward. Both the girls had had the shame of being called bastards when the king discarded their mothers, and were little better than ignored by their father these days. A tactful and gentle stepmother might do much to rearrange this state of affairs. As for Edward — Bess thought him too cosseted and spoiled for his own good; a practical influence in his life would be a very good thing.

'Hmm. Yet gossip has it she is more than taken

with their step-uncle — if that is the correct title for Jane's brother.'

'Tom Seymour?' Bess opened her eyes in surprise. 'I can't see that.'

'Perhaps you think he prefers ladies with eyes like blue lakes and hair like silver with the sun upon it.'

'Backhanded compliments are better than none at all,' Bess smiled. 'But if you want to tell me you admire my eyes and hair, why not just say it outright?'

'I will, if you let me take you away upstairs where we might be alone.'

'Certainly not! I have come down tonight to enjoy myself.'

He frowned. 'You think you won't enjoy the activity I have in mind? That is dismal hearing for a man in love all over again with his wife of five years.'

'Six. . . Do you love me, Harry? In all our heated discussion and — er — what came after last night, you never actually said it.'

Harry kept his eyes on the dancers. He noted that Madrilene had come to the masque dressed in a short white tunic which showed off her lovely legs, and carried an archer's bow. Diana the Huntress was an apt choice for her too. Will Christowe, in divided leather skirt, plumed helmet and massive silver sword, was one of Caesar's legionnaires — also well in character. He said reflectively, 'The night I asked you to be my wife you demanded a similar declaration. Say it to me, you said, so I may take out your words in the years to come when I cannot make you tell me again.'

'You remember that?'

'I have told you, I remember everything you have said or done since the moment we met.'

'Shall I then search in my memories for this particular thing?' Bess asked softly.

Harry, still keeping his eyes fixed on the colourful scene before him, took one of her hands in his. He raised it to his lips and his mouth caressed the fingers. 'Do so,' he said.

'Do you remember what else we spoke of that night? With the moon hanging like a gold coin in the dark sky, and the sound of the sea and wind trying to take our words?' she asked.

He turned to give her a direct blue look. 'I remember. You said you would not wander the boundaries of my life, bearing my children and keeping my house. You see, I am word-perfect — do I get the prize?'

'Not until I get mine, which is to have what you have just described. To be the kind of wife you agreed I should be.'

He removed his eyes from her face. 'We all must adapt, Bess.'

Misgivings slid unwelcome into her mind. Nothing has really changed, she thought regretfully. We have both suffered during our estrangement — Harry more than I would have thought possible — but now it is righted again, he has learned nothing from it.

She said, sighing, 'What did the king want with you earlier?'

He hesitated, then said evasively, 'To reaffirm his friendship, I think.'

'Oh? In what way? And why now?'

'Why not now? Any time is a good time to hear of love, is it not?' he answered, evading the first part of her question.

The king leaned forward a little to peer at them. 'Lady Bess? I believe I feel well enough to attempt the dance. Will you accompany me?'

Bess, startled, rose immediately. 'I would be honoured, sir.'

It was not altogether a pleasurable experience. Henry had been a superb dancer in his youth and middle years; now he was ponderous and heavy, and to partner him hazardous. After some minutes he took her arm and steered her into one of the alcoves. He sat down, breathing painfully.

'Shall I order wine?' Bess asked solicitously.

'No, no, I only wish to talk with you a moment.'

Bess folded her hands in her lap and waited for him to speak.

'It has been in my mind lately,' the king said slowly, 'that I must reward you for your care of my son during his recent illness.'

Bess tilted her square chin. 'No reward is necessary for such an honour, Your Majesty. His little Highness's recovery is reward enough for me.'

'Now, don't be prickly, Bess. Naturally I know that, but. . .in all my dealings over the years I believe none could honestly declare I do not pay my debts.' Bess played with her slim fingers thinking that quite a few men — dead now, or dishonoured — could refute such a statement, but she said nothing and Henry went on, 'Here is what I propose. It has come to my knowledge that your home, your estate, is in the hands of the money-lenders. I intend to redeem it forthwith and present it to you for your efforts on Edward's behalf.'

'Maiden Court? But, sir, I believe it is to go to auction for a vast amount!'

'I hope you do not suggest that any amount could be vast enough to be laid alongside my son's life?'

'Of course not.' Bess's mind struggled with both her joy at what he suggested and what it might mean to Harry, and herself. 'But how could I accept?' she said doubtfully. 'Harry——'

'Harry——' the king smote one hand on his knee '— has no part in this business! I have considered long and hard over how I may please you, and think I have done very well. Now, madam, are you so under that gentleman's thumb that you cannot think for yourself? Or for your two children?'

Bess turned on him the smile which had, over the years, made her so many friends both at court and among the villagers near her home. 'Dear sir,' she said, 'you have an aggressive way with you this night, but I think you are doing this not just for me, or my children. You don't want Harry to go to war, do you? Even though he would be the greatest comfort to you in the heat of battle.'

'I shall be engaged in no heat of battle, Bess,' Henry said irritably. 'But seated on some high ground as an observer. Harry on the other hand, being Harry, will be in the thick of it—so, no, I don't want him there.' The king winced as his leg protested the recent turn about the floor, then shot a look at the delicate profile beside him. 'Now, what is troubling you? Really, some ladies are never satisfied.'

She smiled again. 'Oh, I am well satisfied with your generous offer, but am just wondering how it will affect Harry. I think he wanted to make good his mistakes this time—without applying to any other. I am torn between wishing him to have that satisfaction and being afraid something will happen to him.'

Henry digested this in silence, then said thoughtfully, 'Yes, I see what you are saying, and yet—it seems to me that there has always been someone to pick up the pieces for Harry, and enjoy doing it. Certainly it has been a pleasure for me over the years.'

'You care for him almost as much as I do,' she said softly.

'I can't deny that. He is a hard man to be close to—apparently so open-handed, there is yet a dark side to his nature—both complex and interesting. He is also unpredictable and at times extremely aggravating, but. . .'

'But?'

Henry sighed. Over the long and often turbulent

years he had had many true friends. Most were gone now, but Latimar remained. He said, "Tis the constant thing, d'you see, Bess? The knowing he is there. Always, in so many crises in my life, Harry Latimar has been there. To encourage, to support, often to deride and criticise, but always *there*. I love him, and am not ashamed to admit it, for he is a man worth loving.' He cast a shrewd look at her. 'You and he have had your trials of late. Over a woman. Well, there will always be some woman stalking him, you know—women having such excellent eyesight. . . But since there has been you, lady, no other female can command even one small part of his lasting attention. I hope you know that.'

'I think I do.'

'Good, good. . . Now allow me to give you a little advice: Harry is what he is—you won't change him, and you might—in trying—break a good marriage. One cannot make a high-stepping thoroughbred do the work of a sturdy cobby mare. If you wanted a tabby cat you should not have chosen an entirely different creature. Now——' he laughed at himself '—I have mixed my metaphors, and I an acclaimed poet! Having said all that, I'll finish with this: six years ago I advised him not to marry you. I suppose he will never have told you that. I believed he could do better, but now I am not so sure. You have both proved me wrong. So, this night, and without taking into account that I have made your path easier, I would tell you to take him home, Bess. Take him away from here for a while and see if—intelligent creature that he is—he may work out for himself what is worth having in this life.'

The chamber was noisy; laughter and the sound of dancing feet dominated the warm and stuffy room. But between Bess and the ageing king there was another silence. It was the most personal conversation she had ever had with Henry Tudor. She had never really liked him, often had not respected him, but they had at least one thing in common: they both cared for the same man.

Henry showed that caring in being willing to let his friend go during a period when he probably needed him most. The year had begun in the most dismal way for the king, with the execution of his wife. Mourning her, he also mourned for himself— the massive blow to his heart matched by the blow to his pride in himself as a man. Also, the articulate old poet had a way with words. He had used that tonight to offer her some very good advice. What she made of it was up to her, she thought, rising and curtsying, and crossing the crowded floor to slip her arm through her husband's.

CHAPTER TEN

Two weeks later Harry and Bess were on their way home to Maiden Court. Harry had been outmanoeuvred on three fronts. Firstly, Norfolk — primed by the king — had delicately released him from his military duties. Next, the king had formally dismissed him from the royal court for an unspecified amount of time. Thirdly, Bess had showed him the deeds of their estate, calmly advising him that they were a gift in recognition of her services to the throne. Harry rode under the summer skies on this hot July day with mixed emotions.

Bess had only one thought: I am going home! Back to the place I love the best, in the company of the person I love the best. When they crossed the boundary which separated Latimar land from the neighbouring estate, she looked eagerly about her, noting the abundant fields growing towards harvest, the bordering orchards already ripe with miniature fruit, the general air of tidy and careful husbandry. From the winding lanes she saw the acres of wheat and oats and barley, the men at work in the fields, with a feeling of bursting pride.

In the lanes nearer the house the hedges either side of their path were so high they could have been riding in corridors papered with wild flowers —

waxen hedge roses, purple foxgloves and the gay trumpets of the wild lily.

When they had moved through the spinney and the house was in view, enclosed in its neat gardens and dreaming under hazy clouds, they rode up the incline and looked down on the meadows of buttercups and clover which in turn rolled into the daisy-strewn lawn before Maiden Court.

'The children will be greatly changed from when I saw them last,' Harry said, relaxing his grip on the reins so that Troubadour could crop the sweet grass under his hooves.

'Naturally—they change almost daily at that age, or so it seems to me,' Bess said happily. 'Shall we ride on?'

'In a moment.'

She glanced at him. Surely he was not nervous of meeting his children again? she thought sadly.

In fact Harry was preparing himself for the change from one world to another. From being free to being shackled, or so it appeared to him, although he was ashamed of the thought. There had been shame, he felt, in his dismissal from court. Henry—busy and beset on all sides by worries over the impending invasion—had yet made time to bid him farewell, wished him God speed and embraced him warmly. Even so, Harry had felt of less importance than the youngest foot soldier in the preparing army, for he was going bravely to show his mettle in the coming fight. Latimar, on the other hand, must be protected from such manly activity. Norfolk—too old really for the responsibility he had undertaken, and terrified he might fail again in the operation designed to ingratiate himself with his monarch—had been gracious enough in his tactful release of Latimar. Bess, too, had been almost casual when she had shown him the faded parchment now inscribed with her name, and said lightly that now their future was assured and there was no need for him to place himself in harm's way for anything as paltry as gold to save the roof over their heads.

Nevertheless, Harry could not rid himself of the feeling that he was not unlike a well-tied package: neatly bound up and ready for delivery into the capable arms of his wife.

Both children were in the nursery with their grandmother when their parents arrived. Anne was already tucked up for her afternoon rest and fast asleep. Joan was trying to persuade George to be in the same peaceful state. All morning he had been like a wild thing, racing from one room to another above stairs, clattering noisily down the staircase and out into the dazzling day in another. It was one of those days when Joan almost regretted his abounding health and vitality. Now, when he heard the hoofbeats approaching the house, he ran to the window.

'Tis Mother!' he exclaimed. 'And there is a gentleman with her!'

Joan looked for herself. 'It is your father,' she said sternly. 'And do not think I will not have harsh words to say to him of your behaviour!'

George was silenced both by the threat and by the thought that at last his father had come home. He raised his handsome face to his grandmother and gave her a winning smile. 'May I please come down with you to greet them? I promise I will be good.'

Joan looked at him distractedly. 'Very well, but first I must tidy you.' She seized a brush and George stood patiently as she drew the bristles vigorously through his thick dark hair, lifted a corner of her apron to dab at his face. She took his hand and they walked sedately down the staircase. Halfway down, he wriggled away and took the remaining stairs two at a time, landing at the bottom as the outside door opened and Harry came into the hall. The two male Latimars appraised each other in silence.

My father, thought George. Why, 'tis like looking in the mirror! How tall he is, how wonderfully dressed, how the light sparkles in the fine ring he wears on his forefinger. He stayed quite still, waiting for Harry to make the first move.

Harry was thinking, Myself as a boy! The same unusual height, length of hand and foot, and the ready smile. But I surely never wore that prideful look in my eyes, or achieved that arrogant carriage of head and shoulders! He was suddenly afraid. I always fail — sooner or later — all those who love me. What if I should fail this charming boy? He could not move for this disquieting thought.

Bess, who had come in ahead while Harry handed over their mounts over to the stable groom and gone straight to the kitchens, now opened the adjoining door and came into the hall. She ran across the floor and knelt to embrace her son.

'George!'

George threw his arms around her neck and kissed her on forehead, cheek and chin. 'Mother! You have been away too long. Don't do it again!'

Bess stood up laughing. 'Have you greeted your father yet?'

Harry came slowly to them and held out his hand. George shook it gravely. Bess laughed again, but she was troubled by the distant expression on Harry's face. . . 'What formality! Come, kiss each other.' Harry bent his glossy head obediently and pressed his lips briefly to the boy's upturned face.

Why, they are like strangers, thought Bess sadly. But of course Harry was expecting a baby. We at Maiden Court are used to George's forward ways, but Harry must get to know what is really another person. . . She looked up the stairs and smiled at Joan.

'Mother, I am sorry we sent no word of our coming. We were unsure of our plans until the last moment.'

Joan descended the last steps and kissed her daughter, extended a hand to Harry who looked swiftly into her face before raising it to his lips.

'So,' Joan said, 'I will hurry supper along; you will be hungry.' Joan's answer to all powerful emotions was to feed those around her with all possible speed. She hurried away to stir up Margery and her maids to put on a feast.

'Won't you sit down?' George asked politely. Bess and Harry took seats by the open window. George climbed to the padded window-seat between them and sat, legs dangling. He was wearing only sturdy hose and a loose white linen shirt—Joan had a constant battle to keep him in the voluminous skirts which both little boys and girls wore in these times.

'Where is your sister?' Bess asked, looking at him with pride; he must surely have grown half an inch since she left!

'Asleep. She needs her sleep.' George leaned to touch his father's sleeve, stroking the gleaming silk. 'So soft,' he said. 'I like it.'

'You will be a fop like your sire?' Harry enquired idly.

Not having come across the word before, George asked its meaning. Harry considered, then told him, 'To be over-interested in one's clothing and appearance.'

'You make it sound a bad thing.'

'It is well enough if not carried to extremes,' Harry said lightly. He got up. 'I think I will take a turn around the grounds, Bess.'

'Oh, we will all go.'

'No, you stay here and take some rest. It is warm today.'

When he had gone, George said, 'He is not pleased with me.'

'Oh, darling, of course he is!' Bess's tone was the more fervent to make up for Harry's dismissive one. 'Just a little shy.'

George shook his dark head. 'No, it is not that.'

Bess hardly knew what to say. She must wait and see how the two beloved males in her family worked things out between them.

'We must wait and see,' George echoed her thoughts. Harry's smile crossed his face. 'Perhaps he will take to Anne better.'

Harry did take to Anne. Instantly they were the best of friends. Watching him cuddle his daughter that evening, and in the evenings which followed, Bess found irritation and regret spoiling her homecoming. Perhaps it was because the little girl befitted her age more than her brother did. Anne was still a baby who liked to be carried rather than walk, who was either wreathed in smiles or awash with becoming tears. Her vocabulary, unlike her brother's, was very small, her boundaries limited — in short she was the baby Harry expected to find on his return, while his son was a distinct person, with opinions of his own, complete in himself.

'I cannot understand why Harry is not delighted with him,' Bess said to her mother one August afternoon. 'He is a son to be proud of.'

Joan was sorting linen. It was her custom in the days of summer to lay out on the lawns the bedsheets to bleach in the hot sun. When they were brought in, she scattered dried lavender within their folds before returning them to the deep chests. 'Harry likes people to be as he thinks they should be,' she said. 'What man doesn't? After all, Bess, we at Maiden Court are used to our forward boy, but it must be a shock for Harry to leave a babe in arms and come back to find a child not yet two who could compete with a five-year-old.'

'That should make him even more proud,' Bess protested. 'Instead, he all but ignores George and lavishes attention on Anne. It is most distressing for me as well as my little son.'

'They must sort it out between themselves,' Joan said soothingly. Privately, she thought Bess showed her preference for George too clearly. Perhaps over-compensating for Harry's casual treatment of his son, Bess constantly pointed out his accomplishments, drew the boy to her side at the meal table, and even rode with him before her on the saddle when she went visiting around the estate. George combined both his parents' virtues: Harry's charm and intelligent grasp of any situation, interwoven with Bess's practical nature and gentle perception of others' needs. But even the most promising child could be spoiled by mishandling — and Joan sensed the boy was pulled two ways. He obviously admired his father — what child would not adore a man like Latimar who could by turns be the most amusing company in the great hall, and yet out-ride, out-drink, even out-work any other man within his vicinity? For Harry, previously a little aloof from participating in rural activities, had lately been a vital part in them.

This was the busiest time in any farming community, the effort of the long months' labour about to offer reward to the patient guardians of the soil.

The earth would now give back the hours of toil in an abundant harvest, and in the last weeks Harry had earned his share. Joan, and everyone else, had been forced to review the opinion that Sir Harry Latimar was well enough — an indulgent, if careless, landlord. These days he showed himself capable of putting in as much effort as any man on his estate.

But Joan found it more impossible than usual to decide what went on behind his smiling face, what thoughts were contained in his handsome head. He had come back to Maiden Court a different man from the gay courtier who had left to accompany his king on the royal tour. Of course his mother-in-law knew, from snippets gathered here and there in the conversation between him and Bess, that he had taken the long separation from her daughter very hard, had taken refuge from his pain in indulging in his obsession at the gaming tables, had got himself into an awkward tangle with a lady at court, and had been saved from bankruptcy by his royal master. She also knew that Bess was essentially now both master and mistress of Maiden Court, and this was what worried the kindly, sensible farmwife most of all.

Joan de Cheyne had been a quiet observer of the man her daughter had married for six years now. Naturally, she could not know him intimately, but human nature — whether low or highly bred — and especially in a male, demanded its rightful place. Harry's place, she felt, was to be in the commanding position in any relationship he was part of, particularly that with a female. It was not that he was not in that position here at Maiden Court, it just appeared to Joan that he felt somehow that he wasn't. How she knew this she had no idea, but wondered that sensitive Bess had not picked up the same impression. That she had not was obvious because, apart from her worry over George, she seemed perfectly content.

If Bess had been asked this, she would have agreed that she was. What woman in my position would not be? she asked herself now, kneeling to help lift the fragrant sheets. Maiden Court is flourishing, its land and tenants about to enjoy a wonderful harvest, its mistress loved and cherished by its master. And yet — without being able to put her finger on why, Bess was uneasy.

Harry had said little before they left Greenwich. When she had shown him the ancient parchment proving she now owned Maiden Court, and told him what the king had done, he had said nothing. 'You are pleased, aren't you?' she had pressed him.

'Of course. It never belonged to me anyway.'

'What do you mean?' she had cried. 'It belonged to *us*, and still does.'

'If you say so. Certainly, I think the piece of paper safer with you than with me,' was all he would say on the subject.

He had accepted his enforced release from the planned invasion without any visible struggle also, and had made no comment to her when Henry granted him leave of absence from his court.

'You do want to go home, don't you?' Bess had asked anxiously.

'I want to be wherever you are,' he had said, with all apparent truth. Yet. . .as the year moved on Bess was apprehensive, feeling as one sometimes did before a thunderstorm.

The storm came on a sultry day in mid-September. The family and their servants had been out in the fields all day. There was excitement in the air — country folk took the climax of their labours seriously, but now the harvest was gathered in and there was much to look forward to. The talk was of how well the weather had held, how fine the harvest, and the coming horkey which Lady Latimar intended holding as usual this year in the great barn.

At sunset it was time to go back to the house. Harry lifted Anne on to the saddle before him, Bess took George. Within the cool hall Anne was handed over to Joan to be put to bed.

'You are not tired, George?' Harry asked as the little boy bounded to the table, obviously expecting to take late supper with them.

'No, I slept in the fields this afternoon.'

'Nevertheless, please go with your grandmother.' Harry's tone was curt and George looked at Bess. 'Don't look at your mother,' Harry said sharply. 'When I tell you to do something, I expect to be obeyed. Not a difficult concept for one as advanced as you apparently are.'

Colour flared into George's face. He had been

standing behind his mother's chair at the table waiting for her to be seated; now he turned and made her his little bow.

'Goodnight, Mother,' he said, tears present in his voice, if not his eyes. He bowed again to his father. 'Goodnight, sir.'

He climbed the stairs with such dignity that Bess was torn between laughter and tears. When she heard the nursery door open and close again she said with a catch in her voice, 'Really, dearest, you were a little harsh.'

'Was I?' Harry lifted out her chair and she sat down. Leaning over her shoulder, he filled her glass, then took his seat at the head of the table. Mary, already showing her happy condition in thickening waist and radiant face, bore in the platter of meat. Harry helped Bess, then himself.

They ate in silence, until the table was cleared of all except a bowl of yellow pears, then Bess dismissed Mary to bed and said hesitantly, 'Your attitude towards George is altogether rather strange.'

'You think so?' Harry quartered his fruit, but left it on his plate to pour more wine. 'I find him a little strange. Unnatural——'

'Unnatural?' Bess hastened to her son's defence. 'Why? Because he can hold a conversation? Because he has ideas and opinions——'

'He has an opinion on everything!' Harry interrupted. 'A child should know his place.'

'You are always eager for all to know their place,'

Bess said bitterly. 'This discussion is not about George at all, is it? You are only punishing him for something I have done!'

'What do you mean by that?' Harry demanded.

'You all but pretend he doesn't exist!' she said stormily. 'It is most distressing — for him, and for me who loves him so.'

'It is obvious to all how much you love him!' Harry said coldly. 'You are scarcely from each other's side in daylight hours. The rest of us come a poor second to the young master of Maiden Court!'

'Harry!' she cried, aghast. 'I cannot believe that you are — jealous of a child. And that child your own son!'

'Yes, I am jealous!' Harry said violently. 'I am jealous of anyone you love — especially of those you appear to care for more than myself!'

Bess pushed back her chair and rose. She walked quickly to the door and flung it open. A wave of humid air flowed it, scented with the perfumes of summer and autumn. Harry caught up with her in the vinery. The vines had been a gift from the king and had done very well under their glazed shelter, carefully nutured by Bess.

The light from a rising moon could penetrate here and in passing through the thick green leaves and clusters of fruit cast an eerie light. Bess had had little wooden benches placed in here and often came with her needlework on cool days to enjoy the garden without being exposed to rough weather. She sank on to one of them.

When Harry was in the doorway she said quietly, 'Close the door, Harry; even a warm night can affect the fruit.'

He pushed it shut, then leaned his back against the stout oak. He said, 'I am sorry, Bess, I should not have said what I just did.'

'You should, if it is in your mind. Let us now hear what else has been festering there these past weeks. No——' she lifted blue eyes to his face '—do not say there is nothing, for I will know you lie.'

Harry looked down at the floor, considering her words. The surface was tiled in the old-fashioned Roman way—black and white, black and white. The pattern echoed his wife's clear view of the world, he thought, wishing he had the facility to be so straightforward. His mind was a jumble of half-acknowledged fears.

'I am waiting, Harry,' Bess said quietly.

Harry fingered the ruby in his ear. The gem had been lost at Christmas to Tom Seymour, who had returned it before he left with the advance party bound for Calais. A parting gift, Tom had said, to remember me by. He had also smiled and said, 'You and I have not been the best of friends, Harry. A situation not of my making, but yours. I hope that bearing grudges will not become a habit with you.' The comment had been one of two such barbs; the other had come from Will Christowe, who had sought out Latimar before he rode out with the convoy for Scotland.

'You have the land I love, and the woman too,'

Will had said, made eloquent by the wine drunk to mark the occasion. 'I only wish I thought you deserved either of them.'

Harry left his place by the door and came to the bench. He sat down and took Bess's hand, and also a deep breath. 'You always know when I am troubled,' he murmured, 'almost before I know it myself.'

She looked at him. The greenish light brought out the copper in his hair, and turned his head to bronze. ''Tis a knack which comes with caring so much,' she said.

He straightened her fingers one by one, appreciating their white smoothness. 'You were right when you said our argument was not about George. He is exceptional, yes, although no more so than I would expect any child of yours to be. Tomorrow I shall put aside my petty envy and start again. He is your son and will allow me to do so.' There was a pause, during which they both wondered if what was to follow was either desirable or sensible. Bess decided that it was, if there were to be for them the kind of future she wanted.

'You have said George is not the issue, which means something else is. Pray declare it.'

He doubled her fingers over his. His grip was hard and painful, but she enjoyed it. 'I have not been the best of husbands,' he said thoughtfully. 'I have not been the best of fathers — so far. As to master of this enviable estate — well, irresponsible would be the kindest description any man could give of my conduct. But—if I have failed in all three roles, one saving grace has been mine. For throughout all our time together I have loved you, Bess. Completely and absolutely and seeing no other. I had thought that might be enough for you.'

One strand of her hair, true silver in the odd light, had strayed over his shoulder. He took it between his fingers, feeling its warmth and life. 'But no, it was not enough, for you must demand more. You must—even though our differences were resolved— interfere in my life to ensure that I did not take my rightful place with others of my rank and take arms for my king—and my friend. Very well, perhaps I could accept that—it would have been a sore test for me and probably I should have failed. Now I shall never know. But then I find that you have taken my place as master in my own home. Maiden Court—won in a casual game and ill-regarded at the time—is now yours.' He stopped as the hand in his tensed and looked at her enquiringly.

She had wanted to hear him out without interruption, but now surely she must defend herself! It had not been the way he described—or had it? Will Christowe had informed the king of their problems—she could not have known he would. Or could she? A word from her asking Will to keep Latimar affairs private would have sealed his lips. In the same way a respectful refusal to accept the king's gift of Maiden Court—or her immediate transfer of the deeds to her husband. . . But she had not done any of those things, because. . .because the way it had all turned out had suited her. She bit her lip.

Harry was wondering if he had said too much, or too little, but what he had said had come from the heart of him, painfully and sincerely. Bess stood up.

'Do you not find the difference in court and rural hours very hard to adjust to?' she asked conversationally. 'I do, and could wish for a little entertainment.'

He stared at her. He had done as he thought she wished: opened the dark places in his soul for her to comment upon. Instead, she prattled of useless things! 'What is it you would wish to do?' he asked with studied politeness. 'I can offer no special distraction for you.'

She turned to him in a swirl of pastel silk and shining hair. 'But you can!' she said. 'I have it in my mind to play cards tonight, Harry. Can you accommodate me?'

Back in the warm hall, Bess said, 'I must just look in upon the children. Do you deal our hands.'

'I have no cards,' Harry said, bewildered and quite unable to assess her mood.

Bess walked to the magnificent court cupboard which lined one side of the hall and reached behind one of the tall silver trophies. 'But you do! You left them behind when you went last to court, Harry, but I put them in a safe place for I knew you would want them again. Here. . .'

Harry took the cards from her hand. It was an old set which he used to play with. His friend George

Boleyn's cards, in fact—black and silver and inscribed with the Rochford arms. The shabby plaques held memories both painful and tender for him. He watched Bess go lightly up the staircase while he fingered the painted faces, finding the peculiar comfort the memory of his friend always inspired.

When Bess came down the two hands were dealt on to the polished table. Joan had been down during their absence in the vinery and thriftily quenched most of the candles. She had left one burning in a pewter holder on the square of the newel-post, and Bess picked it up and set it down beside her cards.

'What shall we play for?' asked Harry, taking the chair across the table. He took out his purse and tipped some coins out. 'I can stake you if you wish.'

'I do not wish,' Bess said deliberately. 'For I have my own stake.' She reached into her sleeve and withdrew a crackling parchment. The ancient deeds to Maiden Court lay between them.

Harry half smiled. 'I have no available funds to match those, Bess.'

'No matter,' she said airily. 'We will dispense with the formalities of equal worth. Shall we play?'

Harry picked up his hand and studied it. They were to play the most traditional—and the most deadly—game favoured by two players in court circles: three cards each hand until a previously specified time elapsed. Winner takes all.

'We will play until this candle fails,' Bess said.

'You will keep score and, of course, winner takes all on the table.'

Harry laid the first card; it was matched by Bess. He laid another and won, and another and won the first game. He dealt again. Bess won this time and the score was even. The cards went round several times and each time Bess was the victor. Harry dealt again. Bess lifted hers and said, 'I discard.' Harry marked up the result without comment. He dealt again, again Bess threw in her hand, and the next and again for the following few games. They were nearing the last of the cards now and without speaking Harry put another three before her. She looked at them casually.

'I discard,' she said, placing the cards face down.

'Why?' Harry enquired softly. 'I have an excellent memory, my dear, and feel you have the winning hand.' He reached over and flipped up her cards with one long finger. 'As I suspected. Why have you thrown in such a favourable assembly?'

Bess swallowed.

'If you cheat me,' Harry said gently, 'I will know.'

'I would never cheat you, Harry,' she said, glancing at the candle. It would burn for another half-hour, she estimated. She had always played to win in any game; now she knew that if she won this night she would lose all that was most precious to her.

Harry looked across the table at her, reading her mind. My Bess, he thought, I have sat around many a table and hoped she would win. Now, if she does, it will mark the end of something I scarcely dare imagine. He re-dealt the cards.

The evening drew on. Outside, beyond the dark windows, it was a clear night lit by a giant harvest yellow moon. Beneath this great golden globe the feathered residents of Maiden Court slept in the tall oak trees. On the Latimar land the little woodland creatures were about their business.

The candle was now barely alive in its sea of wax. The score was even, everything rested on this final game. Harry dispensed the cards with steady hands. Each picked up the cards and viewed them. Bess's heart sank, for hers was virtually unbeatable.

Harry laid his first card, she matched it. He laid another and was matched again. The candle-flame wavered as if the devil himself were trying to take it. They both held one card each and Bess put her high card down with a desperate air. The gaudy queen, bold and full-lipped, stared up at them both. Very gently, Harry laid his king upon it, and with a splutter the candle went out.

'I appear to have won,' Harry said. He reached across the table and took up the yellow parchment. 'Maiden Court is mine.' Bess burst into tears.

Harry tucked the papers into his doublet. 'Really, my dear,' he said mildly, 'I have taught you to be a better loser.' Bess put her head down on her folded arms and sobbed. Harry came around the table and touched her shoulder. She raised her tear-stained face and he kissed it.

'Sweet Bess,' he murmured, 'what is this all about?'

'It is about us,' she choked. 'About you and me, and how much we love each other.'

He put his hands on her waist and raised her out of the chair. 'You made five inexcusable errors — in the seventh, the tenth, the fourteenth, fifteenth and nineteenth round——'

'You're impossible!'

'And so are you! Laying our home on the turn of a card! I am ashamed of you.'

'I am sorry. No — I'm not sorry for what I have just done — but I am for interfering as you said earlier. I thought it for the best, truly.'

'I know, I know. Please don't cry. . . I too am glad you made this dramatic gesture tonight.'

'You are? Really?'

'Certainly, for now I know that my luck has turned.' He would have pulled away from her with this light remark, but she held him.

'You did not — I did not allow you to — finish what you were saying in the vinery. Please do so now.'

'It is irrelevant now,' he said, not meeting her eyes.

She turned and began to gather up the cards. Holding them loosely in her hands she said, 'Well, I cannot force you to speak.' She walked to the cupboard and replaced the cards behind the silver. 'Shall you wish for anything before we retire? A cold drink?'

'No...yes, I think I would like a little of your mother's excellent cordial, if there is any.'

'There is a great deal—the blackberries have been wonderful this year.'

When she came back from the kitchens with the beaker, he was standing by the window. From here could be seen the moon-silvered lawns and soft dark outline of the trees sheltering the house. She put the mug into his hands.

'You brought none for yourself? Come, we will share.' He sat down on the window-seat and drew her down beside him. He said slowly, 'There is something I would like to say, Bess, but...' She said nothing; he must find the words for himself. They drank the wine, sip and sip about, and Harry put down the empty mug. 'It is this way... While we were apart that long time it came to me that I missed Maiden Court almost as much as I missed you. Of course that is because you both are so linked in my mind, but I discovered that it is possible for a place to live in one's heart, as well as a person. That is how I feel for our home now—I have taken it with me wherever I went. I lost it, yes, through foolishness, but I felt it to be mine to lose. *My* home—the only home I have ever really had—I am not explaining well, I know.'

'But you are,' she said quietly. 'Do you think I love Maiden Court because it is beautiful and profitable? No, Harry, I love it because it ours. Because even when you are away you are, for me, in every room.' She bent her head and plucked at the embroidery on her skirt. She had sewn the delicate design of spring flowers during her long separation from Harry, and it had painful associations for her. 'Is that why you were so anxious to reclaim it back for yourself? By going to Scotland?'

'I suppose it is. I resented being forced—no, that is the wrong word—*persuaded* away from what I had chosen, however wild that choice. I felt conspired against—by you, by Henry, by circumstances—and although most think me easygoing and flexible, you know differently. I felt you should have known how resentful I would be. . .' He had been looking thoughtfully out into the night, now he looked at her. 'The last year has taught me what I suppose I should have known: that I cannot be without you. You are the reason I rise each morning, walk, talk, breath—*am*.

'In the past it has been enough for me to know that we belonged to each other, that you were here in this safe place where I could be with you whenever I chose—or not, if I so chose. . . Naturally, it was wonderful when you were with me at court; I was proud of you always. *Proud* that you could walk among those perceived to be great, and be admired by them. But when you returned home to Maiden Court, I always felt a burden had been lifted from my shoulders—a desired and cherished burden—but the word, although harsh, seems to fit my feelings.' He moved restlessly on the cushioned seat, so hard for him to express were such analytical thoughts. He went on, 'Then, when we were. . .

estranged, and I had so much time in which to think. . . I suddenly found the flaw in my philosophy. I had tried to fit you into the role I felt to be suitable, but now I discovered it did not suit. It did not suit *me*. I floundered around for months telling myself I was less than a man for feeling I must be tied to any woman's apron strings before I could be happy. 'Twas, you see, the dependency that was so hard to admit—for a man like myself who likes to walk alone.' He smoothed the damp hair back from her forehead, for she was in tears again. 'Going to Scotland, to France, was my final attempt to deny that dependency—to resist an irresistible force, darling.' Her tears, as always, disturbed and restricted him. He said lightly, 'Now you have all my secrets, are you satisfied?'

'Not yet. Forgive me for weeping, but it is the way I am. . . I believe from what you have said tonight, from the way you have acted in the last weeks, that you intend making your life from now on here at Maiden Court. . . For that is what you have decided, is it not?'

Harry released her and stood up. He wandered about the hall, as hard to capture as the capricious breeze drifting in through the open window. The disturbance of air lifted the black hair from his face, revealing his intent dark eyes and vulnerable mouth.

'Tell me about it, Harry,' Bess said quietly. He turned to face her.

'I think I have decided that. At least—it was not a conscious decision when leaving Greenwich, rather the result of my time here. An enjoyable time and a—*positive* time. These are good people here, Bess, here on our land. They have not had the advantages I have had, but they hold as high ideals as ever I was taught in all my years as royal squire and knight. They work the land, they struggle with conditions which take strength and belief, and when knocked back, pick themselves up and begin again. I admire them, and also *like* them. I like Walter Banks for being determined to keep Laks Farm going even though his brothers and eldest son died in the summer plague. I like our own Walter for breaking his back to repair and whitewash the rooms above our stables so he may have a decent place to live with Mary when their babe is born. And I like you for knowing of all their heartaches, but never offering advice or help unless they ask for it. I never thought to like any woman — or at least any woman I desired as well — and 'tis truly a revelation to me.'

Bess accepted this compliment in silence. Let him talk, she thought, torn between pain for his soul-searching and the victorious feeling that at last Latimar could declare himself. She had long suspected that few had ever asked Harry for his private thoughts, few had looked beyond the amusing and convivial persona he chose to present to the world. She said, 'Yes, the life here is good, but there is something else which has contributed to your decision.' She waited.

'True.' Harry looked across the dim room at her. She is with me in this moment, he thought gratefully... 'There was something different in the way the king—the way Henry took his leave of me this time. I have taken leave of him so many times over the years, but this time... I did not think of it especially at the time, but—since—I have pondered his words and found something...final in their meaning. 'Twas as if he did not expect me to come back. Or that he would not come back, I know not which.'

'What was it he said to you?' Bess asked, keeping her voice carefully neutral.

'He said, "Do you wish me luck in my new marriage, Harry?" and of course I said I did. Then he asked me if I wished him well in his venture in France, and I said I did, but with the usual reservations I have for any undertaking of this kind. Then he said...' Harry paused, recalling the scene in his mind. The sun had just dropped out of sight beyond the palace walls, leaving a crimson afterglow which had stained the old king's face and had had the odd effect of obscuring the ravages that time and self-indulgence and cruelty had wrought on his once handsome face.

So he looked when I first saw him, Harry had thought involuntarily. Myself a grubby, timid little boy of eight, and he the golden prince of England who had a taste not only for the masculine provinces of hunting and jousting and chasing pretty women, but also a delicate preference for intellectual pursuits. Young King Henry had come to the throne in his beautiful and vigorous youth. His father had been a clever man, a worthy man, but careful and bound by a limited background. His son would lead England to greatness, make it a dominant force in the world, a country not merely revered for its military strength and diplomacy, but also for its spectacular excellence in the fields of art and music and poetry.

Well, some of these ambitions had been achieved, but along the way gay King Hal had dirtied his hands and reputation and high ideals in various areas. Yet he is still a man deserving the adulation I — and so many others — have accorded him throughout the years, Harry had thought passionately in that moment.

'Yes? He said?' Bess was watching her husband's face.

'Oh. . .' Harry returned to the present. 'He said, "When I am gone, Harry, and laid to rest, as my will has requested, beside my dear Jane at Windsor, I want you to know that another part of the will has made certain the futures of your children, Anne and George. I have asked that it be the bounden duty of my successor to see for Latimar's offspring, and take on my own role as their godparent."

'He said that to me very seriously, and I protested, "But, sire, you have many years ahead in which to watch my children grow," and he smiled. He has, has always had, the most sweet smile. . . "Certainly," he agreed, "but I just wanted you to know this now." Then we embraced and he said a strange thing. He said, "Do not be so often at our court, Harry. We do not expect it, my boy, for it will give us more pleasure to know you to be on your own land, and with the one who holds your heart in the way we could never do."

'It was a curious moment, Bess, as if he stood on a familiar shore and I in the bows of a ship bound for a strange land. At the time I thought: my friend, he knows of my feeling for you and our babes and wishes to make it easy for me to withdraw my support for his war plans, and take you back to Maiden Court. But when I had more time to contemplate his words, they seemed to me to be a... rejection.'

'Oh, no, Harry,' Bess said decisively. 'Not a rejection! More a perceptive declaration. He does, after all, know and love you so well.'

'How can such knowledge account for him virtually telling me I am no longer welcome in his court?'

Bess smiled. 'You will understand, my darling, when you have to tell George he may not eat any more of the sugar sweetmeats he loves so much, but which invariably make him sick.' She watched him consider, and make sense of, her words. He sighed. 'But I shall miss the hurly-burly of court life,' he said slowly. ''Tis such an ideal climate to hide oneself in. Will there be such a haven here, do you think?'

'No, there won't, Harry,' Bess said gently. 'You cannot hedge your bets here at Maiden Court. We deal in real life here—not a hand for a game of cards.'

'What a pity,' Harry answsered wryly. 'I have such a talent for that particular sport.'

'You have a talent for the sport we have here,' she said softly. 'Only give us a chance.'

'And I will be the greatest success?' he asked drily. 'I doubt that.'

'Why should you doubt?'

'From past experience. My life so far is littered with the spectres of my failures.'

'Whom have you failed?' she demanded indignantly. 'No one has ever said such a thing to me. Even those who may not love you, have never said that. Even——'

'Even young Will Christowe? What he did, I think he did for you. At least, that is what he said when I tried to thank him.'

Bess did not agree with him; she remembered what the king had said about so many being willing to pick up the pieces for Latimar. She said thoughtfully, 'Perhaps he was unwilling to admit to a kindness for you — he was rather a black and white young man you know.'

'A perfect match for you, then,' Harry said quietly. 'And set now to be the greatest success.' News of the enterprise in Scotland had filtered through to Maiden Court over the months. As anticipated, King James had refused to sign any treaty which would affect his country's sovereignty and Norfolk had led the English troops on a bloody week-long raid towards Kelso, leaving a shameful path of destruction in his wake. Only a small section of the force had shown a dignified mercy—that commanded by a young half-Frenchman, Lord Christowe.

James had been swift to seek revenge but, even with the superior numbers at his disposal, had come to grief in the marshes of Solway Moss where hundreds of his men were taken prisoner, including the flower of his Scottish nobility, the rout leaving him so disgraced and broken-hearted that he was dead shortly after, leaving his baby daughter, Mary, as queen.

During this time Will Christowe, while acquitting himself brilliantly in the skirmishes, also sent impassioned pleas to Henry, begging him to consider some peaceful solution with an enemy too close to England to be anything but dangerous in the years to come unless pacified. Henry took little notice of these missives, but his acute facility for recognising useful servants noted the contents, admired the diplomatic expression of them, and filed the information away for future use. Soldier-diplomats were rare, and Lord Christowe would make his mark in the years to come.

Bess went to the fire and picked up the poker. She thrust it into the orange-grey ashes, considering her next words. 'I hear the Lady Madrilene,' she said after a moment, 'has left us bound for Spain. If we are to speak of perfect matches, we must consider she was so for you.'

Harry frowned. 'Madrilene? Perfect match or no, she is nothing to me.'

Bess straightened up and turned around. 'Exactly.'

Harry laughed. 'I seem to have determined to spend my days from now on with a very clever woman.' He came to her and put a hand lightly on her shoulder. 'Perhaps you should consider what you are letting yourself in for, though, Bess. You raised Madrilene's name, so I will tell you she said when I bade her farewell—that she would have let me be myself, and you never would.'

'Then she was wrong. It is exactly yourself that I want you to be.' He raised an eyebrow.

'You have been trying to change me since we met, sweetheart.'

'Not change, just become more... You have grown out of the kind of life you led at court, Harry. It is time now to move on—to grow—in another. You spoke of boarding a ship earlier, on course for a strange land. Maiden Court, and your family, are that land and you are now come to safe habour.'

He looked directly into her eyes. 'I also spoke of the court as being a convenient place to hide in, Bess, somewhere my inadequacies would not be discovered. Here they will be only too plain. You have always demanded so much from me and I suspect our son may demand even more—with unpredictable results.'

'We will never ask anything of you that is not there to give. I have always known the worth of you, and so will Anne and George.'

He drew her towards him. 'You always think well

of me, whatever I do; long may you continue to do so. . . Will you not even try to extract a promise from me that I restrain my gambling ways?'

'No indeed! On the contrary, I would have you teach me the secret of your success!'

His lips touched her bright hair, his arms tightened about her. He had an overwhelming sense of coming home. He had resisted that homecoming for so long, while Bess and Henry and others pointed the way. But in the end he had had to acknowledge what he knew to be in his cards, for he had dealt the hand himself. He said, 'There is nothing I can teach you about winning, Bess. You have in the last year taken on a Spanish noblewoman, a court and a king — and the most reckless gambler I know — and vanquished them all to take the dubious prize you hold in your arms now.'

MILLS & BOON

Christmas Treasures

Unwrap the romance this Christmas

Four exciting new Romances by favourite Mills & Boon authors especially for you this Christmas.

A Christmas Wish - Betty Neels
Always Christmas - Eva Rutland
Reform Of The Rake - Catherine George
Christmas Musquerade - Debbie Macomber

Published: November 1994

Available from WH Smith, John Menzies, Volume One, Forbuoys, Martins, Woolworths, Tesco, Asda, Safeway and other paperback stockists.

SPECIAL PRICE : £5.70
(4 BOOKS FOR THE PRICE OF 3)

LEGACY of LOVE

Coming next month

THE ASTROLOGER'S DAUGHTER
Paula Marshall

London 1665

Sir Christopher Carlyon yearned to leave the dissipation of Court, to have again the settled life he knew before the Civil War, but the only way was to accept a disgraceful bet from the Duke of Buckingham. If he could bed the astrologer's daughter, the Duke would give him the manor of Latter—but Celia Antiquis confounded all Kit's expectations. She truly was the chaste woman of her repute and, despite all, how could Kit ruin her for his own gain?

FRIDAY DREAMING
Elizabeth Bailey

Regency England

She did not wish to marry...if she could not marry Nicolas.

And as Miss Frideswid Edborough—familiarly known as Friday—well knew, she could no more marry Nick than fly to the moon. She was plain Friday, a bluestocking, bespectacled miss; not even remotely pretty; as unlike the females Nick's taste ran to as she could be. It seemed then that she was doomed to spinsterhood...But Friday had reckoned without a father determined to see his daughter—sole heir to the Edborough estate—*off* the proverbial shelf...

LEGACY *of* LOVE

Coming next month

CHRISTMAS MIRACLE
Ruth Langan
New Mexico, USA, 1866

Christmas cheer was hard to find on the long, hard trail west. But Lizzy Spooner was determined that her family would not now be defeated by the remorseless winter snows they'd encountered while passing through the mountain wilderness.

For Cody Martin, the spirit of Christmas held little meaning. A grieving man, he had wedded himself to the mountain wilderness, and made it his home. Yet one snow-filled night, a glimmer of promise appeared before him, in the form of one Lizzy Spooner—his own Christmas angel…

ANGEL OF THE LAKE
Ana Seymour
Milwaukee, USA, 1852

Josh Lyman was lucky to have survived the wreck of the S.S. *Atlantic*. But his rescue of Norwegian emigrant girl Kari Aslaksdatter had been proclaimed a miracle—a miracle that plagued him with guilt every time he looked into her trusting blue eyes.

Kari had suffered a blow that robbed her of memory, but somehow she was certain she'd never known a man like the tall, dark American who'd saved her life. Little did she suspect that he would prove to be her greatest challenge in the New World.

PENNY JORDAN

Cruel Legacy

One man's untimely death deprives a wife of her husband, robs a man of his job and offers someone else the chance of a lifetime...

Suicide — the only way out for Andrew Ryecart, facing crippling debt. An end to his troubles, but for those he leaves behind the problems are just beginning, as the repercussions of this most desperate of acts reach out and touch the lives of six different people — changing them forever.

Special large-format paperback edition

OCTOBER   **£8.99**

WORLDWIDE

Available from WH Smith, John Menzies, Volume One, Forbuoys, Martins, Woolworths, Tesco, Asda, Safeway and other paperback stockists.